I0675261

# DRAWN AND QUARTERED

## BLOODY JOE MANNION BOOK SEVEN

### PETER BRANDVOLD

**WOLFPACK**
**PUBLISHING**
— EST 2013 —

# DRAWN AND QUARTERED

## CHAPTER 1

MATT SEVERANCE DREW REIN ON THE SHOULDER OF A low mesa. He thumbed his black hat up on his forehead and gazed northward toward the toy-sized buildings scattered on the sage-tufted plain far ahead, in a bowl hemmed in by the towering peaks of the San Juan Mountains to the west, the Sangre de Cristos to the east, and the bulwark gray shadows of the Sawatch Range to the north.

Twin silver rails ran ruler-straight from that collection of buildings—a larger collection from when Severance was last here and which comprised the town of Del Norte, Colorado Territory. The rails were new, too. They gleamed brightly in the lens-clear light of the Colorado summer.

Severance snorted a dry laugh to himself.

"Bloody" Joe Mannion, town marshal of Del Norte, had always vowed he'd never allow the "consarned iron horse" to befoul his fair town. Not while he still wore the badge, anyway.

*Well, guess who'd won, Bloody Joe?*

Severance knew Mannion still wore the star. He'd

asked when he'd decided to return here...to this home country of bitter memories...two months ago, from where he'd sought refuge from his past, in western Kansas, where he'd broken wild horses for ranchers.

Why was it the bitterest of pasts that always beckoned the most vigorously?

The blaze-faced black stirred restlessly and turned its head slightly and rolled its copper-tan eyes to glance back along their back trail.

"Easy, boy," Severance said, leaning forward to pat the horse's left, sweat-lathered wither. "I know they're back there. Been back there since the roadhouse. We'll see to them soon."

He did not turn his head to peer behind him. He'd seen the curl of dust several times over the past hour. He remembered the quick, anxious looks of the three men standing at the bar when Severance had entered the road-house, batwings clattering back into place behind him. While the barkeep had filled a schooner foaming full and set it in front of Severance, the three men had conferred in low whispers, one man raking a gloved thumb across the walnut grips of the gun holstered low on his right thigh.

Still, Severance had enjoyed the prickly sensation of the beer washing over his tongue and flowing down his throat to spread its coolness through his belly. It had been a long ride up from Pueblo, where he'd spent the night in a bedbug-infested flophouse run by a Chinaman. He'd rebuffed the administrations of the man's not unattractive whores. He'd slept despite the bugs, occasional gunfire on the street, the cloying odor of the midnight oil, and the moaning issuing from the cribs. He'd slept despite the wash of dark memories making bizarre passion plays of his dreams.

*Roy. Eva. Their daughter, Cheyenne...*

*Roy was gone, gunned down by Bloody Joe himself.*

*But what of Eva and Cheyenne?*

Thunder rumbled. A cool wind from the south lifted the black's tail to brush across Severance's back. He looked up and grimaced against the sting of the first few drops of cold rain. Gray clouds with scalloped edges swirled, closing over him, blotting out the sun.

Like the darkest of pasts, the storm had caught up to him.

As would the riders behind him...

He didn't mind either all that much. It was time to confront both. After all, wasn't that what he'd come back for? To take the bull by the horns, so to speak?

To set things right.

He gigged the black down off the mesa and into a canyon he remembered hunting years ago, him and Roy as boys. He knew this country, as Roy had, like the proverbial back of his hand. Soon he was holed up in a notch cave with a fire crackling and the black safely stowed under a stone overhang protected by a large stone escarpment.

It was a well-concealed place, but his stalkers found him. They either knew the country as well as he did, or they'd tracked him here. Maybe both.

"Hello, the camp!" came the cry slicing through the cacophony of thunder, lightning, and slashing rain.

"Ride in easy," Severance called, kneeling by the fire over which he'd hung his battered tin coffeepot from an iron tripod.

He watched the riders—three men riding side by side —move slowly up the pine-stippled slope beneath the cave. The rain slashed against their yellow rainslickers and sluiced off the brims of their hats.

"You can picket your horses with mine," Severance yelled, against the storm's roar, canting his head toward where he'd left the black.

The men rode over and unsaddled their mounts then slouched beneath the weight of their saddles as they clambered up the gravelly slope and into the cave. Severance sat back against the rear wall, legs crossed Indian style, a cup of coffee steaming on one knee. He'd pulled the flap of his own rainslicker back behind the handle of his .44.

"Boy, that coffee sure smells good, friend!" said one of his sodden visitors, slapping his funnel-brimmed, badly weathered Stetson against his thigh. He had a big, square head with thinning, brown hair combed back from a pronounced widow's peak.

The other two agreed.

"Help yourselves," Severance said.

They each dropped their saddles near the fire, fished cups from their saddlebags, and filled them from the gurgling pot. Soon they each sat in a semicircle around the other side of the fire from Matt, their backs to the storm.

Thunder clapped like cymbals. Lightning slashed across the purple sky behind them. The horses stirred, whickering.

No one said anything for a long time. The three newcomers just sat staring at Severance as they sipped their coffee. Matt stared back at them, sipping his own hot mud. They'd each made sure their own hoglegs were within a quick, easy reach. The man on the right wore two, one for the cross-draw on his left hip. He was tall and thin, with a razor slash for a mouth. His eyes were flat and dull. The man to his left was small, thin, and blond. He studied Severance with quick, flashing eyes, his mouth twitching expressively.

He seemed to want to say something for a long time before he said, "Say, you're Matt Severance, ain't ya?"

"That's right," Severance said, and sipped his coffee.

The three pairs of eyes blazed, boring into him.

"Why'd you come back?" asked the stocky man, sitting to the kid's right. He sat leaning back against his heels. He held his steaming cup in his left hand. The walnut grips of his Schofield .44 were revealed by the tucked back flap of his rainslicker upon which the beaded rainwater glistened in the firelight. His black denim jeans were patched at the knees.

Severance avoided the question, asking his own instead. "You boys from around here?"

He knew they were. Having lived here most of his life, except for the last two, he knew most of the cowpunchers and ranchers in this country. He'd seen these three before in one saloon or hurdy-gurdy house or another. He didn't know their names, but he remembered their faces. The faces of these three were a little more worn, a little more lined than they'd been two and a half years ago.

But he'd seen them before. Your average thirty-a-month-and-found cowpuncher. That's all they were, all they ever would be. They'd punch cows until they couldn't any longer and then they'd limp around, mucking out stables or livery barns until they couldn't do *that* any longer. And then only God knew what would happen to them.

It was the life of the western cowboy.

Yes, it's all they were, all they ever would be.

Unless they got lucky...

"Sure, sure," said the stocky gent. "I'm Wayne Fisk."

He canted his head to indicate the little blonde to his left. "This is Titus Willeford. That tall drink of water beyond him is Fred Saturday."

The little blonde smiled. An eager shrewdness shone in his eyes. The tall man's face and eyes remained expressionless as he stared across the fire at Severance.

"You know my story, don't you?" Severance said.

The little blonde's mouth spread a wider smile. "What was your brother's name again? Uh...uh..." He bowed his head and snapped his fingers beside his ear as though prodding his memory.

"Roy," Matt said, his voice flat.

"Roy—that's it!" said the stocky man, Fisk. "Shame what happened to him."

"Dirty, cryin' shame," echoed the blonde. "That's Bloody Joe for you. He'd always rather cart them to town belly down over their saddles than ridin' upright." He gave a dry laugh and shook his head.

"I reckon Roy didn't give him much of a choice." Severance sipped his coffee. It didn't taste as good as it had a few minutes ago. Bile churned in his belly, stirred by bitter memories.

"They say he went bad," said the stocky gent.

Severance rested his cup on his knee. He leaned forward to drop another small branch into the fire, building up the flames against the cold storm swirling around inside the cave from outside. "We both did, Roy an' me," he said, leaning back against the cave wall. He gave the stocky man a direct look. "But I came to my senses. Went back to the ranch and my old man. Roy—he continued down the dark trails."

"You don't say?" said the little blonde, Willeford.

Severance just looked at him. Trouble stirred in those quick, flashing eyes.

"So, then...it wasn't you..." Wayne Fisk said.

"Who was with Roy when he robbed the stage?" Severance said. "No."

"But there were two men..." Fisk said.

"Both masked," Severance said. "The second man wasn't me. And for the record, I have no idea where they hid the money before Mannion and his deputy caught up to Roy at Thunder Mountain."

"The second man got away." These were the first words from the tall man, Saturday, spoken in a dull, flat voice edged with menace. "He'd be the only one who knew where that money is."

"That's right," Severance said, taking another sip from his coffee. "But it wasn't me. Like I told you, I gave up ridin' the long coulees. Whoever the second man was, he wasn't me."

"Probably already come back for the money," Fisk told the other two. "Prob'ly stompin' with his tail up down Mexico-way."

"Sure enough," said Willeford. "Frolickin' with the señoritas in Old *Mejico*!" He slapped his right hand down on his right knee. Then he frowned as though suddenly puzzled. "But then, why'd you come back?"

"To visit my old man."

"Your old man's dead," Fisk said, curling a grim half smile.

"To pay my respects at his grave," Severance said. "To see about the ranch."

"The Half-Moon's been absorbed by Ethel Beech's Triangle Cross," said Fisk.

"I aim to get it back."

"Why now?" Fisk asked. "After two years. Hell, ever'-body knows you didn't have much of a head for cowpunchin'. You preferred..."

"I know what everybody thinks I preferred," Severance said, the taste of gall on his tongue. "But that wasn't really me. That was Roy. My older brother's influence. I'm ready to settle down on my home ground...near the grave of my father. In the cabin I grew up in."

Fisk nodded slowly, sagely, his suspicious gaze drilling deep into Severance's eyes.

No one said anything.

The storm was blowing itself out, the thunder drifting off to the north. The rain was coming down far more gently, and the wind wasn't howling as fiercely as before. The horses seemed to have settled down, as well.

The storm outside was dying. But Severance could feel the storm inside the cave intensifying. He could see it in the hardening eyes of the men sitting across the fire from him.

"You know what I think?" Fisk said quietly, his heavy brows mantling his dark-brown eyes, which now shone with open challenge. "I think you was the second robber. I think that's why you lit out of the country. I think you came back to dig up the loot you and your brother stole."

"I wouldn't think that if I were you," Severance said.

They might have known him before he left. But they didn't know who he was now.

Willeford's nostril flared, and his jaws hardened. "I think Wayne's right. I think that's just what you came back for."

"I think we could get it out of you," said Saturday, in his flat, menacing voice. "If we did it the right way." He hooked a crooked smile that looked like the smile on a snake's mouth, if a snake could smile.

"Don't even think about it," Severance warned.

No one said anything for another full minute.

Then Fisk said, "Don't kill him boys—just drill one in his *guts!*"

The last word hadn't left his tongue before he and the two others went for their guns in a blur of quick motion.

Severance's Colt spoke before any of theirs cleared leather.

*Bang! Bang-Bang!*

All three went flying backward out of the cave, screaming and tossing their coffee and six-guns away before they piled up in bloody heaps at the bottom of the slope.

The horses screamed.

# CHAPTER 2

"GOOD MORNING, MISS JANE. THIS IS SCORPION Charlie crawling up your spine. Time to rise an' shine!"

"Bloody" Joe Mannion, town marshal of Del Norte, walked his fingers up along the spine of his wife's bare back then swept her thick, curly red hair aside and planted a kiss on the back of her neck.

Lying belly down on their bed in the suite of rooms they kept at the San Juan Hotel & Saloon, Jane did not stir.

"Miss Ja-ane," Joe said, frowning down at his beloved, "didn't you hear Scorpion Charlie? It's dang near ten o'clock in the morning. You're burnin' daylight, sweetheart."

Sitting on the edge of the bed which he'd shared with his wife earlier, before he'd risen at six to head over to his small jailhouse and office, locally and whimsically known as Hotel de Mannion, Joe frowned down at the lovely woman in her early forties but with only a few stray strands of silver in her thick hair. Concern grew in Joe. It wasn't like Jane to sleep much over eight even when she'd had a late night which, running a brothel on her second and third floors, and a gambling parlor known as the "Bear Den" on the first, she often did.

Concern grew in Mannion until his heart picked up a fearful beat and he noticed how still she lay, noticed also the tender paleness of her back.

"Jane?" he said, more insistently. "Darling?"

He placed the flat of his hand against her back, hoping to detect a heartbeat. Surely, she hadn't expired on him. Naturally, she hadn't been feeling her old self since she'd taken three bullets to the chest, compliments one sore-headed old rattlesnake of a bounty hunter named Ulysses Xavier Lodge, so Mannion had naturally been concerned. But...oh, God!

"Jane!" he said, fairly yelling and giving her shoulder a hard, anxious jerk.

"Oh!" Jane lifted her chin from the pillow then turned and, using one arm to sweep her hair away from her face, rolled onto her back. She blinked groggily up at her husband. "Oh, Joe...what time is it, darling?" She cast her brown-eyed gaze toward the bright window from which Mannion had drawn the curtains when he'd reentered the suite after his first rounds about the bustling, still-growing town and had a leisurely breakfast in the San Juan's dining room downstairs. "My God, it looks so *late*! Why didn't you *wake me*?"

Pushing up on her elbows, Jane frowned admonishingly up at Mannion.

The lawman heaved a relieved sigh and then gave a dry snort. "If that isn't like you, I don't know what is." He chuckled, thoroughly relieved to be gazing into his beloved's open eyes. For several eternal seconds, he'd believed she'd kicked off, which would not have been one bit fair, given that this was their second marriage— second marriage to *each other*—and he'd seen it as their second and last chance at sharing a good life together.

For sure, they were two people meant to be together despite all their chaotic ups and downs over the past two years, which had only seemed to reflect the passion they felt for each other, cementing the notion that there was no one else for either of them. Not now nor forever more.

"Is what just like me?"

"Never mind."

"Joe, what's wrong." That penetrating gaze. Her eyes widened suddenly. "Oh, you thought..." She reached up and placed her hands on his forearms, gave each an affectionate squeeze. "Oh, Joe. I'm not going to leave you, honey." Jane paused, frowned, suddenly troubled. "I have to admit, though...I certainly can sleep these days."

"Then you should sleep. Get all you need." Mannion planted an affectionate kiss on her forehead and shoved her gently back down against her pillow. "You have good folks working for you. They'll take care of the place."

"You know me, Joe. I can't do that. I always have to have a hand in."

"You're still healing."

"I'm healed. Just tired. That's all, darling."

"Jane?"

"Yes, Joe?"

"Maybe you oughta sell out. I could turn in my badge. We could leave. Find a new place. Hell, with what you could make on the San Juan, we could buy a nice house in Denver."

"That stinky cow town?"

"It's becoming a city. Hell, last time I was there delivering prisoners to the feds, I heard a couple speaking French on Larimer Avenue!"

"*French*...in *Denver*?" Jane laughed and gave his chorded forearm another affectionate squeeze through his red corduroy shirt over which he wore a black leather vest.

Mannion thrilled to the sound of her laughter. No one else laughed like Jane. Throaty, husky yet feminine. What a creature he'd found to spend the rest of his life with. To think he'd divorced her once. Or had let her divorce him. What had gotten into him? Now, he was deathly afraid of losing her. For once you've had a woman like the former Jane Ford...or when you've had her twice, having lost her once...you live in fear of losing her yet again.

For the final time.

"Or we could head west," Mannion said. "To San Francisco, say?"

She smiled up at him, running her hands up and down his arms. "Oh, Joe. You couldn't turn in that badge any more than I could sell the San Juan. My God, what would we do with ourselves?"

"Sit in the sun on a big front porch drinking whisk... er, lemonade." Mannion grinned. He was trying to cut back on his firewater habit. It had never done a man with his naturally fiery disposition any good. It was like pouring gasoline on a smoldering fire. He'd made plenty of mistakes while under its influence. It was a hard thing to give up, though, when it seemed to so nicely file the edges off the world's sharper corners. At least, for a time.

Jane chuckled. "Whiskey or lemonade. I know what we'd end up drinking as well as you do, Joe. No. That's not for us. You'll die in the saddle, you big lug. Me, I'll die kicking a surly jake out of one of the girls' quarters with a bung starter, yelling at the tops of my lungs."

She started to laugh but then she sobered suddenly. She'd kicked Ulysses Lodge out of the room of a girl he'd been roughing up and had had two bouncers chuck him into the street. That was when he'd come back into the San Juan with a gun and shot Jane three times in the chest, damn near killing her. If it hadn't been for the quick, delicate work of young Doctor Ben Ellison, who had later married Mannion's daughter, Vangie, she'd have been a goner.

They both knew that. And were inadvertently reminded of it now.

A pall settled over the room.

Mannion rose from the bed and walked over to the window. He stared down into the street abustle with ore drays, ranch wagons, and mule teams hauling long, unpeeled pine logs to the sawmill to cut into lumber with which to build yet more houses and business establishments that would continue to swell Del Norte until the once-quiet mountain town, which started as a trading post for miners and trappers, was fairly bursting at the seams.

Which it already was with no little help from the iron horse, whose rails split the broad main drag in two equal halves of roughly fifty yards each. The consarned train...

Progress.

Bull hokey.

Trouble is what it was.

*Jane.*

He couldn't help remembering the terrifying limpness of her body in his arms when he was hustling her over to Doc Bohannon's office, knowing that with each running step he took, her life's blood was pouring out of her, taking her farther and farther away from him.

"Your job's more dangerous than mine, darling," Jane said, her voice a throaty cat's purr behind Mannion now. "Besides, he's dead. Lodge is dead. You killed him high up in the Sawatch."

"Oh, I know," Mannion said, embarrassed by his dark turn of thought. Hell, none of this was his first rodeo. He'd always lived a dangerous life. "I just want us to have a good old age together."

He turned his head to gaze back at his wife. Her light brown eyes glistened in the sunlight angling through the window.

"We will." Jane patted the bed beside her. "Right here. And in the house...with Vangie working her horses in the corral out back."

After they'd married the second time, they'd finished building the house they'd started building the first time they were married. It was on the spot of Mannion's first house in which he'd raised Vangie, before Garth Helton's diabolical son and two others had burned him out and kidnapped Vangie. On a night when Mannion was three sheets to the wind, drunk on the Who-Hit-John and reeling from dark memories of Vangie's mother, Sarah, who had hanged herself in their backyard in Kansas only a few months after Vangie was born...

Mannion and Jane spent weeknights in Jane's suite in the San Juan for convenience, since they both worked in town, spending the weekends in their house though Vangie no longer lived there. She lived with her young doctor, Ben Ellison, in a small, neat brick house the doctor had purchased after he and Vangie wed in a double ceremony with Joe and Jane. Vangie still worked her horses in the corral behind the Mannion house, however. Mannion loved to see her out there, clad in her wool and leather cowboy gear, hair loose...as wild as the wind.

Just like always.

Everything changes. His little girl had grown up. But a few things stayed the same, including Vangie's wild and free spirit, so much like her mother's when Sarah was young...before Mannion had virtually abandoned Sarah when he'd been taming raggedy-heeled cow towns from Kansas to Texas, during the years of the great Texas cattle herds making the trip north to the iron horse.

The damnable iron horse...

He couldn't help associating it with Sarah's suicide.

Mannion's smile belied the dark thoughts he couldn't shake. "All right, kid. You got it. We'll stay here."

"Vangie wouldn't let us leave, anyway."

"No."

"You couldn't leave her."

"No, I could—"

Mannion cut himself off abruptly. In the corner of his left eye, he'd spied a familiar figure in the street below him.

A tall, rangy rider on a blaze-faced black gelding was leading three horses with three dead men tied belly down across their saddles. Though they were wrapped in blankets, Mannion knew the rider was leading dead men. Mannion often led such a grisly procession himself—thus his well-earned nickname.

"Joe," Jane said. "Honey, what is it?"

Mannion gazed down into the street, slowly turning his head, tracking the rider as he made his way from Mannion's right to his left, traveling south to north along the busy, dusty main street recently renamed San Juan Avenue. He was on the opposite side of the tracks from the San Juan.

"A ghost from the past," Mannion muttered.

He pushed away from the window.

"Honey, I gotta go."

Mannion kissed Jane quickly then grabbed his hat and left, leaving Jane frowning curiously at the door he'd pulled closed behind him.

## CHAPTER 3

MANNION LEFT THE SAN JUAN AND AT THE BOTTOM OF the swanky watering hole's broad, wooden steps, he swung left and headed north along the boardwalks fronting various business establishments, weaving through the foot traffic already heavy now at midmorning, absently pinching his hat brim to the ladies and nodding to the men he knew.

Having been the top lawdog in Del Norte for the past six years, Mannion pretty much knew all of the natives. A private man, he often yearned to quit here and start fresh elsewhere. But Jane was right. They'd each sunk deep taproots in Del Norte. It was home. Especially so for him now that Vangie had gotten married and bought a house with her new husband, who Joe rather liked though the man hailed from back east and hadn't even known how to ride a horse until Vangie had taught him. Ben Ellison had been educated at Harvard, no less.

Joe didn't hold any of it against the young man.

As he strode quickly along the boardwalks, he shook his head and hooked a dry smile at the notion. Imagine his wild girl, whose only true friends had once been dogs and horses, married to a Harvard grad who had blisters on his hands only where the scalpel rubbed.

Life could take strange turns for a man. Not necessarily unwelcome ones. He'd once been worried about his reclusive daughter. Now he worried no more. Or at least no more than your average father worried about his only child.

Peering ahead along the street, through a veil of passing wagons and horseback riders and roiling dust, Mannion saw the target of his interest, Matt Severance, turn his black toward Mannion's office and jailhouse. The lawman had just picked up his pace when, approaching the Three-Legged Dog Saloon, he heard a man scream from inside the place. There was the staccato sound of boots pounding the floorboards and the wild jangling of spurs before a man went flying through the Three-Legged Dog's batwing doors with such speed and violence that one of the doors was torn off its hinges and went flying with the man across the boardwalk and into the street.

The man was big, burly, and bearded and clad in the ragged, dusty garb of your average grub line rider. The holster on his right hip was empty. The man lay belly down in the finely churned dirt and horse manure, groaning. He'd just started to push up on his hands and knees when another scream issued from inside the Three-Legged Dog. The scream was followed by the clomping of feet moving too fast for the rest of the man to keep pace. He, too, came flying through the doorway, nearly tearing the lone batwing from its hinges, to pile up in the street in a cloud of swirling dust beside the first man.

This man was of average height, sandy-haired, and dressed similarly to the first man. His holster, too, was empty.

The second man had just hit the dirt when a deep, guttural voice rose from inside the Three-Legged Dog. "Anymore cheaters? Huh? Huh? Anyone else cheatin' at cards?"

Mannion, who had paused near the lowly watering hole's entrance to consider the two men now groaning belly down in the street together, smiled. He recognized the voice of his newest deputy, the mountain-sized Cletus Booker, who was not the sharpest tool in the shed but had no need to be.

Mannion had hired Booker for his head-breaking skills, not his proficiency with his letters and numbers or even his ability to get along with others. He'd hired the third deputy, who'd cut his law-bringing teeth in mountain mining towns even more raucous than Del Norte, to help him and his other two deputies—the young Henry McCallister and the middle-aged but still capable Rio Waite—keep the lid on Del Norte, no easy task since the consarned iron horse had galloped straight down the main drag, the Colorado Springs & San Juan Line daily depositing more and more riffraff that tended to linger.

Inside the Three-Legged Dog another man screeched, "Him right there—he's been droppin' pasteboards out of a sleeve rig since last night. I *seen* him!"

"You been cheatin', too—have you, fancy-dan?" roared Booker, his voice echoing off the Dog's mud-brick walls. "Well, we'll see about *that*! Git over here, you *scalawag*!"

"No, no—he has it wrong. Leave me be, ya big ape!"

Grinning, hearing more screams and more clomps of desperately running feet issuing from inside the Three-Legged Dog, Mannion continued forward. He'd just past the saloon's one-doored entrance when yet another man —this one nattily attired in a three-piece suit complete with paisley vest and burgundy ribbon tie—went flying out into the street with a shrill, girlish scream to pile up with the two grub line riders already there.

"Like I done said a thousan' times!" Booker's thunderous voice roared from inside the Three-Legged Dog, "no cheatin' or fightin'! You cheat or fight, you face ol' *Booker*!"

More voices sounded behind Mannion, some in accusing, some in protest of said accusing, but they dwindled quickly, drowned by the even louder cacophony emanating from the main drag as Mannion continued making his way north along the boardwalks. He chuckled and shook his head. In a town like Del Norte, good ol' Cletus was worth his weight in gold-rich ore freshly plundered from the San Juans.

He stepped off the boardwalk fronting John Dunham's Tonsorial Parlor, waited for a supply wagon owned by the Lazy Eight Ranch in the foothills of the Sawatch to pass, then, blinking against the roiling dust, crossed the street, stepping over the consarned rails of the infernal iron horse, and approached Hotel de Mannion just as Matt Severance, standing on the small stoop fronting the small, tin-roofed brick building outfitted with a spacious and well-used basement cellblock, rapped on the front door, canting his head to the door to listen for anyone inside.

"It's locked, Severance," Mannion said, approaching the dun horse standing just off the rump of Severance's black gelding. "My deputies are out on their rounds." He stuck his hand in a fold of the blanket wrapped around the corpse draped over the dun's back and pulled up the dead man's head by a fistful of hair.

He stared down at the broad, fleshy face of Wayne Fisk, a lout who Mannion remembered rode for Norman

MacLean's Turkey Track brand at the base of the Sangre de Cristos. He glanced at the grisly cargoes draped over the other two packhorses. He need not bother checking them. They would be the other two louts Fisk always rode to town with—one named something Willeford and Fred Saturday. Mannion had banned all three from Del Norte for the past two months, for drunk and disorderly —more specifically, for ganging up and beating a man in a back alley after he'd whipped them at cards.

Now they'd shown up dead in the unlikely company of a young man Mannion hadn't seen in over two years— the troubled Matt Severance, whose brother, Roy, Mannion had killed after he and another man had stolen a mine payroll off a stagecoach. The second man had gotten away. The stolen payroll was never found. Mannion believed Roy had buried it somewhere in the San Juans near the base of Thunder Mountain as Mannion and his deputy, Rio Waite, had closed on him and the second man, whom Mannion had never gotten a good look at.

Whether that man had been Roy's brother Matt, Roy's junior by two years, Mannion did not know. He thought it probably was. The two brothers had performed plenty of dirty business together, though most of it had been rustling. They'd been slippery enough to never get caught in the act. They were the progeny of Big John Severance, himself a former highwayman turned shotgun rancher who'd died a drunk on the heels of Roy's death, on the family's run-down Half-Moon Ranch in the first southern front of the San Juans, northwest of Del Norte.

Now he shuttled his gaze back to young Severance who stood at the top of Hotel de Mannion's porch steps, gazing at him sourly. He was a tall, lean, darkly handsome young man; dark-brown hair hung down from his low-crowned, flat-brimmed, black Stetson to well below the collar of his blue chambray shirt. He wore a walnut-gripped Colt .44 low-slung and tied low on his right thigh. He wore wash-worn blue denims under brush-scarred chaps; his neck-knotted red bandanna fluttered in the morning's already hot, dry breeze.

Now he thumbed his hat up on his forehead, glanced at the three packhorses, and said, "They braced me during last night's storm. I shot 'em in self-defense. There were no witnesses, so it's their word against mine. But as you can see, Marshal Mannion, they're all out of words."

Mannion strode to the base of the porch steps and glowered up at the young firebrand. "They may be, but I sure as hell am not."

"I had a feelin'," the younger man said. "I didn't need to bring 'em in, you know. I could have left them in the cave they were in when they tore down on me. Likely never would have been found, their bones strewn about by coyotes and wildcats."

"Most likely," Joe allowed, pursing his lips, nodding, staring up at the young man speculatively. He climbed the porch steps, brushed past Severance, unlocked and opened the door, and went inside. "Come on in, kid. Let's powwow." In his mid-thirties, Severance was no longer a kid, but that's how Mannion remembered him.

He pegged his hat, grabbed two stone mugs off his cluttered desk, and swabbed each out with his index finger. He'd had a cup of mud and a morning palaver earlier with Rio Waite. He took the mugs over to the potbelly stove squatting in the middle of the small office, filled each, and extended one to Severance, who stood just inside the open doorway. The young man looked down at the cup as though he were being offered poison.

"It's been on the rack awhile," Mannion said. "But it won't kill you." He glanced at the chair at the desk his deputies used and which abutted the stone wall to the right of the door that led down to the basement cell-block. "Pull that chair around and have a seat. Naturally, I have a few questions."

"I figured you would." Severance pulled the chair out from the desk, nudged it around with his foot, and slacked his long frame into it, setting his coffee on a knee.

Mannion walked around behind his own desk and eased his creaky but still trim, six four, middle-aged carcass into his swivel chair, which squawked against his two-hundred-plus pounds. He set his cup on his desk, leaned forward, and ran his hands through his longish, salt-and-pepper hair then brushed his fist across his mustache-mantled mouth. The day was young but no day in Del Norte was too young for trouble, and that fact was borne out by the sour-eyed young man sitting across from him and the three packhorses standing outside at Mannion's hitchrack.

Mannion didn't know if Severance had helped his brother steal the mine payroll. Whether he did or not, his return to Del Norte was trouble, just the same.

He drummed fingers on his coffee-stained blotter, and said, "Why'd you come back?"

Severance leaned forward, casting his interrogator a direct look. "It's where I live."

"The Half-Moon's run-down. A few owlhoots have holed up in the cabin a time or two over the past two years, and they didn't make improvements, if you get my drift."

"That's all right. I'll make them. I have plenty of time."

"Your old man's dead."

"I was the one who buried him behind the cabin."

"Then you left. Rode out of here like the wind ahead of a storm. Gone." Mannion lifted his steaming cup to his lips, blew ripples on the surface, and sipped. "Never expected you back. Unless..."

"I came back for the loot."

"Give the kid a seegar."

"If I'd been on that job with Roy, I'd have taken it with me."

"You two split up. Roy was alone with that loot for a full day, while Rio and I trailed him around the base of Thunder Mountain. You likely wouldn't know where he buried it. Just the general area he buried it in. Maybe a place that meant something to you both, from being boys who grew up around there. Maybe you did some wool gathering in Kansas and figured it out."

Severance glowered. "You knew where I was?"

"Sure. I know folks in Kansas. Law*men* in Kansas. I worked there once, long time ago. When I was your age."

"You had me spied on."

"If you want to call it that. You are the main suspect, the *lone living* main suspect, in a holdup that cost the Delacroix Mining Syndicate damn near forty thousand dollars in scrip and specie."

"Why didn't you have me arrested, hauled back here for trial?"

"Not enough evidence, kid. You and Roy were smart enough to wear masks. I never got a good look at you. Suddenly Roy was riding alone, and I saw him clearly through my field glasses...just before he tried to ambush me an' Rio."

"And you killed him." Bitterness shone in the young man's dark-brown eyes framed by the long, straight, dark-brown hair hanging down both sides of his almost effeminately handsome face. He had the distinctive Indian features of his three-quarters Cheyenne mother.

Mannion sat back in his chair with a sigh. "I had no choice, Matt."

"No, you never do."

Mannion had no response to that. He knew his reputation well enough. When the chips were down, he played his cards. That usually meant he ended up hauling dead men to town belly down across their saddles. He didn't mean for it to be that way. Those were just the cards he was dealt. At least, that's how he saw it. Others saw him as bloodier than most, but he couldn't control how others saw him though he always rankled at the "Bloody Joe" moniker. He thought it was cravenly unfair. He was a lawman, a town tamer, for chrissakes.

What was he supposed to do?

Still, he felt a pang of guilt as the young man sitting across from him, who was still obviously grieved by his older brother's death, glared at him accusingly. He'd shot Severance's older brother, a man he'd hero-worshipped. Wrongly, of course. But there it was.

"Just like you had no choice but to kill Fisk and those two other useless scums," Mannion said, hearing the defensiveness in his voice as he canted is head to indicate the horses standing hang-headed outside in the midmorning sunshine.

"You believe me."

"I do."

Severance frowned. "Why?"

"Like you said, you didn't need to bring them in."

"They figured to torture the location of the loot out of me."

Mannion gave a cold smile. "They likely won't be the last."

"Then they likely won't be the last you'll be sending off to Boot Hill, Mannion."

"I see you're wearing your gun tied down these days."

"Makes for a faster pull."

"Been practicing, have you?"

"Yep."

Severance set his coffee, which he had not yet touched, on the desk behind him and rose from his chair.

"You've been planning this return for quite some time, haven't you?" Mannion asked him.

Severance stared blandly down at him. "Yes. I was done runnin' a long time ago. This is my home. I aim to reclaim the Half-Moon."

Mannion sighed. "Hell's gonna pop. You know that, don't you?" Half the county—no, make that the *entire* county or maybe even *most* of the south-central part of the territory—believed Matt Severance knew where his brother Roy had hidden that loot. Forty thousand dollars lying out there in the first front of the San Juans, just waiting to be picked like a fistful of fresh wildflowers, the ownership of which would change the picker's sad life forever.

Bring him up from poor to rich beyond his wildest dreams.

Severance removed his hat, brushed dust from the crown. "About Roy's wife...daughter. Are they still..."

"At Elk Horn Creek? Yes. Leastways, last time I was out that way. I checked in on 'em." Mannion shook his head. "They're not doing very well, I'm afraid. They have a couple of old cowpunchers working for them, but..."

Again, he shook his head. "Eva probably can't trust anyone else. Not without a man of her own on the place and Cheyenne...well, Cheyenne's becoming a woman. Turns a lot of heads when she comes to town, the few times her mother brings her along on a supply run. And that damned loot, of course. Folks wonder if she might not know where it is, though if she did, she likely wouldn't be out there anymore."

Severance winced, set his hat on his head, and slid his dark gaze to the window over Mannion's desk. It was the first show of unregulated emotion Joe had seen on the man's face since he'd ridden back into town. He was trying to put on a brave, determined face but the fates of Roy's wife and daughter had been chewing away at him. No doubt it was as much for them as for himself he'd returned. Mannion couldn't fault him for that.

The fact was, despite the man's rough past, Mannion had always felt a soft spot for him. Not so much for Roy. He believed Roy had turned his younger brother, who'd worshipped the ground Roy walked on, bad. Or at least wild. But deep down Mannion knew that Roy hadn't been so bad, either. They'd both had a rough upbringing —their mother dying just after Matt had been born and an older sister dying from a rattlesnake bite while gathering firewood.

Also, their father, Big John, had been a rough, uncouth man given to drink. Those boys had practically raised themselves. There had been plenty of places for them to go wrong. At least, they'd never killed anybody. The robbers had left unscathed the driver and shotgun messenger as well as the passengers of the stagecoach they'd robbed. They'd just shot the lock off the strongbox, filled a pair of saddlebags, and rode away.

"Well, I'll be heading for the San Juans," Severance said, turning toward the door.

"You know Ethel Beech considers the Half-Moon hers now, don't you?"

Mannion's voice stopped the younger man, turned him back around to face him gravely. "I heard that much. I don't care about the cattle. She can keep them. I aim to trap and break wild horses on the Half-Moon. If she contests me returning to my own headquarters, the place where I was born and where I intend to die and be planted next to Pa, then she's gonna have to rethink it or she's gonna have a fistful of trouble."

"Or you might get planted next to your pa sooner rather than later."

"So be it," Severance said as he walked out the door, calling, "Good day to you, Marshal Mannion," as he crossed the porch.

Mannion heard the creak of leather as the younger man stepped into his saddle.

The thud of galloping hoods dwindled beneath the rattle and squawk of wagon traffic out on the street.

Mannion made a sour look as he stared at the sunlit, open doorway, rammed the end of his right fist down on his desk, and cursed.

## CHAPTER 4

LATE IN THE AFTERNOON, SEVERANCE AND THE BLACK gelding rounded a bend in the trail through the shelving country that comprised the first front of the San Juans. When he saw the wooden bridge that spanned Elk Horn Creek forming a gap in the willows and cottonwoods that lined the sparkling brown water, and the ranch yard beyond the creek, Matt drew rein.

Mannion had been right. Eva wasn't doing well.

There was a dilapidated air to the place, which hadn't been much to begin with. Matt had helped Roy build the small, square cabin after he and Eva, daughter of a neighboring rancher, had been married. By that time, Eva had already been starting to show and her family, being "good Lutherans," had shunned her. Roy had planned on adding to the cabin when more children arrived, but Cheyenne had been all they'd had and after Cheyenne was born, he'd grown tired of ranch work, which he'd actually grown tired of long before he'd bought his own, small spread, and drifted off the straight and narrow path, taking his younger brother along for the wild ride.

A ride that had been irresistible to Matt at the young

age of seventeen, living alone with his drunken father who'd refused to do any real work, instead making Matt and their few lowly hands do it all and taking the willow switch to Matt when Big John didn't think he was doing it right. He fired hands left and right until he could get no one to work for him anymore.

That's when Matt had lit out with the fiery, fun-loving Roy, rustling cattle and occasionally robbing stage-coaches. Not making any real money but more than they made at ranching and at least they were having fun. There wasn't anything quite like the lightning that ran through a young man's veins when they'd succeeded at rustling a half dozen to a dozen head of white-faced cattle belonging to some richer rancher than they and selling them to some corrupt rancher across the border in New Mexico Territory. There were plenty of ranchers in the Black Range and on the south side of the Sangre de Cristos who didn't mind fiddling with the brands of wealthier stockmen from the San Juans.

Roy had neglected his own place. He'd taken too much after the old man.

Now, with his absence, the place had fallen even further into decay. Weeds had grown up along the base of the cabin, and the cabin's roof showed large patches of missing shingles. A shutter on one of the front windows hung askew. The porch running along the front of the cabin listed badly to one side, one of the stone pylons upon which it was perched having caved in on itself.

The small mud-brick bunkhouse, stable, and corral that sat off to the left, with a windmill standing between them and the cabin, had fallen into similar decay. Weeds grew about them all. The bunkhouse needed a fresh coating of whitewash and chinking between the bricks. The tall, narrow log stable, with a hayloft in its upper story, appeared to lean too far to one side, likely the victim of the fierce northern winds of winter. Two old, bandy-legged, gray-bearded men in high-crowned, weather-beaten Stetsons, wool shirts, and baggy denims were just then trying to replace one of the top corral slats, one pounding nails while the other tried feebly to hold the long, peeled pine log in place across the top of two badly leaning posts. A handful of horses—two pintos, a paint, a buckskin, and a lineback dun stood in a semi-circle, watching them skeptically.

A stone jug sat on the ground near the men, attesting that the nature of their trouble wasn't only age.

Severance could hear them barking at each other and laughing.

He gave a wry chuff and booted the black head along the trail, the gelding's shod hooves clomping across the halved-log bridge and into the yard where shadows grew long as the glowing copper orb of the sun had started its tumble behind the San Juan's high, fir-carpeted ridges turning a gauzy blue green now with the fading of the light on their eastern slopes. The two oldsters had heard the black's hooves on the bridge. They turned toward Matt now, frozen in place, watching him warily, suspiciously, one with nails sprouting from between his gray-bearded lips.

An old Spencer repeater leaned against the gate post, ready for trouble though if the graybeards were ready was anyone's guess. Maybe at one time, doubtful they were now. The venal larger ranchers in the San Juan were always trying to crowd the smaller operators out. Now, with the death of Eva's husband, maybe they were leaving her alone. There was much for the taking here, anyway. Severance wondered how much of a herd she had left. He'd seen very few mixed-blood longhorns with the

Elk Horn Creek brand on his way into this neck of the range.

His own spread, the Half-Moon, was on the other side of the low, southern ridge, to the right of the cabin, a two-mile ride as the crow flew.

Severance threw up a placating hand to the old men as he angled the black toward the cabin.

He was twenty feet from the three steps rising to the stoop when boots sounded inside the cabin, the door opened suddenly, and Eva stepped about, bringing a washtub back to toss the soapy water into the yard. She stopped suddenly before she could swing it forward, and the soapy water slopped over the front of the tub and onto the worn floorboards around her feet clad in well-worn men's stockman boots.

Severance drew rein, stopping the black.

Eva stared at him, her sandy blond hair gathered into a loose bun atop her head. She was dressed in denims with a wide, brown belt and a blue-and-green checked wool shirt, the sleeves rolled to her elbows. She probably had to do the work of both of her old, hired men in the saddle, though that was nothing new for Eva. She'd always ridden and roped well, herding and branding and calving from sunup to sundown, sometimes in knee-deep snow and mud.

Anyone could see the hard work she did by looking at her now.

In the two and a half years Severance had been gone, she'd aged a good five. Her sunburned cheeks were hollow, her blue eyes flat and depleted, twin mirrors of raw despair.

Boot clomps sounded behind her, echoing inside the small, dark hovel, beyond the open door. A young woman appeared in the doorway, clad in a white blouse and long, spruce-green skirt, and said, "Momma, you want I should change the sheets on the—"

Cheyenne stopped when her rich, dark-brown eyes found the tall, lean man sitting astride the black facing the cabin. Those dark eyes widened in shock, the strong, lower jaw sagged, and the girl shrieked, "Uncle Matt! Uncle Matt!" She ran out of the cabin, brushing past her still-frozen mother, and clomped down the steps in her gold-buckle ankle boots. As she ran out into the yard, Matt, laughing, swung down from the black's back just in time to sweep the girl, so much taller than he remembered, into his arms.

So much taller and so much more woman than he remembered. He could feel the natural curves and swells of her body as he picked her up off her feet and squeezed her while she hugged him back, her arms around his neck, her face buried in his chest.

"Oh, Cheyenne, my girl! Oh, Cheyenne! It's been sooo long!"

"Uncle Matt! I never thought we'd see you again! Where have you *been*?"

As he set her back down, she pushed away from him and looked up at him with desperation in those lustrous, almond-shaped, dark-brown eyes. She shook her long, straight, dark-brown hair back from her smooth, olive-colored cheeks that tapered upward and spread broadly, exotically, betraying the rich Indian blood of Matt and Roy's mother, a three-quarter Cheyenne from Dakota.

She'd looked so Indian that even as a baby Roy and Matt had called her "Papoose," though Eva had always frowned on the moniker. She'd never gotten along with Roy and Matt's mother, Louise.

"Are you staying?" the girl continued, breathless. She

leaned forward and grabbed a fistful of Severance's black leather vest. "Tell me you're *staying*!"

Matt looked down at her as she gazed up at him crossly, waiting. Her right eye drew slightly inward the way his mother's had when the conversation suddenly turned grave. He didn't remember that himself, but that's how Roy and Pa had told it, and Matt had seen her in his parents' wedding picture, taken in Deadwood back when it was illegal for white men to be there. In the ambrotype, her right eye had been drawn slightly toward the long beak of her Cheyenne nose.

Severance shuttled his gaze over to Eva, who just now tossed the soapy wash water into the yard and held the empty tub down against her right leg, regarding him critically, frowning, loose hair from her bun sliding across her own sun-wizened cheeks in the breeze. She was only a couple years older than Matt, which would put her near forty, and she looked every year of it. The washed-out, sun-dried, work-toughened image of her filled him with sorrow.

She watched him but he had a feeling she wasn't waiting for the answer Cheyenne was waiting for.

Reluctantly, he said, "I'm...staying."

"I'm so glad!" Cheyenne said, throwing her arms around him once more. "I've missed you, you big lug! You're all the family we have—Ma an' me!" She turned to her mother. "Matt's home to stay. Ain't that great, Ma?"

"Isn't," Eva shot back at her daughter. "Haven't I taught you better than that, slaving away at the kitchen table over your letters and numbers? *Isn't* it great?"

Without another look at Severance, she swung around, hung the tub on a peg poking out of the cabin's front wall, to the left of the door, then strode inside to be swallowed up the by the hovel's heavy shadows.

Cheyenne frowned up at Severance. "What has gotten into her? I swear, she can be so colicky at times, Uncle Matt!"

Severance stared at the dark rectangle of the open door. He could hear Eva inside, sliding chairs and knocking pots and pans around.

"Cheyenne, honey," he said, placing a hand on the girl's shoulder, "give your ma an' me a few minutes, will you? It's a little more complicated for her than it is for you. Me returning out of the blue like this."

"I don't see how!" Cheyenne said.

"Trust me," Severance said. "It is."

He gave the girl a squeeze then mounted and crossed the stoop, stepped slowly inside, and drew the door closed behind him. He stood just inside the door. The cabin smelled homey with the aroma of fresh bread, two rich, brown loaves of which sat on a stone plate on the freshly scrubbed table. Eva stood with her back to him, facing the kitchen's rear counter and dry sink filled with dirty cooking pans and mixing bowls.

To her left, a potbelly stove ticked with the fire that had cooked the bread.

To the left of the stove, beyond a square-hewn ceiling support post from which hung a layer of tack to be mended, lay the parlor side of the cabin. Roy's old bull-horn chair was there, facing a hemp rug and the smaller rocker Eva had used to darn socks in the evenings after Cheyenne had gone to bed in one of the two rooms behind blanket curtains in the parlor's rear wall.

Matt had always felt guilty in here.

This wasn't his place. It was Roy's place. He shouldn't be here. He was overstepping his bounds by being here.

But then he'd overstepped his bounds before, and

that's what really bothered him. He just blamed his guilt on the cabin.

Eva stood frozen, forearms resting on the edge of the counter, her head bowed as though in prayer.

"I get it," Matt said, his voice quiet and grave in the nearly silent cabin cloying with heat but buoyed by the smell of the bread. "You don't want me here."

*CHAPTER 5*

EVA TURNED TO SEVERANCE AND CROSSED HER ARMS ON her chest. "What are you doing here?"

Severance had removed his hat. Holding it over his chest, he stepped forward and placed one hand on a back of one of the chairs at the table. "I came to help you and Cheyenne. If you were still here. I didn't know if you would be."

"Where else would we be? Where else would we go?"

"I don't know...I thought...I guess maybe I thought..."

"The loot? Do you think I have it?"

"No," Severance lied. He had to admit he'd considered the possibility that she might have found it. She and Roy had ridden the range together, side by side, tending their herd. She would likely know all the places Roy might hide something of value. After all, he'd been shot a few miles from here at the base of Thunder Mountain, four bald crags jutting up from a deep, twisting canyon in the southwest.

Severance and Roy had roamed there as kids, collecting old bison bones and spearheads. Roy had even once found a dinosaur tooth jutting from the side of the canyon, which had been painted here and there by the ancient Indians. Pictographs, they were called—the stories of many hunts and ceremonies performed under brightly painted moons and stars, some of the stick figure ancient ones wearing bison horns or cloaked in bearskins with the heads still attached. It had been a thrilling place for two young boys to explore when they'd been able to slip away from their pa, to take a reprieve from the endless chores that had embittered them both. Once they'd performed one of their own ceremonies around a fire clad in deerskins and with sharpened sticks as spears.

It had been a fine time, those years growing up with Roy, exploring the canyon around the base of Thunder Mountain.

Bloody Joe had run Roy down near there and shot him. Severance thought it somehow fitting that he'd died there. That's where he'd likely hidden the loot, though Severance had never looked for it. He'd wanted...still wanted...nothing to do with it.

It was as though Roy's wife were reading his mind but taking the snatches of his thoughts out of context.

"Do you have it?" Eva asked.

"If I had it, would I have come back?"

"You said you wanted to help us. Maybe guilt drove you back. Maybe you want to spread some of your wealth around with his family."

"The only wealth I have is a small savings from breaking horses in Kansas. Those wealthy ranchers paid me top dollar. I have nothing...no one...to spend it on."

"You've always been good with horses—haven't you, Matt? It's people you were never all that great with."

Severance turned his head as though from a slap to the face. That's what her barbed words had been like. He could feel the burn of the blow in his cheeks. He found himself gazing out the window to his left. Cheyenne was down near the corral, bantering with the two old-timers, one of whom was sitting on the edge of a wheel-less wagon parked in the weeds by the corral. The other leaned back against the closed gate, laughing as Cheyenne did a little dance for the men, swirling around and holding her skirt out from around her legs with one hand, flinging the other arm above her head, her long hair dancing about her shoulders.

Severance could hear her and the two admiring old-timers laughing.

"Just how I'm gonna do it, someday," the girl told them. "On a stage in New York City!"

"You, too?" Eva said coldly. "Stop staring at her, Matt. She's your niece, after all."

He whipped his gaze back to her. Now it was the burn of anger he felt in his face. "Good God, woman, you know she's more than that to me! We've never talked about it, but have you forgotten?"

She lowered her hands and marched up to him, raised her right hand, brought it back behind her shoulder, then thrust it forward, smashing the open palm against his left cheek. A stinging, burning blow that made his ears ring.

"Don't you ever say that! Don't you even *think* it!"

Her voice broke on the last words. Her lips trembled, a sheen of emotion grew in her washed-out eyes, and she turned away quickly, raising her hand to her mouth, quashing a sob.

Severance was dumbfounded. Good God, she had to know. The girl was the spitting image of him. He took after his and Roy's mother. He was tall and slender, Indian-featured with long, straight, dark-brown hair hanging down past his shoulders. Roy had been sandy-haired, thick-shouldered, thick-waisted, stocky like their father, and he'd owned their father's Welsh-gray eyes. True, he could have passed their mother's looks to Cheyenne, but after what had happened...the unexpected thing that had happened one day at the creek when Severance had come upon Eva picking Juneberries...and they'd taken a swim...there could be no other real explanation for Cheyenne.

Matt and Eva had dated first, before she'd dated Roy. She'd loved Matt first. For some reason, he hadn't returned that love. At least, he hadn't thought he had. Leastways, he wasn't ready to settle down. Still, when he'd ridden up to the creek that day, a few months before she and Roy were married, and he'd found her, young and beautiful and her blond hair bright and shining in the afternoon sun, the old days had flooded back upon him... and then she'd caught the sickness, as well, the wash of tender memories of similar afternoons, and they'd ended up in the tall grass together while the waters of Elk Horn Creek sang across the rocks...

"I'm sorry, Eva," he said now. "I won't mention it again. I didn't know how bad it would hurt you."

She sucked a breath and turned her head to one side to say sharply, "Leave, Matt! Leave us alone! We do just fine on our own, Cheyenne an' me!"

"I'm going back to the Half-Moon. I came back to help you with what little I have. I aim to help you, Eva, whether you like it or not. I can make repairs to the place. You need it or this cabin, the stable...it's all going to sink into the ground. I'm going to do the same to the Half-Moon."

"Hah!" Eva cried through a wicked laugh. "She'll never let you!"

He knew she was talking about Ethel Beech, whose own spread, the Triangle Cross, abutted the Half-Moon to the west—ten thousand acres spread across the first, forested slopes and lush beaver and elk meadows of the San Juan Range. Her husband had been dead for twenty years, but Ethel ran a large, rowdy bunch, determined to protect every acre of what she deemed hers, including every Triangle Cross branded white-faced cow owning the blood of several bulls brought over from Ireland, and to hell with any man she felt threatened by.

And there were plenty. Plenty real but plenty imagined, too.

They usually ended up shot or hanging from trees, left there as a lesson to others.

"She won't have a choice," Severance said.

Eva whipped around, tears rolling down her cheeks but her jaws and eyes hard. She glanced at his holstered Colt, and said, "I see you're wearing your gun tied down now, Matt. If you think it's going to help you against her, you got another thing coming!"

"It can't hurt." Severance tried to sound more determined than he felt. "Goodbye, Eva. I'll be back whether you want me or not."

He set his hat on his head, opened the door, stepped out, and drew the door closed behind him. He drew a breath. He hadn't realized that his heart was hammering. He clenched his fists at his sides and drew another breath, trying to calm himself. He'd thought he was up to the task—of returning here, to see her, Eva, again, and...

"Uncle Matt!"

Of seeing Cheyenne again.

Maybe it was really her and not so much the hidden loot he'd been running from.

She was running and skipping girlishly up from the corral where the two graybeards had gone back to work on another part of the rotting corral. God, how beautiful she was. No wonder she turned heads in town. Hell, she was even turning his head and he was...

What?

Was he really her father? There was a chance he wasn't. Maybe he should just let it be. Let her belong to Roy. Such a hard thing to do, though, when he knew deep down in his bones...to the marrow inside his bones...that she was his own flesh and blood. Not a niece but a daughter.

"Uncle Matt!" she called again as she approached. "Are you going to stay?"

She ran up to him and as he stood by the hitchrack she took his hands in hers, smiling up at him with those beguiling brown eyes that were the very same shade of brown as his, her hair the very same shade of brown as his, as well. She was his, all right. He, hers.

"I'm staying," he said, not so sure anymore. Could he handle all this?

The loot?

Ethel Beech?

Eva and Cheyenne?

Mostly, could he handle the fact he was Cheyenne's father and wanted so very much for her to know yet knowing that he could never tell her because it might alienate her forever. She might see him in an entirely different light. Not as a beloved uncle. But as a man who'd betrayed father. She'd loved Roy. He might not have been much of a father to her. Still, Cheyenne had been devoted to him.

"I'm staying at Half-Moon. At least for a while."

"Good!" She hugged him again. He could feel her lips spread a delighted smile against his chest. "I'm sooo glad!" Suddenly she frowned up at him. "What's with Ma? I'd think she'd be so happy to see you." The light of understanding suddenly shone in her gaze. "It's the money Pa stole, isn't it?"

"You know about that?"

"Of course. I haven't been squirreled away in the cellar, you know?" She gave an impish smile. "Though Ma would love to do nothing more. She won't let me go to town, you know. At least, not very often. The boys...even the men stare at me." She gave a flounce and a toss of her hair, suddenly the unabashed coquette. "Imagine that—little old country girl *me*!"

Matt chuckled uneasily. "Imagine that." He kissed her forehead then removed his reins from the rack. "See you later, little ol' you. I best get to the Half-Moon before dark, see if there's anyone I need to run out of the cabin."

"I've been over there a few times since you've been gone," Cheyenne said, as Matt toed a stirrup and swung up into the saddle. "Actually, many times...since I started riding Queenie, keepin' the stable green run out of her. I help with roundup and branding, though I can't say I like either very much. Yes, I've ridden over to the Half-Moon quite a few times, hoping to see that you've returned. Uncle Matt—you have no idea how much I've longed for you to return!" She frowned again, suddenly. "Ma, she changed after Pa...you know. It's like a light went out of her. I feel so alone!"

She lunged forward and pressed her cheek against his leg.

She looked up at him with beseeching eyes. "Please, don't ever leave us again. I don't care about that money. I don't care if you came back for it. Get it, but just don't leave us again. Ma—she'll come around!"

Severance placed his hand on her cheek. He liked how warm and supple her flesh felt against his. God, how he wished he could tell her he was her father, but he never could. At least, not without risk of losing her.

"I'll be at the Half-Moon, honey," he said. "Come around any time."

She stepped away, smiling up at him. "I'll hold you to that!"

He pinched his hat brim to her then reined the black around and galloped over toward the mouth of the trail that climbed the southern saddle. A few minutes later he gained the top of the saddle then stopped the black to let it blow. It had been a steep climb and before that a hard ride over rough terrain from town. He'd taken his time and explored the old home country a little, his and Roy's old haunts. Now he was roughly a mile from the Half-Moon that sat in a canyon just beyond the next ridge.

The black drew deep of the cooling afternoon air. Suddenly, it held its breath, lifted its head a little, pricking its ears, and whickered. It lifted its head higher, working its nostrils.

Severance leaned forward and patted the mount's left, sweat-lathered wither. "What is it, boy?"

Something had startled the black. It had winded something. Or someone.

Severance just then realized he'd been feeling it, too, since leaving the Elk Horn Creek yard—the sensation that he was being watched, followed. It was the first time he'd felt it since leaving town. When he'd left Del Norte, he'd kept a close watch on his back trail, knowing there could be...probably *would* be...more fools like Fisk, Willeford, and Saturday on his tail, hoping he'd either lead them to Roy's loot or that they'd run him down and torture the loot's location out of him.

He'd known that when he'd ridden into Del Norte with the three dead men, of course. But he wanted to show the world—or at least south-central Colorado Territory—that he had nothing to hide. He wasn't going to go sneaking around, making himself appear even more suspicious. He'd killed those men in self-defense, and he'd hauled them into town and reported the incident to Bloody Joe, all legal-like.

He didn't care that soon everyone within a hundred square miles would know he was back. They'd find out sooner or later. He wanted to be out in the open about his return, and he wanted to make no bones about *why* he'd returned. He'd come back to prove up on the Half-Moon again, to reclaim his home place, and to help his sister-in-law and dau—no, his niece.

He couldn't think of Cheyenne as his daughter. That would drive him mad. She was his niece. He regretted now that he'd had the conversation he'd had with Eva. He shouldn't have mentioned anything about Cheyenne belonging to him. That might have widened the wedge between him and the girl's mother.

He'd made a mistake.

He had to forget about it and move on.

That's what you did in life, he'd learned. You moved on. The longer you lived, the more you moved on.

The black had turned its head to stare up the slope to the west, beyond the saddle. That must be where whoever was following him was. If there was, indeed, someone, and he and the black weren't having a case of the fantods. Maybe the gelding had sensed his own unease after riding west out of Del Norte and was becoming as nervy and suspicious as he himself was.

He saw no movement on the slope to his left which rose toward the crest of the ridge touched with the salmons and pinks of the growing dusk. Crows cawed up that way, halfway between him and the ridge crest. Severance could see three or four of them winging up out of the forest and then out across and over the narrow canyon to the south, where Elk Horn Creek cut through the ridge and then curved along the canyon and out into the broader valley to the west.

The cawing of the crows was the only sound beyond the faint soughing of the cooling breeze and the rustling sounds it made in the pine and fir crowns, the soft thuds of falling pinecones.

Had someone flushed the crows?

His unease growing, Severance nudged the black on across the saddle and then down the steep slope, taking the old, switchbacking horse trail that connected the Elk Horn Creek headquarters with that of the Half-Moon. A half hour later he crested yet another, lower saddle and gazed down at the Half-Moon cradled in a bowl-like canyon hemmed in on three sides by steep mountain ridges. The wooden blades of the windmill turned lazily, making an unoiled screeching sound that Severance could hear from even a hundred feet above. A sad-looking place. As sad or sadder than that of Eva's place.

The shutters were closed over the cabin's front windows—those shutters that remained, that was. The front door stood one-quarter open, nudged back and forth slightly by the breeze. Shadows filled the hollow in which the yard sat, darkening the stable, corral, small bunkhouse, privy, woodshed, and blacksmith shop flanking the long, low log cabin. The corral gate was open wide, left open by the place's last tenants, likely drifting highwaymen—probably rustlers preying on the herds of the wealthier ranchers in the area, like Ethel Beech.

The creek that ran along the base of the opposite ridge, straight across the hollow from Severance, glinted with the pinks and ochres of the setting sun.

He gazed down at the cabin in which Big John Severance had raised his boys in the years after his wife died. If you could call it "raising." Matt had been told his father had been a better man before they'd had to plant Louise. Her death had soured Big John. No one had told Matt this, but he'd always sensed that Big John had blamed her death on him, Matt. It had been after Matt had been born that she'd died. It had been a problematic delivery, one from which she'd never fully recovered.

She'd died a few days before Matt's third birthday.

Severance nudged the black ahead.

As it started down the ridge, something whistled past Severance's left ear to slam loudly into a tree bole behind him.

The crack of the rifle sounded half a second later.

The black whinnied and pitched.

*"Oh, hell!"*

Severance managed to grab his 1873 Winchester carbine just before he went rolling off the black's left hip to strike the ground with bone-crushing savagery.

## CHAPTER 6

EARLIER, JUST AFTER MATT SEVERANCE HAD LEFT Bloody Joe's office and the rataplan of the man's horse had been drowned by the wagon and horseback traffic, Mannion heard men conversing loudly out on the street.

Again, he cursed. He knew what all the ruckus was about. You bet he did.

What else?

He heaved his weary body up out of his chair and walked to the window. Several men, likely having spilled out of several nearby saloons, were standing at the mouth of a cross street on the other side of San Juan Avenue, staring north along San Juan, the direction in which young Severance had just galloped as though his black's tail was on fire.

More voices rose, slightly more muffled with distance, to Mannion's left. He cursed, moved to the door, and stepped out onto his stoop. He peered south along San Juan Avenue and cursed yet again when he saw more men standing outside a café, some having spilled out onto the street and staring in the same direction the others across the street from them were.

North, where Matt Severance's dust was still sifting to mingle with that of a large lumber dray drawn by six beefy, sweat-lathered mules, the bearded driver, Whitey Newcomb, standing in the driver's boot and popping a blacksnake over the team's backs to keep them moving amid the distractions all around them. As the mule team and dray drew up even with Hotel de Mannion, Whitey turned to Joe, half the man's craggy face with wide, bulbous nose shaded by the brim of his weather-hammered tan sombrero, and shouted, "Say, Joe, wasn't that Matt Severance that just rode past me like he had a whole war party of top-knot hungry Utes powderin' his back trail?" He hooked his gloved thumb over his left shoulder.

Mannion threw out a dismissive hand. "Oh, mind your own business, Whitey!"

Whitey's bearded lower jaw dropped as he and the mules and the dray trundled on past the jailhouse. "I'll be hanged if you ain't more colicky than you usually are, an' that's *galldang colicky*!" The mule skinner gave a disgruntled chuff and turned his head forward and he and the mules and the dray drifted on up the street in the direction of Del Norte's two lumberyards.

As he did, five men from the far side of the street quickly mounted horses tied to two hitchracks out front of the Three-Legged Dog Saloon and the Red Rock Inn beside it while two more men mounted horses at the rack fronting the Continental Café. One of the two men fighting to get himself seated in his saddle while his cream Barb, as excited as its rider was, it seemed, trotted out into the street, shouted, "Hold on, Bill! Hold on, Nash—me an' Chic's gonna join you!"

As Carlton "C.B." Blanchard swung up onto the Barb's back, he and the cowpuncher Mannion recognized as Pinky Streiber galloped on past Mannion, heading north into the dust of the other five who were powdering Matt Severance's trail.

Mannion had stepped out to the end of the porch, and was yelling, "Hold on, dammit! You men stand down! Dammit, you listen—those are *orders*!"

He might as well have been yelling at a solid stone ridge wall.

All seven were seeing dollar signs in their eyes and even if they hadn't been so excited and single-minded, they wouldn't have been able to hear Mannion because a second lumber dray, this one driven by Whitey's partner, Lyle Black, passed in front of the yelling lawman. All Mannion could do now was stare after the fast disappearing seven, curse, and ram his clenched right fist into the palm of his left hand.

He'd expected trouble the moment he'd laid eyes on Severance, but he hadn't expected it to come this quickly!

"Say, Joe," came another voice. "Was that not Matt Severance I just seen—"

Mannion's senior-most deputy cut himself off abruptly. Walking toward the jailhouse beside Mannion's junior-most deputy, the tall, slender young Henry McCallister who had outgrown the somewhat derogatory nickname of "Stringbean," Rio Waite had seen the woolly eyeball his boss had swung his way. As he and Henry stopped at the bottom of the porch steps, Rio glanced at the taller, slenderer, younger deputy, and said, "Yep, yep, somethin' does indeed tell me that was who we thought it was, Hank."

For some reason known only to Rio, he'd recently taken to calling the younger deputy Hank. That nickname, Henry didn't seem to mind, knowing it was meant to be somehow endearing. It was Rio's way to act endearing when he felt endearing. He was a man true to his feelings in that way, though he was also a still right capable deputy, so Bloody Joe didn't mind. Rio also loved cats and his fat black-and-white mouser, who came trimmed with a natural black bowtie, kept the basement cellblock scoured of rats and mice, though he often hauled his trophies upstairs to show them off to the paid employees in the main office. Sometimes they were only half dead and still screeching, and he'd paw them around and play with them at his leisure, which made Buster give proud curls to his tail.

Mannion glanced at the three horses whom Severance had tied to the hitchrack fronting the jailhouse and was about to have young McCallister lead them off to the livery barn, but just then he saw the local odd-job boy, Harmon Haufenthistle, step out of Dunham's Tonsorial Parlor directly across the street, a dog-eared wish book in his hands. Harmon was a twelve-year-old towhead, deeply tanned, who did more work in a day than most full-grown men around Del Norte.

Mannion stuck two fingers between his lips and whistled.

Harmon had just stepped off the boardwalk fronting the barber shop. Now he swung his head toward Mannion, who beckoned him over. Young Harmon grimaced. The twelve-year-old was a workhorse, and he wanted everyone to know it. There wasn't a job he ever accepted without complaint. It was his way of nudging up his fees.

When he'd worked his way across the dusty street without getting trampled, he stepped up to the bottom of the porch steps, nudged his leather-billed immigrant hat up on his forehead, powdery white above the deep, nut-brown tan below it, and said, "What is it, Bloody Joe?

I'm supposed to get Mister Dunham's orders over to the Post Office muy pronto, before the midday train arrives."

"I have a more important job for you, son."

Mannion flipped the kid a silver dollar, which glinted in the sunshine just before young Harmon expertly snapped it out of the air with a hand clad in a fingerless leather glove. He peered down at it, unimpressed, then looked blandly up at Mannion, who knew that young Haufenthistle mostly worked for nickels and dimes.

"I want you to take these three horses over to the livery barn. Have Dave Scallion fetch the undertaker for the three men they're carrying, but before you do that, have him saddle ol' Red for me. Lead him back over here muy pronto. I got business with the old fella."

"I seen Matt Severance ride into town with that fresh beef," Harmon said, hooking a thumb over his shoulder to indicate the three blanket-wrapped cadavers. "You goin' after him, Bloody Joe?"

Young Harmon was not only Del Norte's workhorse, but he was also its primary spreader of gossip. There were very little doings in town that Harmon didn't know about, and he usually knew about it first.

"What do you think?" Mannion said. "Hurry up, Harmon. Have Red back in ten minutes and there'll be another buck in it for you."

Harmon rolled his eyes and shoved the wish book at McCallister. "Hold on to these for me—will you, Henry?" He gave a ragged sigh then began untying the dead men's three mounts from the hitchrail. "It's always 'Hurry here, Harmon!' 'Hurry there, Harmon!' 'An' when you got that done, oh, Missus Owens needs some fresh goat milk for the little urchin she just dropped last week!'"

Again, he rolled his eyes. As he led the three horses carrying their stiff cargoes south along San Juan Avenue, he kicked a horse apple, and said, "There ain't enough hours in the day for some fellas, I tell you..."

Looking after the boy, Rio said, "Don't you think that might be an older man's job, Joe? Cartin' off dead men."

"Hell," Mannion said. "In some ways, young Harmon's older than all three of us put together."

The other two chuckled at that.

"You want I should ride with you, Marshal?" Henry McCallister asked Mannion. "That's quite the posse that went after Severance."

"No, I want you both to stay here and *discourage* anyone else that decides to ride out after that loot."

"You think that's what he's back for, Joe?" Rio asked.

"I don't know what he came back for, exactly. Not sure he does. But everyone else who knows about him and his brother is going to believe he's back for the missing payroll loot."

Mannion swung around to head back into the jail office. He'd just unlocked the chain that ran through the cocking levers of the three rifles in the wall-mounted gun rack when Rio Waite stepped into the office behind him and rested his double-bore twelve-gauge on his shoulder.

"What if he is back for the loot, Joe?"

Mannion removed his prized Winchester Yellowboy repeating rifle, ran an appreciative hand over the barrel and brass receiver then locked the padlock securing the chain to the rack.

He swung around to face his middle-aged deputy clad in dungarees, a gray wool shirt, neckerchief, worn brown leather vest to which his star was pinned, and funnel-brimmed Stetson even more worn than his vest. Rio's walnut-butted Colt .44 hung low off his stout right hip, and his sagging paunch caused both the belt holding up his pants and the one attached to his shell belt to bend forward until they faced the floor. Rio had warm eyes and a fleshy, craggy, patch-bearded face—the face of a man, a former cowpuncher and ranch foreman, who'd run the river and climbed the mountain more times than he could count on both hands.

He'd talked of retirement a time or two, but Mannion had talked him out of it mainly because he knew Rio himself wasn't ready. What in hell would he do without rounds to make with that double-bore gut-shredder of his? Sit around some boardinghouse playing cribbage with a couple of other old farts, listening to the clock tick away the last of his days?

After the life he'd lived, Mannion couldn't see him doing that. Didn't *want* to see him doing it.

Mannion pondered the question of Matt Severance's return, frowning, then found himself saying, "You know, Rio—I don't think he is back for the loot."

As he walked over to his desk, removed a box of .44 shells from the second drawer down on the right, above the one in which he kept a whiskey bottle for emergencies, Rio said, "You don't say."

Mannion thumbed .44 shells through the Yellowboy's loading gate. "I have no idea why I don't, but I don't. Just a sense I got. If he was back for the loot, I don't think he'd have rode to town with those three MacLean riders he shot. They braced him for the loot."

"Figured as much. Also figure they ain't gonna be the last."

"That's what I told him. Still, he's headed back to Half-Moon." Mannion levered a round into the rifle's action, off cocked the hammer and, holding the rifle barrel up atop his desk, turned to Rio. "I aim to see that he gets there. He's got a mission. I got a feelin' it's a worthy one. Not that it won't get him killed, but I'd kind of hate to see it."

"Yeah, I know what you mean, boss," Rio said, opening and closing his gloved right hand around the neck of the shotgun resting on his thick, age-slumped shoulder. "I would, too." His voice owned the same pitch of wonder as Mannion's had.

Joe grabbed a grub sack off a shelf, a black jacket off a wall peg, and headed for the door. Through the window over his desk, he'd spied Harmon Haufenthistle leading Joe's saddled bay stallion, Red, up to the jailhouse. As Rio stepped back, yielding the doorway, Mannion said, "Keep the lid on things while I'm gone, and try to keep anymore treasure hunters from riding into the San Juans."

He crossed the porch and started down the steps, tossing another dollar to young Harmon, who once again snatched it expertly out of the air. He looked down at it as though he'd just been thrown a horse apple. The shaver would make a mighty formidable gambler one day.

"You got it, Joe," Rio said behind Mannion. "Don't worry about nothin'. We'll keep the crabs in the bucket, Hank an' me."

## CHAPTER 7

RIO WAITE STOOD ATOP THE PORCH STEPS, WATCHING his boss, Bloody Joe Mannion, put the steel to his prized bay stallion, Red, and gallop northward along San Juan Avenue. Mannion's senior deputy had a dreadful feeling deep in his guts. Like a knot tied in wet rawhide and set out in the sun to dry...and tighten...and tighten.

Nothing made men more unmanageable than the craving for lost treasure.

Not women, horses, poker, or land.

Treasure.

So many had flooded the San Juans around Thunder Mountain looking for that forty grand in payroll loot and had come up dry. Things had settled down in the months after Joe had killed Roy and that second, mysterious rider had gotten away. Treasure hunters had turned over every rock in that area of the San Juans, looked behind every tree, *inside every knot in every tree*, scoured every nook and cranny...and ridden out hang-jawed and empty-handed.

At least, as far as Rio knew.

Now seven more had ridden out on the heels of Matt

Severance himself, who most in the area believed had been that second rider who'd gotten away.

Who else could it have been?

Roy and Matt had been close. They'd rustled cattle and held up stagecoaches together. Always just them, the two brothers, riding side by side. Everybody knew that the wild-assed Roy had turned his younger, adoring brother bad.

No, that second rider had to be Matt.

On the other hand, Bloody Joe had a good sense about things.

When he thought things through and came up with an opinion, that opinion was usually right. Maybe Matt hadn't been that mysterious second rider, after all.

But if not him, *who*?

Rio winced and shook his head as he continued staring off to the north, where Joe and Red had disappeared, heading north before swinging westward onto the trail that would lead him into the first shelving cliffs, dikes, and mesas of the first front of the San Juans. A big, mysterious range. After he and that second rider had forked trails, Roy had led Joe and Rio on one hell of a wild ride, trying to shake them from his trail. There was a broad area in which he could have squirreled away that loot.

Both Rio and Joe thought he'd had those overstuffed saddlebags on his horse when they'd run him to ground in that devil's playground country at the base of Thunder Mountain. But they'd never gotten a good look at the man or the horse, and he'd been riding fast, nearly killing his mount. They might have been wrong.

That loot could be anywhere.

*Forty thousand dollars...*

Rio chuckled dryly to himself.

Hell, the notion of all that cash even made *him* swoon. What a fella like himself, poor most of his life, could do with that kind of loot. Hell, he could pull his picket pin and head for San Francisco, live high on the hog in his last years. Hell, he could...

*No, no, you damn fool*, he chastised himself silently. *Don't you get started, you old devil. You got a job to do.*

He turned to close and lock the office door and get started on another set of rounds with the intention of discouraging anymore would-be treasure hunters, but just as he grabbed the steel knob, he heard a muffled meowing.

He left the door standing wide and strode back into the office, his spurs chinging, and grabbed the key to the cellblock door off the nail in a stout ceiling support post. Again, came a muffled meow as he twisted the key in the lock. When he drew open the stout wooden door, which had a small, barred window in its upper half, there sat the jailhouse mouser, Buster, sitting atop the stairs of the basement cellblock, gazing up at Rio and curling his tail impatiently.

In his thick, black-and-white fur coat complete with black bowtie, Buster always appeared like nothing so much as a fancy-dan decked out for a ball with all the pomp and circumstance, but with no such ball to attend. Not out here in the dusty, tall-and-uncut wilds of Del Norte, at least. So, he hunted mice in Hotel de Mannion's basement cellblock instead.

"*Meowww*," said Buster again, casting his copper gaze up at his sixty-three-year- old master, who'd rescued him from a back alley when he'd been just a wisp of a little orphan hiding from two hunting coyotes in a pile of brush and discarded lumber one early morning behind the jailhouse.

A dead mouse, bloody and mangled, lay before him.

A trophy on display.

Buster's payment for a bowl of cream.

Rio chuckled then stooped to pluck the mouse up by its tail.

"You done good, my boy. Real good. Come on in, an' ol' Rio will fix you right up!"

"Meow!"

Buster slinked into the main office, folding his body, tail raised, against Rio's stovepipe boots, giving the dangling mule ears a playful nibble.

Rio tossed the mouse in the trash then closed and locked the cellblock door. He had two prisoners down there, a pair of drunks that young Hank had brought in overnight. They were dead asleep. He'd fine and release them later—a pair of German miners from the Cloud Tickler up in the San Juans. They'd gotten into a scrap over a Chinese doxie in Ma Sherman's place down by Pine Creek, the low-rent end of Del Norte. They likely wouldn't be able to pay the fine—they'd likely had their pockets emptied by Ma Sherman herself—so Rio would just read to them from the Book, so to speak, and ban them from town for two weeks.

That's usually how Bloody Joe played it. Joe had been town taming and lawdogging for most of the past twenty-five years, after a stint in the frontier army fighting Apaches, and he knew you couldn't sit around and wait for a circuit-riding judge to come around and settle petty offenses. He usually only summoned the judge for murder. Under most circumstances—and sometimes even for murder—Bloody Joe had no problem playing judge, jury, and, if need be, executioner.

Thus, his nickname: Bloody Joe.

"Brought in a fresh batch of cream just this mornin',

Buster," Rio said, prying up a floorboard with a pocketknife.

He kept Buster's cream in a small, corked, stone bottle under the floorboard and in a cool, little hole. When he'd poured out a pie pan of fresh cream, and Buster had hunkered over it, lapping to his purring satisfaction, Rio grabbed his double-bore barn blaster, went out, closed and locked the office door, crossed San Juan Avenue, and headed south along the opposite side of the street, keeping his eyes and ears skinned for trouble.

It didn't take him long to find it.

First, hearing a scuffle in the Black Cat Saloon, he went in and broke up a fight between two half-dressed doxies who'd apparently been drinking all night and well into the morning. One accused the other of slipping into her room and pilfering her "kitty," which was the cache where the *doves du pave* stowed away their earnings. The girls were going at it pretty good, trying to claw each other's eyes out while half a dozen men stood around, enjoying the show.

Rio knew both girls. He knew most of the working girls in town and had a pretty good rapport with them all, being sort of an uncle figure, so it didn't take him long to settle them down and shepherd them off, having buried the hatchet, holding hands and sobbing, to their separate rooms.

Next, he intervened at Wilfred Drake's Mercantile when he came upon two small-time ranchers, brothers from Texas, pushing around a Norwegian Honyocker from Kansas, who was proving up on his homestead claim on land the ranchers considered their own. Rio called in his double-bore to settle the matter, which it was right effective at doing. He waited while the two rancher brothers finished loading parched corn into their wagon, cursing the deputy under their breaths, and rattled on out of town before Rio depressed his double-bore's hammers, pinched his hat brim to the flushed and indignant squarehead, whose name was Andersson, and continued his stroll.

He was just approaching the north front corner of Miss Jane's San Juan Hotel & Saloon when he saw a man standing with his back pressed against that corner of the building, arms crossed on his chest, the sole of one boot pressed up flat against the front wall of the building, as well. His hat pulled down over his eyes, he appeared to be asleep on his feet, but as Rio approached, the man thumbed his hat up onto his forehead, gave Rio a dubious look, then sort of rolled around the corner of the San Juan and disappeared into the break between it and the Won Ton Café, which had an opium den out back, on the other side of a dry wash.

Just before the man had slipped into the narrow gap, Rio had glimpsed and recognized his face. Ed Colvin. A known cardsharp, though he dressed like a thirty-a-month-and-found cowpuncher. He and his partner, Bob Sugar, could fleece an entire saloon before any of the *fleecies*, usually drunk by midnight, which was when Colvin and Sugar customarily went to work, realized their pockets were turned inside out.

Rio had banned both degenerates from town for a month two weeks ago.

"Hey!" Rio said, increasing his bandy-legged pace, the mule ears of his stovepipe boots jostling wildly. "I say, hey there, Colvin! I seen you! *Stop!*"

Rio himself stopped at the mouth of the fifteen-foot, trash-strewn, sage-stippled gap between the buildings. He'd just glimpsed Colvin disappear around the San Juan's rear corner.

"Dang it, Colvin, I seen you! Don't think I didn't!" Rio strode angrily down the break between the buildings, holding the double-bore up high across his lumpy chest. As he stepped around the San Juan's rear corner, hot on Colvin's heels, he said, "I told both you two that you was—"

He cut himself off abruptly, realizing his mistake.

For just then he heard a man chuckle behind him and turned his head just in time to see Colvin's seedy partner, Bob Sugar, step out from behind a pile of moldering lumber leftover from when Miss Ford had renovated the San Juan. Sugar rushed toward Rio, raising a six-gun, butt-forward, and gritting his teeth in anticipatory delight. At the same time, in the corner of his left eye, Rio saw Ed Colvin step out from the San Juan's rear wall, also grinning like the cat that ate the canary.

They had Rio in whipsaw.

A damn trap he'd walked right into.

While Sugar slammed the butt of his .44 down against the back of Rio's head, Colvin jerked the double-bore out of the deputy's hand and flung it away. The smashing blow to Rio's head buckled his knees but Sugar caught him under both arms and held him while Colvin, grinning through gritted teeth, his dark eyes flashing with shrewd malevolence, smashed first his right fist into the deputy's bulging belly, then his left fist, then his right again before giving a loud grunt as he buried the left one even deeper than the others.

Sugar released Rio who dropped to his knees, trying to suck air into his battered lungs. Not managing it, he fell forward, striking the ground on his chest and belly. Colvin kicked Rio onto his back and crouched down over him to blow his whiskey breath into the deputy's face, as he said, "That there's for two weeks ago, old man. You come after us again, you're gonna get more than what you just got. Far more! Understand, you washed-up old mossyhorn?"

There was more than whiskey on the man's breath. There was the cloying, burnt pepper smell of opium. The two had likely been partaking of the midnight oil served in the dark, smoky den behind the Won Ton.

Then it was Sugar's turn to crouch down over Rio, who was breathing like a landed fish, hearing his breath rake loudly as he tried to get a complete one into his lungs, to bark into Rio's face: "Don't you know when it's time fer the rockin' chair, old man?"

He flung an arm out as he buried the toe of a boot in Rio's side.

Then Colvin and Sugar turned away and strode off around the far side of the San Juan, gone.

Leaving Rio to lie there, helpless, sucking air into his lungs and gritting his teeth against the crushing pain in his head that caused Fourth of July firecrackers to flash in his eyes. His ribs grieved him where Sugar had buried his boot.

When he finally got a couple of somewhat complete breaths into his lungs, he used them to yell, albeit hoarsely, "Rio...y-you...you...damn...old...*fool!*"

And smashed the ends of both his clenched fists into the ground beside him.

## CHAPTER 8

"Rio!" a familiar voice shouted. "Rio! Rio! You all right?"

Rio had rolled onto his belly and pushed up onto his hands and knees. He'd gotten that far, anyway. Now he turned his head to see Junior Deputy Henry "Hank" McCallister run toward him down the gap between the San Juan and the Won Ton Café, holding his Winchester repeater in one hand, clamping his tan slouch hat on his head with his other hand, a wing of his sandy-red hair sliding across his freckled forehead.

Rio could see several gawkers standing at the alley mouth behind the younger deputy, gawking at the older deputy down on his hands and knees, having had the stuffing stomped out of both ends of his flabby old self.

His foolish old self.

With emphasis on "flabby," "old," and "foolish."

"Oh, hell," Rio said, his face warming with humiliation, to add to his other string of sundry complaints—namely, the pounding in his head and the aching agony in his ribs. He'd finally gotten his wind back, at least. Or most of it. His lungs felt half as large as they had before he'd been pummeled in the guts.

"Rio—what in hell happened? Someone said you got jumped!"

"Oh, hell!" Rio said again as Hank leaned his rifle against the San Juan and crouched to help the older deputy to his feet.

Getting his feet set unsteadily beneath him, Rio leaned forward and drew air in and out of his lungs, still feeling a little dizzy and a whole lot creaky. His ribs ached like hell, and his head felt as though he'd had a rusty railroad spike driven into it.

"We'd best get you over to Docs Bohannon and Ellison," Hank said, keeping a gloved hand on the older deputy's left shoulder.

Rio shook his head. "I don't need a sawbones."

"You sure, Rio? You don't look so good."

"I haven't looked good in thirty years, kid. I don't *feel* too good to go with my lousy looks," Rio said, and spat grit from his lips. "But..."

"But what?" Hank said, frowning, deeply concerned. "What is it?"

Rio scowled up at the younger man. "How my creaky old carcass feels ain't nothin' compared to..." He let his voice trail off as he glanced again at the dozen or so gawkers gawking from the alley mouth.

"*What?*" Hank prodded. "Ain't nothing compared to *what*, Rio?"

"Dammit, Hank, ain't you ever been jumped before?"

"Why, sure. Sure, I have. More times than I care to remember," the younger deputy added with a dry laugh.

"Well, it's...it's just..."

"What?"

"It's *embarrassing*, kid!" Rio barked out at the younger

man. He glanced again at the gawkers then turned back to Hank and, lowering his voice, added, "It's damned embarrassing. Especially when you done as dunderheaded a fool thing as I done. I should've known Colvin an' Sugar was settin' a trap. I shoulda seen that right off. An' I would have...hell, I probably would have a few years *back*!"

Rio stumbled around and picked up his hat, reshaped it, and stuffed it down on his head.

"Colvin and Sugar?" Hank said.

"Two cardsharps I kicked out of town two weeks ago." Rio stooped to pick up his shotgun then ran his gloved hands over the beloved weapon, brushing off the sand and gravel. "I kicked 'em out of town two weeks ago for a *month*!"

"Oh, you did, did ya?" Hank said. "Well, you just let me go find them two an'—"

"No!" Rio set the double-bore on his right shoulder and turned to face the taller, younger man. "You stay out of it." He thumbed himself in the chest. "I'm gonna settle it. Me. They kicked the stuffin' out of me. I'll settle it!"

"All right, all right," Hank said. "Whatever you say, Rio."

"Now, get out of here. Leave me alone. I'm gonna go on into the San Juan an' have me a bracer."

"All right, Rio," Hank said, hiking a shoulder.

He was about to turn away and head back toward the alley mouth where the crowd was finally dispersing, thank God, when Rio grabbed his arm and turned him back around. "Not a word to Joe, all right?"

Hank studied the older man for a moment, then smiled and nodded. "You got it, Rio. Not a word to the marshal."

"Not a word to no one." Rio glanced at where the crowd was slouching away from the alley mouth. "Least-ways, no one who don't already know, anyway."

"You got it, Rio," Hank said.

Then he walked with the older deputy to the alley mouth where the two forked trails and Rio climbed the San Juan Hotel & Saloon's broad front steps and pushed through its two stout, wooden front doors. He stopped just inside the tony place and, holding his head high and suppressing the pain in his head, ribs, and gut, strode toward the mahogany bar and polished backbar mirror running along the wall on his left.

"My God, Rio—you're either hungover or had a mountain fall on you! Which is it?"

"Why, I thank you, Miss Jane," Rio said, removing his hat and taking a courtly bow. "I appreciate that. And here I was thinking I looked ready for a debutant's ball."

"Depends on which debutante," said the pretty redhead and Bloody Joe Mannion's wife two times in a row. Rio thought that if a man was going to marry the same woman twice, you could do far worse than having that woman be the former Miss Jane Ford.

Standing behind the bar, running a dry white towel around the inside of a dimpled beer schooner, clad in a fine, low-cut, lace-edged, robin's-egg blue silk gown, Miss Jane looked the aging deputy up and down, taking in the especially unkempt appearance of his humble attire, the sand and gravel still clinging to his shirt, vest, and dunga-rees, his five-pointed deputy's badge barely clinging to his vest. "I *am* hoping the other guy looks worse...?"

Rio set the shotgun on the bar and slapped his left hand down on the bar beside it. "Not a chance. I doubt they even wrinkled their clothes. They took me to the woodshed, Miss Jane, and it does grieve me to confess that shameful fact, though I doubt I'd confess it to anyone but you. Whiskey, please. A big, big beer to chase it into my aching belly with!"

"Coming right up."

Jane filled a schooner with a thick, tan ale, scraped the excess foam off the top with a flat stick, set it in front of Rio, one of only four men standing at the bar. The other three were businessmen. Two stood together at the bar's far end having a loud discussion over a recent vote by the Del Norte town council while the third stood ten feet to Rio's right, absorbed in *The Weekly Courant* while nibbling a breakfast sandwich and nursing a beer with a bright orange egg lolling at the bottom of the mug.

Jane filled a shot glass from a bottle she hauled down from a high shelf with the help of a stepping stool, expertly slid the glass across the bar until it just barely nudged the schooner.

"Ahh," Rio said, lifting the shot glass between sausage-sized thumb and index finger in salute. "Here's to ya, Miss Jane." He tossed back the entire shot, set the empty glass down, picked up the schooner, and took three hearty drafts before returning the mug to the bar, as well.

He sighed deeply.

"Nothing like a top-shelf shot of Who-Hit-John and a good ale after you've had your fat gut as well as your pride severely pummeled." Rio gave the woman an ironic wink.

Jane was still holding the bottle. She refilled the shot glass, eyeing the old deputy with concern in her deep, brown eyes. "On the house, Rio. Tell me what happened."

"You won't tell the marshal?"

"What Joe doesn't know won't hurt him." She winked.

"I made a blame fool out of myself."

"Haven't we all?"

"Oh, sure, but this is a thing I wouldn't have tumbled for oh, say, two or three years ago." Rio turned sideways to the bar and leaned his left elbow on the edge of it. He raised the heavy schooner to his lips, sipped, and set the schooner back down on the bar. He pressed his right index finger to his temple, and said, "I think I might be gettin' a little mushy in my thinker box. You see, a fella I got crossways with a couple weeks back led me into the gap between your place and the Won Ton. I followed him like a baby duck followin' its mother. I shoulda known it was a trap. An'...sure enough, it *was*!"

"How bad, Rio?"

"Oh, hell, I'll live." Rio glanced around to make sure no one was listening. Then he leaned a little closer to Jane, who turned her head to one side and leaned a little closer to Rio. "They took my shotgun away from me! They laughed. They left me lyin' in the damn alley, an' they laughed as they walked away."

Rio picked up the shot glass, tossed back half, and set the glass back down on the bar. He swallowed, winced against the burn of the liquor as well as his chagrin, and shook his head. "Hank saw me like that. Fumblin' to get up like some turtle some lousy kids turned over on its shell for a prank!"

"Did Henry go after 'em?"

"No. He doesn't know who they were."

"Who were they?"

"I'll never tell." Rio smiled coldly down at his beer. "I'll settle up with them two myself. I'll find 'em. They stick to the lower rent business establishments in Del Norte, to the Mescin and half-breed sides of town. They find easy marks in them kind of places. Oh, I'll find 'em, all right. And you wanna know what I'm gonna do...?"

Rio let his voice trail off. He'd been glowering down at his beer while he'd been talking, but now he turned to Jane to find her no longer where she'd been standing, right across the bar from him. In fact, she was nowhere in sight.

She'd disappeared as though into thin air.

"Miss Jane?" Rio said, looking around.

"Miss Jane!" said the businessman standing to Rio's right—Hans Butler, a clerk at one of the town's two banks, the Stockman's. He jerked his flushed face framed by shaggy gray muttonchops to Rio, and said, "She fell! She's behind the bar!"

As Butler start hurrying down the bar toward Rio, Rio said, "Miss Jane!" and ran to his left. He ran around behind the bar. Sure enough, Jane was on the floor. She lay on her back, her gown and hair in disarray, pale hands, fingers curled inward, flung out to each side of her head lying in the pillow of her copper read hair. She was frowning and moaning and moving her head from side to side.

"Miss Jane!" Rio said again, his old heart hammering as he dropped to a knee beside the woman and placed his thick hand on her narrow right shoulder. "Miss Jane, what happened? You must've fainted!" He glanced up at the clerk crouching beside him, and said, "Fetch one o' the sawbones from Bohannon's office!"

"Ohh, Miss Jane, Miss Jane!" Rio cooed, looking down the bar for another apron. Seeing none, he heaved himself to his feet and looked around the saloon. He saw none of Jane's usual bouncers, either. All the other customers in the room were either peering at him and Jane from the other side of the bar or had gathered in a clump behind him, a hushed roar of concern rising in the room.

"I need to get her upstairs!" Rio said.

He wasn't quite sure how he'd manage it in his condition, but he'd manage it, by God. He crouched beside Jane again, snaked his left hand beneath her neck and slid his right arm between her lower back and the floor. Grimacing against the throbbing in his head and the creaky weakness in his knees, Rio rose with a grunt, lifting Jane up off the floor as he did.

He swung around, and yelled, "Make way! Make way, gents. Comin' through with the lady of the house!"

The handful of other customers scrambled out of the way as Rio hurried down the bar then around the end of it and hurried through the main drinking hall toward the stairs running up the room's rear wall, near a potted plant, a baby grand piano, and a large oil painting of a nearly naked black woman lying in a meadow of deep green grass, a white horse lowering its head to sniff her hair. Rio was breathless when he reached the bottom of the stairs, but he shook his head against his weakness, cursed his age and the way he'd let his old body go to lard, drew a deep breath, and marched up the stairs with Jane moaning softly in his arms.

As he clomped up the stairs, spurs jangling, grunts issuing from deep in his throat, he glanced down at Jane. How pale she looked. He'd noticed it as soon as he'd seen her standing behind the bar, but he'd been so absorbed in his own complaints he'd failed to mention it or even to reflect on it in anything but a vague way.

Now here she was, limp in his arms...

He heard several men climbing the stairs behind him. One hurried past Rio. It was her manager, Howard Dean, who pulled a ring of keys out of his pants pocket.

"Jane's door will be locked—I'll open it!"

Dean must have been in his office and came out when he heard the commotion and saw Rio carrying his boss up the stairs. He glanced over his shoulder then turned his head forward and wagged it, clucking his dismay. "I've been worried about this very thing. She's been so frail and weak. She hardly ever eats anything!"

Gaining the second-floor landing, Dean turned right to half run, half walk along the second-floor hall, sorting through the keys on his ring. When Dean unlocked the door to Jane's suite, Rio carried the woman into her bedroom. Dean pulled back the covers, and Rio eased her onto the bed. He gazed down at her, his old ticker beating frantically both from the climb up the stairs and anxiousness.

She was no longer making any sounds. Earlier, it appeared she'd been trying to open her eyes, but she was no longer moving. Her head was turned slightly to one side, lips slightly apart, red hair screening her face.

"Miss Jane?" Rio said, giving her shoulder a slight shake. "Miss Jane?" he said again, louder.

He looked at Dean crouching to his left. The two men shared a haunted, terrified look.

Rio grabbed Jane's shoulders and gave her a hard shake, yelling, "*Miss Jane!*"

DEAN LINDQUIST OTT

## CHAPTER 9

SITTING ASTRIDE RED UNDER A SPRAWLING CEDAR ON A low, rocky dike six miles west of Del Norte, Mannion stared through his field glasses, adjusting the focus.

As he did, the seven men and seven horses milling on the next dike beyond him, roughly seventy yards away, came into focus within the single sphere of magnified vision. All had dismounted and loosened their horses' saddle cinches to rest the mounts, which they'd pushed hard trying to keep up with Matt Severance. Severance was on a better horse, however, one he'd likely broken himself—he'd always been known as a horse man, even while growing up out here in the San Juans—and he'd outdistanced them.

But one of the seven had been a tracker for the army back when the Utes were still running off their leashes in this neck of the frontier, so they'd managed to stay on his trail. That man was Bill Wade, the oldest of the seven. Old enough to know better.

The other six, younger men rode for two or three other ranches in the area.

And now as they stood smoking and conversing and

occasionally casting their hopeful gazes to the west, where the blue-green slopes and stony peaks of the San Juans jutted against a clear, blue western sky, they had dollar signs in their eyes. Mannion knew most of them. He'd had most as guest in Hotel de Mannion a time or two. Yeah, he knew most of them—raggedy-heeled punchers who, barring finding that lost mine payroll, would likely spend most of their lives doing just what they were doing now.

Riding for thirty-a-month-and-found until they could no longer climb into their saddles. After that, God help them.

Mannion cursed and returned the glasses to their baize-lined case. He reached back to return the case to a saddlebag pouch then drew the big Russian .44 revolver holstered for the cross-draw on his left hip. He ratcheted back the hammer as he raised the long-barreled, silver-chased hogleg high above his head and sent a round singing skyward.

All seven drovers swiveled their heads around quickly at the Russian's echoing report. To a man, they closed their hands around holstered six-shooters.

"Keep 'em pouched!" Mannion yelled, and holstered his own, smoking revolver. "I'm coming over!"

He clucked Red down off the dike, across the flat, sage-stippled gap where a few gnarled cedars and junipers grew, and then up the dike upon which the seven other riders stood, watching him with sour expressions beneath the brims of their weathered Stetsons. All seven kept their guns holstered. All seven kept a glove hand over the grips of those holstered guns while they grabbed the reins of their ground-reined horses to hold the mounts in place, as they'd started at the roar of Mannion's six-shooter. The men's eyes were hard, flat and, sneering.

Mannion drew rein atop the dike.

One of the seven horses sidled off to the left of the tightly grouped seven riders and gave a nervous whinny. Then one of the others did. Red answered with a whicker and shook his head.

Mannion eyed the men each in turn, his own hard, uncompromising features a mask of bitter disgust. He could tell from their glassy eyes they'd been drinking all night. They were brimming with bottle bravery, general nastiness, and greed.

A bad combination.

"What're you dunderheads doing out here? You really think that if Severance knows where that loot is buried, he's going to ride right to it? You think he doesn't know you're on his back trail?" He picked out Bill Wade— short, potbellied, stoop-shouldered, his thick, black beard liberally laced with gray. "Is that what *you* think, Bill?"

Wade kept his eyes on the ground. He was the only one of the seven who looked sheepish. He toed a rock with the tip of his boot and removed his hand from his holstered Schofield.

"You go to hell, Mannion!" barked Nash Mullen, who rode for the Circle P not far from here. He was a tall, lanky man in his early thirties, his face badly pitted from teenage acne. He'd ridden for most of the outfits in the area at one time or another after his sixteenth birthday. He never lasted on any of them for long. "You ain't got no business out here! An' you sure as hell got no business pokin' your nose into ours!"

"Besides, Mannion," added Pinky Streiber, sitting his black beside Mullen's steeldust, encouraged by Mullen's bravery, it seemed, "you're outgunned seven to one. We ain't in Del Norte and you don't got one of your deputies to back your play!"

"We could shoot you right off your damn horse, an' no one would ever know where your bones were picked and strewn!" added yet another one of the seven—Carlton "C.B." Blanchard, another yellow dog clad in drover's attire including a blue neckerchief with white polka dots, a black Stetson shoved far back on his head, and leggings so worn that his faded denims shone through in places. He was short and sandy-haired and scrappy—another one who'd ridden for most of the area's ranches, though he never stayed for long in one place.

Mannion had turned the key on him more times than he could remember. When drunk, Blanchard lost all sense of himself and could turn a saloon into little more than matchsticks in minutes if Mannion or one of his deputies didn't get to him first. Joe knew the contrary little man, pushing forty but still owning the air of a rebellious teenager, had wanted to kill him for years. He'd just lacked the courage to try. Out here, with the odds looking so good, Blanchard was considering it. The gloved hand closed over his .44's handle twitched eagerly, and a shrewd, anxious flush had moved up into the man's long, narrow, coyote face.

Joe grinned coldly. "Pull it, Blanchard. Go ahead!"

Blanchard glared at him. The flush in his cadaverous cheeks grew. The others slid their gazes to him and then back to Mannion sitting his bay stallion ten feet from where the others stood, holding their horses and regarding him skeptically.

"Go ahead, C.B.," Mannion said, swinging down from Red's back. "You've been wanting to for years. Here's your chance." Joe walked toward the little, curly-headed man, throwing his arms out to both sides, making himself a clean target. "Didn't you hear Pinky? I'm outgunned seven to one!"

"We got him, boys!" Pinky screamed suddenly, standing to the far right of the seven-man pack.

A wild look on his face as he stretched his lips back from his teeth, Pinky jerked his six-gun out of its holster.

The barrel hadn't cleared leather before Mannion's own cross-draw Russian was in his hand and spitting smoke and flames.

Pinky screamed and dropped his gun, which bounced off the toe of his right boot.

He stumbled back, clutching his bullet-torn arm and glaring at Mannion. As he did, Blanchard saw his own opportunity. He jerked his own .44 out of its pouch. Mannion swung his still-smoking .44 against the side of the man's head. Blanchard fired, the bullet whistling wide as he stumbled sideways. Mannion smashed his big Russian against the man's head once more.

Bones yelped and dropped.

"Mannion, you crazy son of a bitch!" he howled, clutching his left temple with both hands.

"He shot me!" Pinky screamed, down on both knees and staring at the blood oozing from his right arm, just above the elbow.

He lifted his spade-shaped chin to glare, red-faced, at Mannion who stood before the group, feet spread a little more than shoulder-width apart, in open challenge. The five, still-standing men had stepped back and spread out a little, regarding Mannion and the two men he'd taken to the woodshed in quiet exasperation.

Joe held the Russian in his right hand, half out from his right side. His wolfish gray eyes were hard and commanding beneath the brim of his high-crowned, broad brimmed black Stetson while the breeze chewed at the end of his red, neck-knotted bandanna.

"Anyone else?" He paused a few moments, waiting. His gaze burrowed into a tall, mustached man standing at the rear of the pack wearing a long, cream duster. "What about you, Turnbuckle? You look like you got an itchy trigger finger."

Max Turnbuckle, who'd ramrodded the Forty Aces outfit in the Sawatch Range before the ranch had been bought out by English investors, glared darkly at the lawman, then removed his hand from the bone grips of the Colt Peacemaker low-slung off his right hip. He thrust his right arm and accusing right finger out toward the lawman, staring down at it as though aiming down a rifle barrel. "You're plum crazy, Mannion. I always heard it but now I see it right here today!"

Rage burned inside Mannion.

He marched forward, toward Turnbuckle. As he drew within three feet of the man, Turnbuckle's eyes snapped wide. He opened his mouth to protest but not before Mannion buried his stout Russian barrel-first in the man's solar plexus.

Turnbuckle jackknifed, gave a great "WHOOSH" of displaced air, and dropped to his knees. In the corner of his left eye, Joe spied a man reaching toward his hip. It was the lowly puncher from Missouri, Nash Kingman. Mannion wheeled, clicking his Russian's hammer back once more.

Kingman had his old-model Remington out of its holster.

He froze with the hogleg's barrel about six inches above the leather he'd jerked it from. He looked from his own gun to Mannion's, cocked and aimed at Turnbuckle's belly, the silver-chased revolver resembling nothing so much as a snake about to strike.

Mannion gave a shrewd grin.

"Ah...ah...," Turnbuckle stammered, looking down at his six-gun once more. "Ah, no...now, don't you...don't you shoot me, Mannion!" His gun hand shaking, he thrust the Remy back down into its holster and jerked his hand away from the handle as though from a hot potato. He took one stumbling step straight back, half turned his head to one side, stretched his thin lips back from stained, yellow teeth, and raised both hands palm out in supplication.

"Don't shoot," he begged, quietly and with some chagrin on his bearded face.

He closed his eyes.

Mannion glared at him, kept the Russian cocked and aimed at him.

The others stared back at the lawman, anxiously, as though they'd suddenly found themselves in the midst of an escaped circus lion. A hungry one. A man-eater. The only one making any noise was Pinky Streiber. Still down on his knees, the coyote-faced puncher said, "I'm hurt, boys. I'm hurt real bad. Like to bleed dry. Someone fetch me back to town. I need to see a sawbones!"

Mannion said to the group in general, jerking his cocked Russian, "You heard the man. He needs a sawbones. Get him back to town and don't none of you ever come out here again."

The five standing men just stared back at him.

Then Max Turnbuckle said, "For chrissakes!" and heaved himself to his feet. He picked up his hat, set it on his head, then went stumbling toward one of the horses standing nearby, eyes wide with nerves, shifting their weight from one hoof to another, chewing their bits.

Turnbuckle climbed onto a stout bay, reined it around, and spurred it down off the dike and back in the direction of town, his duster winging out to each side in the wind of his passing. Drumming hooves faded to silence.

One of the other men helped Pinky to his feet and over to his horse. While Pinky was helped onto his zebra dun, the others turned away from Mannion and mounted their own horses. A minute later, Mannion stood alone atop the dike, watching the six riders gallop down off the dike and back in the direction of Del Norte.

He heaved a relieved sigh and holstered the Russian.

Still, concern weighed in him. The current storm might have passed, but more fools would ride out here, looking for Severance and the payroll loot. Joe turned to gaze west into the rugged foothills of the San Juans and chewed the ends of his mustache. Should he continue following Severance?

Judging by the route he was taking, south of the trail that would have led directly to the Half-Moon, he was heading for the Elk Horn Creek ranch of his sister-in-law and Eva Severance's daughter, Cheyenne, who was the spitting image of Matt's and Roy's mother, Louise. The spitting image of Matt himself, for that matter.

Mannion had wondered about that back when Matt and Roy had been making pests of themselves and sometimes more than pests, known stagecoach robbers and rustlers though Mannion had never been able to gather enough concrete evidence against them to arrest them. He'd wondered why Roy's daughter had turned out looking more like his younger brother than himself.

Now, Matt was heading for Elk Horn Creek.

Mannion pondered that.

Anyway, that he was heading for Elk Horn Creek was

reason enough to leave him alone now. Let him visit his family in private. After a few days, Mannion would ride back out and check on him.

"Yep," Joe said now, reaching for Red's reins and toeing a stirrup, "I'm needed back in town, Red. Getting late. I'd like to get back before..."

He let his voice trail off as the crack of a distant gun report sounded in the west, almost straight out from where he and Red stood atop the dike. He turned to gaze in that direction. Elk Horn Creek lay farther south. The Half-Moon was nearly straight west, cross-country from Mannion's current position.

He frowned, pondering on that lone rifle report that had echoed briefly but had fallen to silence now.

Concern and curiosity nettled him.

That concern grew when another rifle cracked distantly, straight off in the direction he was staring, toward where several hills and mesas and the first steep slopes and of the San Juans rose, misty with the deep blue greens of fir and pine forests touched with the salmons and pinks of the approaching dusk.

That shot was followed by another and then gunfire was fairly crackling like Fourth of July fireworks. Those weren't the shots of game hunters.

Those were the shots of men shooting at men.

And they were coming from the direction of the Half-Moon.

Mannion toed the stirrup again, pulled himself up into the leather, reined Red away from the direction of town, and booted him down off the dike, heading straight west into the heart of the battle he had a feeling was only the start of all-out war.

## CHAPTER 10

SEVERANCE ROLLED TO HIS LEFT, HARDENING HIS JAWS in fury as he levered a live cartridge into his Winchester's breech.

Another bullet plowed into a sage shrub inches to his right, sending a stem of the shrub flying. As Matt rolled up behind a rock roughly the size of a grave marker, yet another bullet caromed in to hammer the backside of the rock. The bullet's shrill spang was followed closely by the thunder of the rifle that had sent it. That report joined the echo of the first two, the echoes dwindling as they vaulted skyward.

Severance rolled onto his belly and, keeping his head low, edged a look around the rock's right side. He could see four men hunkered down along the base of the ridge, partly concealed by rocks and cedars. Beyond them, across the creek that curved around the front of the canyon in which the Half-Moon sat, he saw four horses tied in the cottonwoods lining the creek's other side.

Matt cursed.

He'd been so damn absorbed with scrutinizing the Half-Moon headquarters, the motley collection of old, log ranch buildings, that he'd let four riders steal up on him from his left flank, from out in the broad valley in which the Animas River curled down from its headwaters in the San Juan's higher reaches. He'd gotten careless when before he'd ridden back here to his old home country, he'd promised himself he wouldn't.

He knew he'd be a target.

"You damn fool," he growled at himself, pulling his head back behind the rock just as one of the four men at the base of the slope took another shot at him. The bullet cut through the air where his face had just been to plow into the ground beside him, ripping a deep groove in the sage and short, blond grass.

As the crack of the rifle reached his ears, Matt said, "You should've stayed where you were if this is all the better you can do!"

With that, he quickly rose to his knees then leaped to his feet and ran hard to his right. As the rifles crackled at the base of the slope, sending bullets screeching around his head, he dropped down the mountain slope but slanted north and westward, followed the gentle curve of the declivity in the direction of his ambushers. Soon he was in heavy junipers peppered with a few fragrant cedars.

He stopped in the center of the mountain growth, on the backside of a large, moss-speckled, granite boulder. On both sides of the boulder, there was a slight gap between the rock and the evergreen shrubs. Down on one knee, Severance stared through the gap toward where the shoulder of the slope curved to the west. If the shooters came for him, that's likely where they'd come from.

If they came for him—he knew they would—he'd make them wish they hadn't.

He chewed his bottom lip and caressed his Winchester's hammer with his thumb, waiting.

The only sounds were the wind sloughing down the valley from the higher peaks, rattling the leaves of the cottonwoods on the other side of the stream, and the caws of distant crows likely spooked by the gunfire. The air was cooling, and the evening shadows, limned with the golds of the fast-approaching dusk, grew long.

Footsteps sounded from nearly straight out away from Severance.

He heard strained breathing.

The crunching footsteps stopped, and then a man's voice said something Matt couldn't make out. The man sort of half whispered.

Another voice said a little louder than the first one: "All right."

Gazing through the gap between the boulder and the junipers, Severance slowly clicked the Winchester's hammer back to full cock. A shadow moved along the ground ten feet away from him. Then a thick-set man in a cream wool shirt, suspenders, and floppy-brimmed, clay-colored hat stepped slowly out from around a large, dead pine that had been split by lightning many years ago, when Matt was just a boy. He remembered smelling the aroma of brimstone and burning pine where he'd lain awake in his bedroom. The top, charred half of the pine lay straight out from the fire-blackened tree that thrust out its stubby, black branches like the arms of a dead man pleading for salvation.

At least, that's how the pine had always appeared in Matt's younger eyes. Now it was just a lightning-struck tree.

He watched his stalker push through some evergreen shrubs that had grown up around the pine's charred bole.

As the man moved toward Severance, Matt gave a cold grin and took aim. The man stopped suddenly, eyes widening in his bearded face. He'd seen the rifle aimed at him from the side of the rock; maybe the dying rays of the sun had glinted off the barrel.

He gave a startled grunt and raised his own Winchester but did not get the butt plate pressed against his shoulder before Matt's own long gun thundered, punching a hole through the dead center of the man's shirt, knocking him straight back off his feet. The man, already dead, threw his rifle high in the air but not before triggering a wild round skyward.

"Oh, hell!" Severance heard another man yell softly, somewhere ahead and to his left.

Matt moved quickly to the rock's left side and fired a round through the gap, his bullet drilling through the back of the other man who'd come around the left side of the pine but was now retreating. Or trying to. Severance's bullet took him between the shoulder blades and punched him belly down on the ground where he shivered as he died.

A bullet slammed into the rock so close to Matt that both his ears rang painfully.

Matt whipped around to see another man standing atop the slope to his left, just then jacking another round into the breech of his Henry rifle. Gritting his teeth, Matt jacked a live round into his Winchester and fired. He jacked and fired two more times, sending that man flying backward, spreading both arms wide, his hat tumbling off his shoulder just before he disappeared down the other side of the ridge.

"Hold it," said a soft, darkly menacing voice behind Matt.

Matt wheeled, jacking another round.

He held fire.

The black-clad man who'd snuck up behind him and was standing between two cedars, aiming down the barrel of his own 1873 Winchester, had him dead to rights. The man frowned suddenly. The frown grew more severe on his clean-shaven, lightly freckled face.

Incredulously, the man said, "Matt?" He lifted his head slightly, his dark-blue eyes cast in disbelief. "Matt Severance." It wasn't a question but a surprised declaration. Then he steadied the rifle in his hands and canted his cheek down against the rear stock once more. "Drop the rifle, Matt!"

"You first, Garrett." Matt grinned. He'd taken advantage of the man's surprise to aim his own weapon at the man's pale blue shirt between the flaps of his black vest strung together with strips of black rawhide.

Severance gritted his teeth against the painful ringing in his ears from the bullet the man on the ridge had slammed against the boulder.

Garrett Beech kept his Winchester aimed at Matt.

Matt kept his own Winchester aimed at Beech, who, the only son of Ethel Beech—the largest, most powerful rancher in this neck of the San Juans—was several years younger than Matt.

"What the hell are doing back here?" Beech bit out.

He had a V-shaped, fair-skinned, lightly freckled face that didn't tan so much as turn pink. Trimmed, pale-blond sideburns slid only an inch down from beneath the narrow brim of his low-crowned, black hat. His eyes had always been an off-putting cobalt blue. Severance had always thought they'd betrayed an inner lunacy in the kid, who was a man now. Severance had known Garrett when they'd been boys working the same free range, branding together with hands from the other area ranches, also riding together during the fall gather when all the cattle from the various outfits were cut from one big, scattered herd. A few times, he, Garrett, and Roy had explored the big canyon at the base of Thunder Mountain.

Matt had never cared for Garrett Beech, whom he'd seen as spoiled and arrogant. Because he was her only child and because his father, Owen Beech, was dead, killed by a business rival when Garrett had been young, Ethel Beech had always pretty much given Garrett free rein. She'd spared the rod and spoiled the child, to Matt's way of thinking. He didn't really know the man, though. Roy had known him better though Garrett was even younger than Matt. Matt knew Roy and Garrett had had a falling out in town in one of the saloons or brothels, likely over a girl or a card game. Matt couldn't recall which. The two had been too much alike—big-headed, swaggering, young men—to not have locked horns.

Both had been proud, wild, young men. Easy to rile.

"What the hell do you think I'm doing back here, Beech?" Matt said, easy to rile again now himself, keeping his own Winchester aimed at his opponent. "I'm here for the loot! You gonna try to take it from me?"

Garrett Beech stared at him.

"Here's a question for you," Matt said, keeping his right index finger curled taut across his Winchester's trigger, finding it hard not to jerk it back in light of Beech's attack on him at his own headquarters. "What the hell are you doing bushwhacking me on my own property?"

Beech stared at him again for several seconds.

He said, "It's not your headquarters anymore, Severance. My ma has staked a claim to it."

"She has no right to stake a claim to something she didn't pay for."

"She had no chance to buy it. You left. Just abandoned it, remember?"

"Yeah, well, I'm back," Matt said. "As you can see."

"I didn't know it was you." Beech depressed his Winchester hammer and lowered the weapon, looking a little chagrined. "I figured you were some nester who'd moved onto your old place. Or rustlers. A few have holed up here over the past two years."

"I'll probably find them buried in shallow graves."

"I doubt you'll find them at all." Beech smiled coldly, his flat, cobalt eyes glinting devilishly in the fading light. "You know how Ma is. An' she gives the orders."

"You tell your ma for me to leave me alone. I don't care about the cattle. But I'm movin' back."

"What the hell are you gonna do out here if you don't run cattle?"

"I'm gonna trap horses out along the San Juan. Bring 'em back here, break 'em slow, and sell 'em high." Matt grinned. In the wild country along the San Juan River, several herds of mustangs still ran, as free as the Ute Indians who once populated that wild country.

Garrett Beech studied him critically. "I know you're good with horses. You were the best around the San Juans for that. But I don't believe you came back for that. You came back for the loot. I can see it in your eyes."

"What do you see in my eyes?"

"I don't know." Beech studied him again, his colorless brows mantling over those vaguely crazy eyes. "A kind of wildness. Sort of like ol' Roy."

"That's what happens to hunted men. They get a little wild. *Dangerous*. You can tell that to your ma."

"Oh, she'll know that soon enough. As soon as I ride back to the Triangle Cross with three of her men...three of her *best* men...slung belly down across their saddles."

"If they were the best she has, she's in trouble." Matt leveled a steady gaze on Garrett Beech and gave his head a single, warning wag. "Tell her not to crowd me, Garrett. If she does, there'll be hell to pay. She'll lose more than those three men." He canted his head to indicate the ridge where the third man lay.

Beech gave a caustic snort. "Boy, you have gone wild, haven't you. Challenging Ethel Beech! All right, I'll tell her. But, like you said, Matt, there's gonna be hell to pay."

"I'll be right here, waiting to pay it in lead!" Severance brushed past Beech and began climbing the ridge to look for his horse. "Now, if you'll forgive me, I have a cabin to get in order."

"Fine," Beech spat. "I'll be gatherin' my dead!"

"You do that. Ride here again, and there'll be more to gather!"

## CHAPTER 11

Miss Jane's bedroom door opened, and the tall, handsome Dr. Ben Ellison stepped out. He held his black leather medical kit down low in his right hand. He wore a solemn expression as with his left hand he peeled a bow of his wire-framed spectacles off his right ear and then the one off his left ear and stuffed the spectacles into the breast pocket of his broadcloth jacket, which he wore with a white silk shirt and burgundy foulard tie.

Rio rose from the straight-backed, brocade-bottomed chair he'd been sitting in, his hat in his lap, listening to the hollow ticking of the clock on the wall across from him, above a stone statue of two wild-eyed grizzlies up on their hind legs and locked in a battle to the death. The details in those two bruins—their bared teeth, tongues, enraged eyes, and the fur standing on their humps—made them appear so alive that Rio thought he could hear their bugling roars echo around the room.

Having been a guest here to this suite which Miss Jane shared with his boss, Bloody Joe, Rio knew that Miss Jane had bought the statue on a trip to Europe. It had been sculpted by a fellow from Austria whose name was Lusenberg or some such and who'd traveled in the American West as a guest of Jane herself. Later, she'd visited the sculptor in Europe, bought the sculpture, and had it shipped here to Del Norte.

Jane had lived an amazing life. She had the finest things in her suite of rooms here in the San Juan. Seeing such trimmings, reflecting on such civility and refinement, always humbled Rio though he enjoyed being around them, seeing how the other half lived, so to speak. How they appreciated life.

And Jane did surely appreciate life. Especially now that she was married once again—for the final time, hopefully—to the still wild and untethered though middle-aged Bloody Joe Mannion. Rio hoped she'd be able to continue enjoying that life. For a while there, just after he'd delivered her to her bed, he'd thought she'd given up the ghost.

But then she'd murmured and turned her head from one side to the other, and Rio's own heart began beating again.

For a while there, Rio had thought she was dead and beneath the shock of that possibility, he tried to imagine how he would deliver that bit of horrific news to the man who loved Jane Mannion more than life itself—Bloody Joe. He tried to imagine the world in general and Del Norte more specifically without her in it, and both places seemed very bleak, indeed.

She was like the diamond in the stick pin, Jane was. What would the pin be without the diamond?

Rio stood nervously, worrying the brim of his battered hat with his fingers, not liking the expression on the doctor's pale, handsome face. Ellison seemed to have trouble looking Rio in the eye, and that troubled Rio even more.

The learned, cultivated young man—he was only in his late twenties, Rio thought—had just opened his mouth to speak when hurried footsteps sounded in the carpeted hall beyond the main door to Jane's suite. The footsteps grew louder, fell silent, and were replaced by two quick, hard knocks on Jane's door. Before Rio or Ellison could say anything, the door opened and Joe's daughter, the former Vangie Mannion, poked her head into the room, her worried eyes finding her husband, who'd been her husband as of only a few months ago.

"Ben!" the young lady, all of nineteen years old, exclaimed. She came into the room and kicked the door closed behind her with her right foot clad in a dusty, manure-rimed stockman's boot. "What happened? How is she? I'd just driven up to Mister Drake's Mercantile for feed when Mister Drake himself told me Miss Jane had fainted!"

"She fainted, all right," Rio said, giving the brim of his hat a good workout with his nervous fingers. "Couldn't believe what I was seein'. Don't think I ever been more worried about anyone in all my years!"

"Hi, Rio," Vangie, short for Evangeline, said as she walked past him and stepped up to Dr. Ellison still standing in front of Jane's closed door. "Ben," she said, placing a hand on her husband's right arm, "what happened? I can tell by your expression it's not going to be good."

What a contrast were the two standing before him, Rio vaguely noted. The tall, handsome doctor decked out in his tailored suit and the young woman in her wool shirt, wide leather belt, and blue denim trousers with buckskin sewn into the seat and the insides of the thighs. A horse girl was Vangie Mannion. Practically since she'd first started walking, she'd preferred the saddle, Joe had once told him. Now the pretty young woman wore her hair in a French braid at the back of her head and beneath her low-crowned, flat-brimmed tan Stetson.

"Why don't you take a seat, honey?" the doctor said, stepping up close to Vangie and resting his left hand against her suntanned right cheek.

"Oh, it is bad!" Vangie said. "Come on, Ben. Out with it. Rio and I can take it standing up."

"Sure, sure, Doc," Rio said, impatient to hear the news, however bad it might be. "I'll take it standin'." He heard the dread in his voice; it made him feel even more dreadful.

"It's her heart," Ellison said, drawing in a ragged breath. "I'm afraid that when that crazy bounty hunter, Lodge, shot her—three times in the chest—it weakened her heart." He shuttled his grave gaze between Rio and Vangie as he said, "It's not beating as it should. Not as strongly as it should be, and it seems to be skipping beats now and then. I'm afraid the loss of blood and the shock of those three bullets, one of which is still lodged in her ribs, too close to her heart to be removed, has weakened the cardiac muscle."

"That's her heart?" Rio asked.

"Yes," said the young doctor, dropping his gaze to the floor between him and his young wife staring up at him, speechless for the moment.

Vangie swung around to face Rio.

They shared a worried look and then Vangie turned and walked several feet into the parlor area of Jane's suite, to Rio's right. Near a low, round table standing at the *V* formed by two overstuffed leather sofas, she turned back around to face her husband, her brown eyes pensive, deeply worried.

"What does this mean, Ben? Tell me she's not...for

God's sake, Ben...for Pa's sake if for no one else's...tell me Jane's not..."

"I don't know," Dr. Ellison said, with an air of incredulity, wincing a little, dreadfully. "I really don't know, honey. What I do know is that she has to stop working so hard. She can't keep putting in twelve-to-fourteen-hour days. Good Lord, when I come in for breakfast, she's downstairs, helping the bartenders and servers. When I come in for supper, she's here, freshly bathed and in a different gown, ready to take on the evening. She can't work such long hours, and she needs to eat something now and then."

"I noticed she's gotten awful thin," Rio mentioned.

"I've noticed it, too," Vangie said. "I'll do what I can." She paused and then shook her head slowly, and said, "Pa...he's gonna be so worried."

"I know," the young doctor said.

He walked over and placed a kiss on Vangie's forehead. "She's awake. You can go in and see her." He glanced at Rio. "Both of you can. But just for a minute. I have to fetch my carriage from the livery. Mrs. Peterson is going to deliver her baby this afternoon, and Doc Bohannon is up at the Cloud Tickler, setting a leg."

He squeezed Vangie's arm. "I'll see you later, honey. Sorry I didn't have better news."

"Thanks, Ben. See you later."

The doctor nodded at Rio then left the suite.

"Oh, Rio," Vangie said, a sheen of emotion showing in her eyes, "I don't know how I'm going to tell Pa. He's been a changed man since he and Jane married again. He's been so optimistic...energetic. If he loses her..."

"Now, now, young lady," Rio said, walking up and squeezing the young woman's arm and dipping his chin to stare into her eyes, "let's not put the cart before the mule. Sure, it wasn't good news, but that lady in there is still alive. And she's strong. We both know how strong she is. Now, let's poke our heads in and say hi an' let her know we're backin' her play. Who knows?" He shrugged and gave Vangie an encouraging smile. "It might even help."

Vangie brushed a tear from her cheek with the back of one hand and returned the deputy's smile. "Okay, Rio," she said, choking back a sob. "Okay. Let's do that."

Rio thrust out his hand holding his hat, indicating the door to Jane's bedroom. "After you."

Rio followed Vangie slowly, quietly into the bedroom in which Jane lay in a large, four-poster bed with a green velvet canopy. The room was in deep shadow relieved only by the clear western sunlight peeking around the edges of two sets of velvet drapes.

Rio followed Vangie up to the side of the bed.

He hated how small and frail and pale Miss Jane appeared against the whiteness of the sheets and the deep red of the heavy quilt covering her. She almost appeared dead, her pale hands resting one atop the other, on the red quilt. Her thick, curly red hair was fanned out across the pillow behind her head.

She appeared to be sleeping, her chest rising and falling slowly.

Vangie turned to Rio, hesitantly, and whispered, "Maybe we'd best leave, Rio. Visit her later. She looks like she's—"

Jane's voice cut her off abruptly. "Mmmm...now that's a voice that always cheers me." Jane's mouth twisted a smile and then she opened her eyes and turned her head slightly, casting her gaze between her stepdaughter and the stocky deputy standing to Vangie's right, holding his hat over his double belt buckles straining against the pot gut the deputy was not proud of. "And you, Rio...a sight for these sore eyes."

"Me?" Rio said. "Pshaw! Now you're just funnin' me, Miss Jane."

Smiling tenderly, Jane shook her head slowly, looking from Vangie to Rio and back again. "I've never seen two more welcome and beautiful faces. Let me...let me just..."

Jane lifted her head from her pillow, sort of half sitting up, placing her hands flat against the mattress to each side of her and grunting as she struggled to slide up a little higher on the bed.

"Oh, Jane," Vangie said. "Please, you're—"

"Do me a favor, honey, and prop both pillows up behind me, will you?"

"Here, here," Rio said, hurrying around to the far side of the bed to grab one of the two other pillows.

When he and Vangie had propped both pillows behind Jane, between the broad, carved oak headboard and Jane's head and back, Jane said, "There, now...that's better. I don't have to stare up at you. Ridiculous! You'd swear I was an invalid or something, taken to bed in the middle of the day!"

She glanced to her left, at the two long, arched, windows along the draperied edges of which shone the lens-clear sunlight of early afternoon.

"Now, now, Miss Jane," Rio said. "You have to rest. Doc Ellison—he said—"

"Rio, I am sorry to have been such a pest. Good Lord, how worried you must have been! But as far as what the good doctor said, I'm stronger than he thinks."

"Jane," Vangie said, placing both her hands on Jane's left forearm, "you have to take it easier. Your heart's weak. You can't work so many hours, and you need to eat!"

"I eat when I'm hungry, darling. And I am not weak. I have full faith in your husband, my sweet, but like I said, he doesn't know me. He doesn't know how strong I am. I'll be *damned* if I'll let that crazy, maniacal bounty hunter kill me now nearly a year later after his first attempt! A year after Joe hunted him down and sent him back to the hell that spawned him!"

"Oh, dear, Miss Jane..." Rio said.

"Jane, please," Vangie beseeched her stepmother, "you have to settle down. You're getting all riled up!"

"And one more thing." Jane placed her left hand over one of Vangie's and cast her and Rio a hard, commanding look. "I'll not have one word of this mentioned to Joe. Do you understand. Not a word! Not now or *ever*!"

CHAPTER 12

MANNION CROSSED THE SHALLOW STREAM SLOWLY, keeping Red in check, looking around carefully, one hand on the butt of the big, right-side Russian.

He hadn't heard anymore shooting for the last two miles or so of his ride from nearly straight east. Now, as Red crossed the stream and climbed the low bank into the Half-Moon headquarters, he saw no sign of any trouble, either. No sign of the men who'd been shooting.

In the last, watery, lime-green light of the late-summer dusk, he saw one horse standing at the hitchrack fronting the long, low, shake-shingled cabin, the right side of which formed the small part of an *L*. The large, fieldstone hearth was on that side of the cabin. Gray smoke rose from it, unspooling nearly straight up in the still, early evening air toward a couple stars kindling to life in the dark-green firmament turning darker by the second.

The door flanking the porch running along the front of the cabin was propped open with a white porcelain pot with a red rim. As Mannion approached astride Red, the blaze-faced black gelding watched the newcomers as well, giving his tail quick, anxious switches spaced about three seconds apart.

The animals weren't the only ones watching Mannion approach, the lawman saw now, as he drew rein to the right of the black.

Matt Severance stood just inside the cabin's open doorway, both hands wrapped over the end of a broom he held straight up and down before him. Joe hadn't seen him till now because the dark shadows filling the cabin had concealed him. Now he could make out little more than Severance's silhouette, the blue handle of the broom catching the last light of the setting sun.

Mannion removed his hand from the walnut grips of the Russian.

Severance leaned the broom against the wall to his right then strode out of the cabin to stand at the top of the worn, gray porch steps. "Here to arrest me, Marshal Mannion? I haven't dug up the loot yet, so you'll be lacking evidence to convict me with."

"I heard shooting."

"I just added three more notches to my pistol grips."

"Cleaning up right well."

"Can't say as I wasn't expecting it."

"Anyone I'd know?"

"Three of Ethel Beech's men."

"Ouch."

"Well, she still has her precious son."

"Garrett was here, too?"

Severance nodded.

Mannion stretched his lips back from his teeth, scowling. "What is it about you? Don't you bathe? Barring smelling you in the area, how in hell did they know—"

"They just happened to be riding through and spotted

me. They didn't know it was me. Thought I was someone nesting here, I reckon. Garrett still likes to shoot first and ask questions later."

"Just like his ma," Mannion put in.

"Chip off the old Ethel block, Garrett."

Again, the lawman scowled. "Those two have been a burr in my bonnet for years. Owen before them. I don't mind them hanging a rustler now an' then. Rustlers know the risk," he added, narrowing one eye pointedly at the former rustler, Severance. "But when so-called nesters turn up missing, I figure they been thrown to the wolves. And that there ain't right."

Severance chuckled. "If Ethel Beech hasn't understood the meaning of free range by now, she never will."

"You think she's gonna let you stay here?"

Severance shrugged. "It's my place. Still got the deed locked away in the bank."

Again, Mannion narrowed an eye. "You sure about that?"

Matt gave a dry chuckle. "Well, no, I reckon I haven't checked on it lately. I reckon a mouse might've crawled into the safety deposit box, chewed it to shreds."

"Or one of the bankers might have used it to light his cigar." Mannion looked around at the shabby outbuildings flanking the shabby cabin, which was in desperate need of a new roof. "You got your work cut out for you here."

"I have all the time in the world, Marshal."

Mannion grinned. "I must say I admire your optimism. Ol' Ethel might keep you occupied dodging bullets."

"If she sends her men around, she might get the Half-Moon back, but she's gonna pay a heavy price for it."

Mannion looked at the gun rig low-slung on Severance's right hip. A vagrant breeze caught the young man's long, dark-brown hair, cast a few wisps about his smooth, dark cheeks, moved it about his broad shoulders.

"You come out here to nursemaid me, Marshal?" he asked.

"No," Joe said. "I came out here to cut trouble off at the pass."

"I can't be that much trouble. I'm only one man." It was Severance's turn to narrow a pointed eye. "And I do not have any idea where Roy hid that loot."

"You're still trouble."

"If she kills me, your trouble's over."

"Funny thing about trouble," Mannion said. "It's kind of like a wildfire. Once there's a spark in dry grass and timber, it can get outta hand mighty fast. Spread to where you never expected."

Severance pursed his lips till his cheeks dimpled fatefully.

Both horses lifted their heads suddenly, pricking their ears.

Red whinnied and shifted his weight beneath Mannion.

"Now what in the hell..."

Mannion let his voice trail off. Just then he heard what the horses had heard—the sounds of an approaching rider.

"Oh, no," Severance said.

Mannion followed the younger man's gaze to the fir- and pine-stippled ridge east of the ranch yard. The hoof thuds grew louder as a horse and rider followed the switchbacking trail down the ridge through the darkening trees. It was almost dark, but there was just enough green light left in the sky that Mannion could see the rider on the long-legged roan was of the female persuasion. There were too many curves for a man; long hair danced about her shoulders clad in a brown leather vest with jostling whang strings.

There was really only one girl it could be.

Mannion said, "I'll leave you to powwow with your niece."

Severance shot him a vaguely suspicious look. That look told Mannion, who hadn't realized his tone might have been odd, more than words could have. It told him he might be right about his own uncertainties, though who Cheyenne Severance belonged to was none of his business. That was a bit of trouble he couldn't help young Severance with.

"Tread cautiously out here, son," Mannion said, pinching his hat brim. "I'll stop out again in a few days to check on you."

"No need, Marshal," Severance said, as Mannion reined Red around.

"Just the same," Mannion said, and booted Red into a trot back toward the stream glinting dully in its bed before the dark cottonwoods. Several stars had kindled to life between the distant western peaks. He passed young Miss Severance just as she and the roan reached the bottom of the ridge, the roan blowing and fighting the bit, the girl watching the lawman dubiously from beneath the brim of her cream hat.

Mannion threw her a wave, crossed the stream, and trotted through the faintly rustling cottonwoods before swinging east toward home and Jane.

———

Matt stood on the porch, watching the girl put the roan into a lope, riding from the base of the ridge toward the cabin.

As she drew within thirty feet, the roan blowing, the hooves thudding loudly in the otherwise quiet ranch yard, Matt stepped down off the porch. He smiled. What a lovely lady she'd become, her long hair blowing straight back behind her in the wind.

He wished he hadn't invited her out here now, though. He hadn't anticipated the intensity of the danger.

Cheyenne drew back on the reins sharply, and as the roan locked up its legs and skidded to a stop, she curveted the mount expertly. She removed her hat and shook her head, tossing her hair, then set the hat back on her head and, breathless, said, "I heard shooting! I wanted to ride over right away but Ma wouldn't have it. 'Let him fight his own battles,' she said. I waited till she went to bed. She turns in early. Then I saddled Queenie."

Cheyenne reached forward to touch the stock of the Winchester carbine jutting up from its sheath. "Figured you could use some help."

*No*, Severance thought. *No, no, no, no!* This was one complication he hadn't expected. She'd grown up and she wanted to be involved in his life, which was what he wanted more than anything. But not now. Not like this! Especially not after the dustup of nearly an hour ago.

The admiring smile faded quickly from his lips as fear and concern bucked against him hard. He stepped forward. "Cheyenne, you can't come here. I'm sorry I invited. You can't *be* here. It's too dangerous. We can't be together. Not away from the Elk Horn Creek headquarters. Especially not here. I think the danger will pass eventually. But for now, you have to stay home. Least-ways, you have to stay away from me."

"Don't worry—I can shoot. Pa started me on it, an' after he...well, I kept practicing. I've run rustlers off our range three times over the past two years!"

Severance walked up to the sweaty roan mare, curled his fingers around the cheek strap of the horse's bridle. "You have to let this horse rest before you head back home. Come down from there. Let's loosen his cinch and let her drink, and you and I will go inside."

"Oh, come on, Uncle Matt. Don't be an old woman about this! You're gonna need help!"

Severance took a quick look around, suddenly feeling several pairs of eyes on him. Eyes burning down on him from the near ridges cloaked in darkness and mantled by stars. He was probably imagining it, but then again, there'd been enough time for his return to the Half-Moon to have spread halfway around the county. He needed to get the girl inside.

"We'll discuss it in the cabin," he said, trying to maintain his calm. "Swing down."

With an incredulous sigh, Cheyenne swung down from the saddle.

"Go on inside."

"I'll lead Queenie over to—"

"Cheyenne, go inside!" Severance couldn't help yelling at the girl, taking another paranoid look around though it was suddenly so dark he couldn't have seen would-be ambushers if there were really any out there.

The girl gave a groan of deep frustration, clenching her gloved fists at her sides. "All right, all right! Hold on." She slid the carbine from its boot, gave her uncle a foxy grin, then mounted the porch steps.

His heart beating anxiously, Matt led the roan over to

the stone tank at the base of the windmill. He slipped the bit from the mare's teeth and loosened her latigo, letting the strap hang toward the hard-packed, barren ground. Then, looking around again, compulsively, he hurried back to the cabin, mounted the porch, and stepped inside just as Cheyenne lit the hurricane lamp he'd set on the table to the right of the door—the table at which he, Roy, and his father had shared many a meal.

Their father usually in truculent silence, taking liberal sips from a tin cup flavored with whiskey. After supper, the old man would slouch off with a stone jug to his bedroom in the cabin's rear addition, where the bedrooms were, leaving the boys to clean up after the meal and lay out the fixing for the next day's breakfast. Then Matt and Roy would spend the evening sharpening knives or mending harnesses, a never-ending chore.

Or, when they were sure their father was asleep, they'd slip quietly out of the cabin, stifling snickers and all-out laughter, punching each other playfully. They'd saddle their horses and light out on the outlaw trail, most times returning home just before Big John rose well after the sun was climbing up behind the high, dark humps of the Sangre de Cristos in the east.

"There," Cheyenne said, waving out the match and turning up the wick. "That's better." She returned the mantle to the lamp and looked around. "Oof! Leastways, I thought it was better."

"Don't worry," Severance said. "I just got started."

Cheyenne sniffed the air and made a face. "Smells like unwashed *men*!"

"I'll continue airing it out tomorrow."

Severance pulled the door closed and set the locking bar in place.

He went around the cabin, drawing the flour-sack curtains over the windows.

"Have you had anything to eat?" Cheyenne asked.

"Not yet," Matt said, drawing the curtains over the window near the hearth, in which a low fire snapped and crackled. He'd made coffee over the fire and set the pot on a flat stone in the hearth to keep it warm.

"Do you *have* anything to eat?"

She was standing near the table, looking around the shadowy quarters distastefully. Dust and cobwebs clung to everything. The smell of mouse droppings laced the smell of rancid sweat.

Matt walked to the table, slid the curtain aside from the window left of the door, and peered out anxiously, holding up a hand to block the lamp's reflection in the warped glass. "I have some beans and bacon in my saddle-bags. Figure to shoot a deer tomorrow then, after I've made the cabin livable, I'll head to town for stores."

He closed the curtain and turned to the girl staring up at him with concern. "First things first, though. As soon as that roan has had a good blow, I want to get you safely out of here."

Cheyenne glanced at the coffeepot then turned to one of the kitchen shelves and hauled down a couple of stone mugs. She looked into each, made a distasteful expression, then blew out the dust.

"First, let's have a cup of coffee. I have something I need to talk to you about, Uncle Matt."

Severance frowned. "Oh? What's that?"

Her watched her walk over to the hearth and use the ancient leather swatch to fill both mugs from the pot. She returned to the table, both mugs smoking in her hands. She set the mugs on the table then sat down in a creaky spool-back, hide-bottom chair, curling one leg beneath the other.

"Sit down," she said, a beguiling smile spreading her pretty mouth, showing the ends of her fine, white teeth.

Frowning at her curiously, Severance pulled a chair out to the girl's right, his back to the kitchen part of the cabin. He wanted to face the window and the door, in case trouble came calling beyond them.

"All right," he said, "I'm sitting."

Cheyenne sipped her coffee, set the mug down, rested her elbows on the table, and leaned over her smoking mug, sliding her head up close to Matt's. The lamplight danced in her brown eyes.

That beguiling, coyote smile in place, she said softly, "I think I know where Pa hid the loot."

## CHAPTER 13

SEVERAL DAYS LATER, JOE MANNION DRIBBLED chopped Durham tobacco onto a wheat paper troughed between his thumb and index finger.

He'd drawn his makins sack closed with his teeth, stuffed it back inside his corduroy shirt, and had just started rolling the paper closed when in the distance he heard the rapid *CHUGA! CHUGA! CHUGA!* marking the approach of the infernal, narrow-gauge train of the Colorado Springs & San Juan Line that trundled up the eastern front of the Rockies from Colorado Springs to the mountain mining towns of Salida and Gunnison before boomeranging back down Monarch Pass and angling south through Del Norte. From there, it completed its horseshoe route by trundling back down the canyon of the Colorado River to the burgeoning town of Pueblo, which, like Colorado Springs, sat at the eastern foot of the Rockies.

The ermine-tipped Pikes Peak looming over Colorado Springs, ever-growing, as well, could be seen from as far away as Julesburg in the far northwestern part of the territory.

Both towns nestled at the eastern base of the mountains, spaced fifty miles apart, were growing fast, as was the whole damn territory.

"Ah, shit," Joe said, carefully rolling the quirley closed with both big, brown index fingers and thumbs. Bits of tobacco spilled from both ends of the cylinder. He blamed it on the train, the reverberations of which he could feel through his boot soles.

"What'd you think, Joe?" Rio Waite sat beside Joe on a bench outside of the brick depot platform in the heart of Del Norte. He was desultorily spinning his hat between his spread knees. "It wasn't gonna come? It always comes! Might be late...might sometimes be *two hours* late depending on what's fallen over the rails or if it got held up or not. But, hell, one thing you can always count on—aside from the moon, stars, and the spite of a persnickety woman, that is, ha-ha—is the train always comes."

Rio gave a dry chuckle.

He enjoyed ribbing his boss about the train because he knew how badly, unabashedly Joe hated it. Had hated it since the Colorado Springs & San Juan Line had first been surveyed, its course plotted so that after months of Mannion's dark, tooth-grindingly dreadful anticipation the tracks were laid by dozens of Americans, Mexicans, Chinese, Blacks, and big, bearded, grunting Scandinavians right down the middle of Del Norte's main street.

The dragon-like pants grew louder as the long, caterpillar-like contraption came around a bend south of town, out from behind a steeply slanting tabletop mesa. The diamond-shaped stack of the black locomotive, trailed by the red-and-gold tender car, issued a long, thick, wavering guidon of black coal smoke that dissipated into the otherwise pure mountain air behind the caboose.

Mannion hated the smoke most of all, for, like too many of the train's passengers, which included con men, horseback highwaymen, footpads, swindlers, fakes, frauds of both sexes, as well as pistol-packing cardsharps and regulators lured here by competing, large businesses including ranchers and miners, remained long after the locomotive and the tender car had pulled the rest of the infernal, fetid, filth-belching contraption back down the mountains to the plains.

The rumbling grew louder as did the locomotive's dragon-like pants:

*CHUGA! CHUGA! CHUGA! CHUGA!*

Then, as the train formed a straight line a quarter mile from town, Mannion ground his teeth against the two short whistles followed by one long, especially grating one, which signaled the depot manager and the porters to prepare for action. The signaling wouldn't stop there, of course, the lawman knew. Oh, no, the engineer would keep belting out that series of whistles as though no one within miles of Del Norte had heard the first set.

Mannion imagined the big, broad-shouldered graybeard, Mike Donnelly, standing at the locomotive's controls, grinning with wolfish delight and winking at his fireman, Dwight Free, as he pulled the lever to sound those infernal horns that likely caused rockslides in all three of the surrounding mountain ranges. Or so Joe, in his hatred of everything to do with the damn contraption, imagined.

It sure as hell threatened to knock loose the fillings in his teeth.

He'd been about to fire a lucifer to life on his thumbnail but now he dropped the match and the cigarette into his shirt pocket to save for later. He couldn't enjoy the smoke now, not with that big, miserable iron contraption rattling, thundering, and clickety-clacking into town, sending great pillowing waves of smoke billowing against the false facades on both sides of the street, making women and men on the boardwalks or in passing wagons or on horseback cover their mouths and noses with their neckerchiefs.

Mannion hated the way people on both sides of the street, including gaudily, half-dressed soiled doves, spilled out from the buildings onto the boardwalks or second- or third-floor balconies, smiling and waving at the train's crew and passengers gathered on the platforms at the front and rear of the two passenger cars.

The big, black locomotive screeched past Mannion and Rio, slowly stopping, the engineer, Mike Donnelly, grinning down from his high perch at the town's top lawdog, showing his big, yellow horse teeth beneath his red, soup-strainer mustache as he cut loose with the two shorts and one long, long, long final whistle for Mannion's benefit.

"Oh, fer chrissakes!" Mannion snarled up at the engineer. "You blow that one more time, Mike, I'm gonna blow you outta there!" He patted the grips of the big Russian holstered for the cross-draw on his left hip.

The locomotive, obscured by the steam issuing from the iron beast's pressure release valves, drew to a stop roughly a hundred feet to Mannion's right. As it did, Donnelly, who'd turned his head to track the two lawmen with his grinning gaze, yelled, "Oh, come on, Joe! There's no stopping progress. You know that!"

Mannion cursed and cowed Rio, who'd started to chuckle at the engineer's remark, with a look.

Then both lawmen turned their attention to the

passengers stepping down from the two passenger cars—men and women of all ages, shapes, sizes, and races, including two big Chinamen with goatees and clad in the rough dungarees and hobnailed boots of miners as well as two nuns, one of which was carrying a wicker cage in which a copper-red chicken with a single, blood-red comb clucked at the crowd bustling around it. Porters who'd hurried to set stepstools onto the platform for the detraining crowd milled among the small horde as several young boys hocked burritos or ham sandwiches out of wheelbarrows, dogs barking at their heels.

Mannion waved the steam and coal smoke away with his hat and glanced at Rio. "You see anyone we should give a little extra attention?"

Joe and Rio usually met the train when it was due. It was another way Mannion tried to cut trouble off at the pass, so to speak, discouraging obvious trouble—especially men wearing too many hoglegs or overly cagey-looking cardsharps, many of whom Mannion recognized from his years town taming from Kansas to Texas, back when he and the West were relatively young and maybe not quite as jaded.

Ah, hell, who was Bloody Joe kidding? He'd been born jaded.

"Nobody stands out this mornin', boss," Rio said, scowling curiously at the two nuns walking past him and Mannion, a porter in a red wool uniform trimmed with gold stitching following along behind them with an over-filled luggage cart. The nuns conversed in Irish brogues so heavy as to be nearly unintelligible to Mannion. "I would like to know what that sister is doin' with that Rhode Island Red, though." The deputy raked the tip of his index finger up and down his lips. "Hmm."

"Good morning, gentlemen!" said a familiar woman's voice beneath the din.

Mannion turned to see his lovely wife striding toward him and Rio through the crowd, her beguiling and always welcome visage intermittently obscured by wisping coal smoke and steam. The former Miss Jane Ford was clad to the nines, as usual. This morning she wore a spruce-green gown with billowy sleeves and a white shirtwaist trimmed with lace the same copper orange as her hair. The shirtwaist was low-cut enough to offer just enough of a peek at the former Miss Ford's opulent, freckled cleavage to make any man with red blood in his veins stop and take notice.

Well, maybe two notices, Joe silently opined with an uneasy chuckle aloud.

He couldn't help feeling jealous at how enticingly his wife dressed, but he knew it was all part of the business. The San Juan Hotel & Saloon had to present well in its entirety, and that meant Jane's girls as well as the madam herself had to present well, as well. Enticingly well.

They always did.

What really boggled Joe's mind was how well the madam presented even in bed. How many women in their early forties looked even better with their clothes off than on?

Well, Joe's beloved did.

"Good morning, honey," Mannion said, feeling himself blush like a schoolboy as he pushed to his feet.

He removed his Stetson and leaned down to give his lovely wife a heartfelt kiss on the lips. He didn't use to cotton to public shows of affection. They'd embarrassed him. But Jane had changed that about him. She'd changed many things about him. The most important thing she'd changed about him was that he'd learned to make room in his life for more than just work. He'd always made time for Vangie, because he knew it was his uncompromising, single-mindedness about his job that had helped drive Vangie's mother, Sarah, over the edge. For that he would forever feel guilty and had no doubt he'd pay for it one day, when he bowed his head before his Maker.

But while still standing upright on this side of the sod, he knew he had to make room for romantic love in his life, as well. He had to make room for a woman lest he should spend the rest of his days alone and lonely, now that Vangie was married—driven only by obsession for his work, which did not make a man complete.

The love of a good woman did. A woman to grow old with. A woman whose warm lips would be there, pressed against his, to send him off into that long, last, frigid night...

"Good mornin', Miss Jane." Rio had also gained his feet, and now he pinched his hat brim to the woman, whose thick, curly, copper-red hair spilled over her shoulders and glinted in the bright, midmorning sunshine.

"You were up and gone by the time I woke," Mannion told Jane. "And I didn't sleep in by any means." He chuckled, again uneasily though he wasn't sure why. Regarding his true love, he'd been feeling uneasy for days. "What's got you rising so early these days, my love? Are you breaking in a new cook or something?"

"No," Jane said, smiling as she gazed up at her tall husband. "I just feel the need to appreciate every minute, every hour of every day. That's all. Besides, I do have a whole lot of work to do. I'm just on my way over to Mrs. Harrison's Dress Shop to order material for new dresses for my girls. I've sent for a tailor from Leadville, a famous one at that—a Mister Goldstein, originally from New York City—to sew them right here at the San Juan. My poor doves haven't worn anything new in well over a year, and that needs to change. They always feel better about themselves when they wear new things, as do I. *Then* I need to put in an order at the grocery store. The larder at the San Juan is nearly empty and I'll be hosting a wedding party at the end of the month, one whose elaborate menu includes oysters, elk with mint sauce, roast duckling, and chateau potatoes!"

Mannion shared an incredulous look with Rio. "What in holy blazes is chateau—"

Jane laughed, tipped her picture hat up with one white-gloved hand, rose onto the toes of her elastic, side-button shoes, and gave her husband an affectionate kiss on each cheek, patting his broad chest. "With that, gentlemen, I bid good day to you both, for this lady is off!"

Jane kissed Rio's cheek in parting, raising in flush in *both* the deputy's craggy, patch-bearded cheeks, then continued her way through the crowd, striding off up the street to the north.

Both men turned to watch her go.

Mannion winced. "She works so hard."

"That she does, that she does," Rio said, staring after the lady with concern in his eyes.

"Does she look all right to you, Rio?"

Rio snapped a surprised look at his boss. "What's that, Joe?"

"Jane. Does she look all right to you?"

"Ah, well, well—how do you mean, Joe?"

"I don't know. She looks a little pale, doesn't she? A little...I don't know...*frail?*"

"Hmm," Rio said, running his index finger down his lips again and staring off toward where Jane had just turned the corner at the end of the block. "Well, maybe just a tad. Burns it at both ends, Miss Jane does."

Mannion's senior deputy gave an uneasy chuckle. He seemed to want to say something more but settled with, "She always has, you know, Joe. Likely always will, I'm afraid."

"Rio?"

Rio looked up at his boss.

Joe studied the older man suspiciously.

"Is there something...about Jane...that I should know. I mean, do you know something—"

Just then a gun blasted down the street to Mannion's left.

It was followed by a girl's shrill scream, which, in turn, was followed by two more quick, roaring blasts and a man's shouted curse.

## CHAPTER 14

"HOLY CRAP IN THE NUNS' PRIVY!" MANNION SWUNG around to face south. "That's comin' from the All-Nighter!"

"Where else?" Rio said, grabbing his trusty double-bore up from where it had been leaning against the bench between him and his boss.

Mannion broke into a run, shoving through the mixed crowd of milling townsfolk and train passengers. Behind him, Rio worked to keep stride, holding the shotgun up high across his chest.

"Another war's broke out at the All-Nighter, sounds like, Joe!" said Earl Pilgrim, standing in the double open doorway of his Emporium Dance Hall and rolling a sharpened matchstick between his lips.

Mannion ran ten more feet then made a hard right to push through the batwings of one of the lowliest watering holes in town, one which seemed to serve the dregs of Del Norte society, if you could call it "society." Despite several more pistol blasts and more screams in the place's second story, two Mexicans and one half-breed slept face down on a table to Mannion's right, near a player piano and under a large, faux gilt framed, badly faded oil painting of a naked blonde riding bareback atop a coal-white horse through a forest along the shore of a placid lake.

The painting had so many bullet holes in it, it looked like someone had used it for target practice.

More pistol blasts, and still the slumbering trio did not stir.

"They're really goin' at it, Joe!" said a short, sharp-faced man standing behind the bar to Mannion's left. George Pyle, owner of the place, held his hands over his ears. "Drovers out to the Barbed Wire and guards from the Cloud Tickler fightin' over the girls!"

Just then two men clad only in longhandles appeared at the top of the stairs that ran up the center of the fetid place's rear wall. One appeared in the hall to the left of the stairs. The other appeared in the hall to the right of the stairs, each with a six-shooter blasting away in his hand. They were so drunk that each fired at each other three times from ten feet away, gritting their teeth and cursing, before the one on the left managed to drill a round into the shoulder of the man on the right.

The man on the right bellowed and stumbled backward, firing his next round into the ceiling, falling and grabbing the balcony rail on his left with that hand. The man on the left ducked as another, unseen gunman fired from farther down the hall, beyond the wounded man.

The man on the right returned fire.

Mannion ran across the room, kicking chairs out of his way—several customers were huddled behind over-turned tables—and stopped ten feet from the bottom of the stairs. He aimed his left-side Russian up at the man on the left side of the balcony. "Hold it right there, Haney! Drop that hogleg and kiss the—"

Joe cut himself off as the man he recognized as Charles Haney, a backshooting toughnut from Texas who worked as a guard for the Cloud Tickler, swung his smoking Colt over the balcony, angling it down toward Mannion while gritting his teeth and pinching up his eyes in drunken fury.

Mannion shot him once, twice, three times, knocking him back against the unfinished pine-paneled wall. Haney lowered his six-shooter and shot himself in his right, bare foot.

He lifted his chin and sent a shrill wail caroming toward the ceiling above him. Then he stumbled forward into the balcony rail, which wobbled precariously but held. Haney wailed again then tumbled straight over the rail. He turned a single somersault in midair before landing belly down atop a table littered with beer bottles, shot glasses, playing cards, and money in the first-floor drinking hall. The men who'd been sitting at the table were pressed up close against the saloon's rear wall, beneath the balcony and out of the path of wayward lead from above.

Two more quick blasts sounded from the far left side of the hall.

Two more shots hammered from the hall's far right side.

Mannion glanced at Rio standing behind him, looking a little green around the gills but holding his double-bore at port arms. Joe canted his head, indicating for Rio to follow him up the stairs. Then Mannion turned to the top of the stairs, and shouted, "You men stop your consarned shooting and throw down your weapons! This is Joe Mannion, marshal of Del Norte, and I'm coming up there to clean your damn clocks!"

With that, Mannion moved quickly up the steps,

holding both big Russians now, one aimed toward the left side of the balcony, the other aimed toward the right side of the balcony.

"Go to hell, Mannion!" came a man's shout from the balcony's far right side. "This ain't your fight. We'll settle it our ownselves!"

The voice of the shouter was more than a little slurred from drink.

Mannion could hear several girls sobbing down the hall on his right. Seemed as though one of the two factions, either the Barbed Wire cowpunchers or the Cloud Tickler guards, were hoarding the All-Nighter's doves.

When Mannion was two steps from the top of the stairs, a door opened down the hall on his left. A man poked his head out of the room one room down from the end, on the hall's left side. A revolver was thrust out of the room, as well. Joe threw himself belly down atop the balcony as two bullets screeched over him toward the balcony's far right side.

Mannion rolled onto his right side and hurled two slugs at the shooter, who howled and dropped, drilling another round into the floor. Joe turned as another man stepped out of a room at the opposite end of the hall from the last one, and, nearly as naked as the day he was born, clad in only a beard and a shabby bowler hat, a fat stogie protruding from between his lips, marched toward the lawman, extending one long-barreled Colt and a pepperbox revolver straight out before him.

The Colt bucked once, sending a bullet screeching over Mannion's head and making a pinging sound as it punched through the window at the far end of the hall behind him.

The nearly naked man had lowered his head a little to

aim down the pepperbox just before Mannion emptied both his Russians into his broad, naked, fleshy frame, the man's breasts jostling and the loose flesh at his haunches doing the same as he twisted around and stumbled backward half a dozen steps, triggering the pepperbox into the ceiling before he fell sideways out the window at that end of the hall.

The screech of breaking glass as well as the shooter's last, dying cry filled the hall just before the man dropped out of sight, his hat tumbling into the hall he'd just vacated. There was the final, punctuating sound of crunching wood as the dead man landed on packing crates or some such pile in the alley on that side of the building.

Mannion stared over both smoking Russians at the broken window.

The girls were still sobbing. Two or three, it sounded like.

He considered reloading his pistols, but no more heads or guns poked out of either the room ahead of him or behind him. It was over, it seemed. Whatever in hell *it* was.

In Del Norte these days, you just never knew.

He let the barrels of both Russians sag to the floor.

"Whew!"

He glanced behind him.

No sign of Rio.

He got a knee under him, then both knees, and heaved himself wearily to his feet.

He saw his senior deputy sitting on the stairs, roughly halfway down from the top. Rio rested his back up against the rail to Mannion's left as the lawman faced the saloon's first floor, where men were just then starting to rise from behind the tables they'd cowered behind. Rio had one leg stretched out along the step before him. His Greener lay on the step above. He had both hands wrapped around the spools of the rail behind him. His chest and bulging belly rose heavily as he breathed.

Sweat glistened on Rio's face.

"Rio," Joe said, moving quickly down the stairs to drop to one knee beside his deputy. "What happened? You hit?"

Rio bunched his lips and cheeks.

He drew a ragged breath.

"Nah, nah," he said, and drew another deep breath as he lifted his uncertain gaze to Mannion. "Just think...I lost my nerve's all...Joe."

He gave a bitter smile.

———

A HALF HOUR LATER, MANNION SAT ON THE PORCH OF the jail office, in the hide-bottom chair in which Rio usually sat, his fat, black-and-white cat, Buster, purring on his lap.

Only now Buster sat on Mannion's lap. But Buster was not purring.

Mannion could tell the cat was as concerned as he was. Buster sat stiffly, staring at the closed jailhouse door behind which Dr. Ben Ellison was checking out Rio, whom Mannion had helped back over to the jailhouse after the dustup in the All-Nighter. On the way over, Joe had summoned young Harmon Haufenthistle to fetch one of the town's two doctors, and it was Vangie's medico husband who'd rolled up in his red-wheeled, leather two-seater chaise a few minutes after Mannion had gotten Rio into his office and into his chair and poured him a tin cup of water from the olla hanging on the porch.

Mannion had taken a seat out here on the porch, with Buster, to give the doctor and Rio some privacy while the young sawbones examined the man.

Joe feared heart attack, though Rio had insisted he was fine and had even tried to laugh off the whole affair. But Mannion was having none of it. He'd wanted him checked out.

Now Del Norte's top lawman ran his hand down Buster's broad back. Joe could see the worry in the cat's eyes as he stared at the door behind which Mannion could make out the quiet discussion the sawbones was having with his senior deputy.

"It's all right, Buster," Joe said, running his hand down the cat's back once more. "Ol' Rio's tougher'n whang leather. You know that."

The cat glanced up at him but then, twitching one ear and then the other, listening intently to the murmurs from within the jailhouse, returned his worried gaze to the closed door.

Presently footsteps sounded from inside.

The door opened.

Dr. Ben Ellison stepped out, placing his crisp, black bowler on his head. He drew the door closed behind him and turned to Mannion, giving a reassuring smile. "You can see him now, Marshal. I think he'll be all right. It was just as we in the profession call a case of nerves. Should pass before long. Maybe give him a day or two to go fishing."

He strode down the porch steps and set his medical kit in his carriage before untying the reins from the hitchrack.

Joe sat watching the medico turn his buggy into the street and shake the reins over the back of the handsome steeldust in the traces, heading south toward where he shared an office with Doctor Bohannon, whose practice he would take over when the older doctor retired in the spring.

Buster turned his gaze to Mannion.

"Meow," the cat said, commandingly.

"All right, Buster." Joe heaved himself to his feet while the cat dropped to the porch floor with a thud. "Let's go check on the old fella. Nerves," he muttered to himself, running a hand across his chin and lower jaw. "Didn't know Rio even had any..."

He opened the door and Buster ran in ahead of him, launching himself up onto the desk that abutted the wall to the right of the door that led down to the basement cellblock. Rio sat at the desk, staring dully at the wall before him, both beefy arms stretched across the desk littered with newspapers, old wanted dodgers, cups, and overfilled ashtrays. A cribbage board and a deck of pasteboards was shoved to one side.

Rio and the younger deputy, Henry McCallister, often played cribbage between their rounds about the town.

Buster walked up before Rio, brushed his nose against Rio's nose, arched his tail, and purred. Rio ran a hand down Buster's back and turned to Mannion.

"The doc tell you I'm a damn coward?"

Mannion closed the door then leaned back against it, crossing his arms on his chest. "I've known some cowards in my day, Rio, most of 'em in the army"—he narrowed an eye at the deputy as he added levelly—"an' you ain't one of 'em."

"I've lost my nerve, Joe. I didn't want you to know, but I got lured into a trap the other night. Got the stuffing stomped out of both ends. Never shoulda walked into that whipsaw. Shoulda smelled it from a mile away."

Rio shook his head and then closed his hands over his

face, drew a deep breath, and let it out slow. He rolled his eyes up and sideways to regard Mannion staring expressionlessly down at him. "Don't trust myself no more. Lost my nerve. That's what happened in the All-Nighter. Halfway up the stairs, my heart started hammerin' an' my knees went weak. Thought I was about to pass out. Couldn't climb another step. My feet turned to lead."

"Turned out I didn't need you, anyway, Rio."

"But what if you did?"

Mannion didn't know how to answer that. He said nothing.

Rio ran his hand down Buster's back and smoothed out his tail. The cat was purring. Facing the wall before him, Rio said, "I reckon I come to the end of it, Joe."

"No, you haven't. Don't say that again, Rio. You've come to *something*. We all come to *something*. A hill that's hard to climb. You'll climb that hill and you'll be even stronger once you've reached the other side."

Rio ran his hand down his face. He looked up at Mannion, a sheen of emotion in the older man's eyes. "You think so, Joe? For real?"

"For real."

The emotion in Rio's eyes grew. "Joe, I'm ready to turn in my badge. I'm ready to retire."

Mannion stepped forward and hiked a hip on the edge of Rio's desk. He crossed his arms on his chest and gazed down at the older man incredulously.

"And do what?" He canted his head toward the building's rear wall. "Sit in your cabin and watch Buster chase mice? Watch the sage grow off your front stoop?"

"I thought maybe I'd pan for gold."

Mannion threw his head back and laughed.

He sobered and regarded his deputy once more.

Buster was purring as Rio stroked his back.

"You think I'm never scared, Rio?"

Rio chuckled. "No, Joe. No, I don't."

"Well, you're wrong. Sometimes I get so damn scared I can't sleep nights. Thinkin' about all that can go wrong. Jane...Vangie...hell, even the young doctor. A bullet drilled through my back when I'm riding after rustlers or bank robbers or some such, leaving Jane and Vangie alone. Christ, we're all standing on the edge of one high ridge, my friend, looking down."

"And what do we do about it, Joe?"

"We go about our business."

Rio just stared at him.

"Courage is being scared to death and still climbing aboard that bronc that damn near killed us."

Rio scowled up at Mannion and closed his left hand around the badge pinned to his cracked, leather vest. "You're not gonna accept this, are ya?"

Mannion shook his head.

Rio gave the purring Buster's back another tender stroke. "Well, hell, then."

## CHAPTER 15

MATT SEVERANCE REMOVED THE LOCKING BAR FROM over his cabin door and leaned it against the wall. He tripped the latch and drew the door open slowly, half expecting a bullet to come caroming in from one of the near ridges.

But it was quiet out there in the sun-drenched yard. Quiet save for the birds, that was. Chickadees, nuthatches, mountain bluebirds, cardinals, every kind of sparrow you can think of, and, somewhere on the ridge rising to Matt's left, crows were thoroughly enjoying the start of a brand-new day. Well, not entirely brand-new.

He dug his timepiece out of his vest pocket and flipped the lid.

Damn near ten o'clock.

He'd been working so hard for the past week that he'd slept the sleep of the dead. He'd awakened an hour ago and, having fixed the old supply wagon and driven to town the day before last, laying in a good supply of stores with which to fill the larder, he'd cooked himself a big breakfast of ham, eggs, fried potatoes, and toast with strawberry jelly. Then he'd dumped his dishes in the wreck pan, filled the sink from the pump, and went to work, scrubbing every pot, pan, plate, fork, and knife until they shone in the sun angling through the kitchen's sashed window.

Big John had built the cabin over a well he'd dug himself, back when he and their mother had just been married—back when he was still in the spirit of such backbreaking work.

That had been when Ma, the former Louise Stump, had been pregnant with Roy.

Big John had met her when he'd been in his early twenties and working on a ranch in Kansas. Her family were farmers who lived in a dugout along the North Fork of the Solomon River. Her mother was a full-breed Cheyenne originally from Dakota. Her father was half Arapaho. They'd been dirt poor. Pa had bought Ma for six horses he'd trapped and broken himself in his off-hours down along the Cimarron River. He'd felt the western pull, as had most young men his age back in the years before the war, so they'd packed up their few belongings in tow sacks, saddled two horses, rigged a packhorse to haul trail supplies, and rode west into the Rocky Mountains, hunting and fishing and following their noses till the ground they were on felt right.

Then Pa had filed a claim in the land office in Salida —Del Norte had been nothing more than a trading post for mountain men and buffalo hunters in those days— and he and Ma had commenced to build the cabin while Ma was already showing with Roy. It was a nice place they'd built on. The buildings used to reflect that pride and the dreams of the man and woman who'd built them.

Then Ma died and everything started to gradually go to hell.

Matt looked distastefully down at the boards of the

porch steps before him. They all needed to be torn out and replaced. Before winter settled in, he needed to mix up some chinking and slather it in between the logs all around the cabin, for in many places daylight shone through. When he had the cabin tight, he'd go to work rebuilding the corral, because most of that had gone to hell over the long years of neglect, as well. He couldn't house broncs in there while he was gentling them. Hell, he couldn't house Shetland ponies in there now. They'd bust a whole section down with a single kick.

All in good time.

Severance had all the time in the world.

At thirty-seven, he was still a relatively young man. Leastways, he was strong. And he was determined.

He'd prove up on his homegrown, his father's and mother's land, now *his* land. It would once again reflect the pride and dreams of a Severance, and so would his successful horse ranching business. He had kin nearby, too. He had a daughter nearby. He might not ever be able to tell her that he was her father, but he knew it. And at least from the distance, he'd watch her grow up. With any luck, she'd marry a boy from one of the area ranches. There were getting to be more and more of them now. Maybe she'd stay here, and Matt could watch her kids, his grandkids, grow up.

What of Eva?

Maybe he could make amends with her. Maybe they...

*No, don't think about that*, he admonished himself. *One step at a time. Stick with the fixing up of the place, the porch, the chinking, the cabin's roof, the corral...*

*One step at a time.*

He sipped the coffee steaming in his hand and then turned to look around the inside of the cabin. He'd cleaned it out nicely, hauled out all the trash, and scrubbed it down—the floor, the cupboards, the walls, and even the ceiling, ridding the place of every inch of years of dust, grime, and fire soot. He'd aired out the rugs and wool blankets and washed his bedding and all the quilts he could find, some of which had been sewn by his ma, though most of hers had long since gone to tatters and been discarded.

*Ah, the years do pass. But I'm here. I'm home. And it feels damn good.*

He took another sip of his stout, black mud.

His eyes drifted to the table, freshly scrubbed clean with soap and a brush following his king-sized breakfast. His gaze settled on the folded leaf of paper there, beside the hurricane lamp in the table's center.

He turned away from the paper as he'd turned away from the other thoughts that, if he dwelled on them too long, would become like goat head thorns under a camp blanket—chafing, tearing, gouging.

He winced, helpless against the memory of what Cheyenne had told him she'd found among her father's papers, in a footlocker Roy had kept at the foot of his and Eva's bed. It was a mining claim that Roy had filed at the land office in town. According to the description of the land on the claim, the mine was somewhere near the base of Thunder Mountain, in that devil's playground of a canyon in which Bloody Joe had shot and killed Roy.

Had Roy hidden the money on his claim?

Suppose he'd started work on the claim, maybe even built a shed to sleep in and for storing his equipment? Cheyenne had said that over the past few years before he'd died, her father had spent several days away from their cabin after calving every spring and just before and after the autumn roundups. Matt hadn't known about it, because those times had been busy for him and Pa here at the Half-Moon.

Roy had been very quiet and mysterious about what he'd been doing. By that time, he and Eva's marriage had disintegrated to the point that they had mostly stopped speaking to each other. He believed that it was guilt for her brief affair with him, Matt, that had soured their marriage. Perhaps she'd even confessed the tryst to Roy. Maybe that's why Roy had become all but alienated from him, as well.

Of course, Cheyenne didn't know what had soured her parents' marriage. But she believed that because her mother and father were no longer speaking, or maybe just out of pure paranoia, her father never told her mother of his workings around Thunder Mountain. She believed that he'd been spending that mysterious time away proving up on his claim so he could acquire a patent for it.

Then suddenly he stopped leaving for prolonged periods in the spring and fall. Possibly, the curious and precocious girl opined, it was his disappointment at having found no gold that turned him back to rustling and holdups.

Still, however, what better place to stow that forty thousand dollars than at the claim he'd given up on?

There, he'd easily find it when he returned for it. If he'd stowed it anywhere else in that canyon, he'd likely never be able to find it again. The west was peppered with such treasures, simply lost like the proverbial needle in a haystack.

If the claim was well-concealed, no one else would likely ever find it.

Roy hadn't even told Matt about the claim.

That made Matt think that somehow Roy had discovered Cheyenne wasn't his. Either Eva had told him or he'd just seen how, day after day as the child had matured, she'd more and more come to resemble her "uncle."

Guilt like a rat chewed at Matt's guts as he gazed at the folded paper.

How could he have done what he'd done—allowed that meeting with Eva sixteen years ago at Wolf Creek to turn into the forbidden debacle it had become? She and Roy had been married only a couple of weeks. Matt sensed later that Eva had been having cold feet. He knew she'd still loved him. Maybe he'd still loved her, as well, and that's why it had gotten so out of control, and they'd stripped, swam, and frolicked as they had when they had been going together.

His eyes returned to the paper.

That was why Roy hadn't told him about the claim.

Somehow, he'd learned that Cheyenne wasn't his but Matt's.

It was just like Roy not to say anything but to harbor those hurt feelings, that hatred, that jealousy and humiliation all those years.

It was why Roy hadn't involved him in the payroll robbery, as well. Matt had chosen to walk the straight and narrow by then. Still, Roy would have at least asked him, at least tried to get his younger brother to join in the "fun," which was what Roy had always called it.

Matt eyed the paper.

He'd tried not to think about it after Cheyenne had produced it and told him about it, but it had chewed on the edges of his consciousness at night. This morning, he'd busied himself with a big breakfast, trying to distract himself. Still, it was there.

Had Roy hidden the loot at his claim?

Was forty thousand dollars just lying out there, at the bottom of some exploratory hole, somewhere around the base of Thunder Mountain?

Before he returned to the Half-Moon, Matt hadn't thought about the money. He'd been glad he didn't know where it was. He'd focused all his attention on clearing his name, of trying to convince people he'd had no part in the robbery.

No, he hadn't thought about the money.

Now, after Cheyenne's visit the night before, he couldn't get it off his mind.

Cheyenne had looked for it, but the description of the location on the claim certificate was too technical. Even if it hadn't been, that devil's playground was infamous for getting folks lost. The light and shadows played with a person's mind until they had no idea what direction they were heading in. Riding through the canyon at the base of Thunder Mountain was like riding through a maze that kept changing. It was an illusion, of course, but it seemed so real, perilous, and horrifying.

Cheyenne had ridden down there once and got lost nearly right away. She'd spent a panicked few hours trying to find her way out and when she finally did, she'd vowed never to attempt looking for her father's cache again. At least, not without the help of someone who knew the area well.

Like Matt, who'd explored it with Roy when they'd been fearless boys.

Matt stared at the folded paper on the table, but what he was seeing were the badlands around Thunder Mountain. If anyone could find Roy's claim, he could.

His heart quickened its pace.

He just now realized that a cold sweat had broken out

on the back of his neck. A single bead trickled coolly down under his shirt, along his spine.

He hardened his jaws against his anxiousness. Against his own innate greed.

*You can't do it,* he silently told himself. *You came back here to make things simpler, not to complicate matters. Not after all these years to return to the outlaw trail.*

*What would you do with that money if you found it?*

*You'd have to leave, of course, if you wanted to spend it.*

*And folks would believe that you'd come back for the loot and had lit off with it. Someday, someone would hunt you down.*

*You could never spend it. At least not anywhere nearby. You'd have to change your name, find a whole new identity, a whole new way of life...*

*But...would that be so bad...?*

*What about Cheyenne and Eva?*

*You'd have to take them with you.*

"No!" he heard himself grate out through gritted teeth, clenching his fists at his sides.

"No, what?" came a voice from outside. A female voice. "I haven't even announced myself yet."

The voice brought Matt back to the here and now. It was like climbing up from the bottom of a deep well. He felt badly disoriented. He turned slowly to the door, frowning. He hadn't heard anyone ride up.

Cheyenne?

No, it hadn't been her voice.

Matt set his cup of now-cold coffee on the table and swung around to step through the open door and onto the rickety stoop. His heart lurched when he saw the pretty blonde sitting the handsome, long-legged brown-and-white tobiano stallion only a few feet from the porch.

She raised a black-gloved hand to shield her eyes from the intensifying rays of the climbing sun, and spread her red, bee-stung lips to show fine, white teeth as she said, "Well, hello there, stranger. You've returned to the scene of the crime, have you?"

# CHAPTER 16

"HELLO, JODI," SEVERANCE SAID, GIVING THE GIRL A warm smile as he stood facing her from atop the porch steps, the condition of which he felt ashamed of. But then, he felt ashamed of how poorly the entire place looked—especially to a pretty girl, the daughter of a neighboring rancher, Karl Miller, who'd once been close friends with Matt's father, Big John. "You've grown up, too," he mused aloud.

He remembered her as the feisty, awkward girl, a young teenager trying to prove she could do the work of any man on roundup and during branding. He'd also seen her from a distance a few times at her family's Triple Seven Ranch, when he'd worked breaking horses for her father—usually very late or very early in the year, when he and Big John had needed extra cash.

He hadn't known Jodi beyond that, for she was a good fifteen years younger than he. In fact, he couldn't remember exchanging more than a handful of words with the girl. Before he'd lit out from the Half-Moon two years ago, he hadn't seen her on the range for several years. He'd figured her parents were trying to make a lady out of her and marry her off to some wealthy rancher's son, or maybe the son of a businessman in town. Karl Miller had always been well connected.

The young woman frowned. Curly, yellow hair spilled across her shoulders clad in a soft, brown deerskin dress over a red-and-brown checked shirt, the tails of which were tucked into a long, light-tan riding skirt to which wisps of dust and weed seeds clung. A cream hat, its rawhide thong snugged against the underside of her chin, sat on her pretty, pug-nosed face with sparkling hazel eyes.

"Too?" Jodi Miller said. "Ah, you've seen your niece."

She smiled again, those hazel eyes holding on his. Was he just being paranoid or had she given "niece" a little emphasis, subtly announcing that she knew Cheyenne was more than his niece. Did that mean this entire neck of the San Juans knew?

He kicked the thought out of his mind, and said, "Time marches on."

"Was that what the 'no' was about?"

Severance frowned. "The 'no'? Oh, that." He felt the warmth of embarrassment rise in his cheeks, remembering the exclamation he'd fairly shouted at himself inside only a moment ago, staring at that damnable mining claim of Roy's. Commanding himself not to go after the money like every other damn fool cowpuncher or mule skinner in south-central Colorado had already done. "A rat. Trying to rid the place of them but I keep seeing one more."

"Ah. Get a cat."

"I might just do that."

"Come riding with me, Matt?"

Again, Severance frowned.

She turned her head to take in the country, her thick,

curly hair jostling about her shoulders, before she returned her sparkling gaze to him, smiling. "Beautiful day."

Suddenly, he saw an underlying brittleness in her smile. He hadn't seen her for years. He'd heard she'd married but her husband had been killed in an accident of some kind, and she'd returned to the Miller Triple Seven. Now, she was suddenly here at the Half-Moon, wanting to go riding.

Anger rose in him. He tamped it down, gave what he hoped would come off as a reluctant smile.

"I'm sorry—I can't, Jodi. Too much work to do."

Again, she raised a hand to shade her eyes. "Pa would like you to break some horses for him."

"He would?"

"Sure. Just like old times. He said you were the best horse breaker in the San Juans. He got top dollar for the ones you broke years ago."

"I'm surprised you even remember that."

"It wasn't all that long ago."

Severance just stared at her. Suspicions swirled inside him, but he wasn't sure he could trust them. Maybe he was just being paranoid and this pretty girl, fifteen years his junior, really did want to go riding with him, fifteen years her senior. Maybe Karl Miller really did want him to break horses for him. One thing Matt did know—he could use the extra cash.

Just like old times.

"Matt, I know what you're thinking. I'm not here about...about the money. The money you an'—" Abruptly, she stopped, shook her head. "I mean about the mine payroll. I don't care about that, if that's what you're thinking. I just thought..." She glanced off again then returned her gaze to his and he could no longer see anything phony in it. "I just thought you could use a friend. As I could." She leaned forward against her saddle horn, drew a deep breath, regarded Severance levelly. "I'm a widow. Did you know that?"

"I heard. I'm sorry."

"I could use a friend, too."

"I'm sorry, Jodi. Like I said, I have—"

"I know, I know." She straightened in her saddle. This time her smile was both brittle and phony. "You have work to do. What shall I tell Pa about *his* offer?"

"Tell him I'll think about it. I have to get a few things done around here first."

"All right, then."

The pretty blonde smiled, pinched her hat brim, neck reined the tobiano around, and booted the horse into a hard gallop through the yard and across the creek and into the cottonwoods beyond where they disappeared for a few seconds before reappearing again on the trail curving south along the broad valley carved over the centuries by the Animas River. Horse and rider disappeared behind the southern ridge and the horse's thuds dwindled until there was only the sound of the birds and the breeze in the Half-Moon yard.

Severance stood on the porch, staring across the creek at the cottonwoods and their flashing silver leaves, feeling suddenly very lonely. He looked at the high country jutting before him, the high, bald crags and the long slopes troughed with canyons and carpeted with pines and firs beckoned.

He did need a ride. But he needed to ride out alone, to be alone with his thoughts. His return home had become far more complicated than he'd anticipated.

He returned to the cabin and looked once more at Roy's mine claim on the table. His hands grew hot. He was about to pluck the claim off the table and stuff it into his pocket for safekeeping. But he knew that if he had the claim on him, he wouldn't be able to resist the temptation to ride over to Thunder Mountain, five miles as the crow flies away from the Half-Moon, and begin scouring those canyons that troughed down the sides of the steep, craggy formation's pedestal-like base, looking for Roy's claim. He didn't need that temptation. He must stay pure in his motives for returning to his home country, though for the life of him he couldn't clearly remember just what those motives had been.

Part of him wished he'd ridden out with Jodi Miller, after all. She might have been the distraction he needed, even if the young woman's own motives were likely anything but pure. But then, whose motives were ever pure, when you got right down to brass tacks?

Severance stuck the claim in the hollow of a ceiling beam in which his old man, who'd lost his trust in banks in his latter, alcohol-sodden years, had kept his own savings. Matt had had a feeling that ever since he'd returned to the Half-Moon, he'd been being watched from one of the surrounding ridges. Probably closely watched. That could have been paranoia, too, but better safe than sorry.

He adjusted the saddlebags he'd draped over his left shoulder, picked up his Winchester, left the cabin, and headed for the stable and corral in which he'd housed the black.

A little over an hour later, after a refreshing ride through the broad canyon of the Animas and up a steeply sloping side canyon, Matt put the black up onto a broad, open, sun-washed ridge crest. From here he could see down the gently sloping ground before him and across a broad twisting canyon the jutting hulk of Thunder

Mountain, which was four bald, granite crags jutting high against the cerulean sky from a forested pedestal with deep, rocky chasms running vertically down its sides. Thunder Mountain and the main canyon skirting it, carved by an ancient, long-defunct river, was a wild tangle of a country, and many a man searching for gold or silver had become forever lost in it.

Years ago, Matt and Roy had found the bones of a man strewn about Spanish armor including part of a conquistador's helmet and what remained of a Spanish spear, both of which the boys had hauled back to the Half-Moon as keepsakes. Another time, they'd found more human remains around the mouth of a shallow mine as well as the bones of what Roy opined was a donkey. The gold-seeker and his pack animal had likely been killed by a wild cat or a grizzly. Judging by the bits of clothing and hide clinging to both sets of bones, the pair's demise had happened between five and ten years earlier.

Each set of grisly findings, spaced roughly a year apart, had sent both boys scrambling back out of the canyon skirting Thunder Mountain and back to the Half-Moon with a bad case of the "creepy-crawlies."

Severance smiled now at the memory as he sat the black on the open stretch of gently sloping ground with steep, forested ridges rising on three sides around him and the somehow malign-looking formation of Thunder Mountain jutting straight ahead of him, appearing much closer than it really was, thrusting those four bald crags high against the sky, as though to give God a jeering poke.

Matt was glad he didn't have Roy's claim with him.

He couldn't resist visiting Thunder Mountain. If he had the claim, however, he might not have been able to resist the urge to put the black ahead and down into the canyon to try and match up the description of the mine's location with a nook or cranny in one of those secondary canyons scoring the pedestal beneath the jutting crags.

Yeah, he'd leave it there.

Better yet, he'd burn it.

Cheyenne might not forgive him, but that was all right. She already had a lot to not forgive him about. She just didn't know it. Besides, he'd be doing her a favor.

The black, who had lowered his head to crop the fescue and needlegrass growing in these high climes, a good ten thousand feet above sea level, suddenly lifted its head and rolled its eyes around warily. It twitched its ears and gave a near-soundless whicker deep in its chest.

"What is it, boy?"

But then he heard it, too.

He whipped his head around as the thuds of several slow-moving horses touched his ears. The hooves making crunching, thumping sounds in the forest duff of needles and old leaves grew steadily louder as Severance watched a dozen or so riders ride slowly up the ridge he'd climbed a few minutes ago, the heads of the horses appearing first and then the heads of the riders—all twelve riding side by side, roughly ten feet apart.

When the horsebackers gained the top of the ridge and they rode out of the pine and fir forest, the lead rider —the only one not wearing a Stetson and sitting her cream mare in the middle of the pack—held up a black-gloved hand.

"Hold on, you men," said the ratcheting, crone-like drone of Ethel Beech, matriarch of the Triangle Cross. She turned her pale, cadaverous face with large, crow-like, inky black eyes to her son, Garrett, riding to her left and holding a Winchester carbine across his saddlebow. "That him, boy?"

She turned her malignant gaze to Severance, and added, "Haven't seen him in years." She drew out the "years" so that in her smoker's rasp it sounded like the long, slow squawk of unoiled hinges.

"That's him, Ma," Garrett Beech said. He nudged the brim of his black hat a little higher and smiled malevolently. "That's Roy's brother, Matt. Come lookin' for his loot!"

## CHAPTER 17

SEVERANCE REINED THE BLACK AROUND TO FACE THE crow-like matriarch of the Triangle Cross and her gun-hung punchers spread out to each side of her, the black-hatted and vested Garrett sitting his dun to her left. Ethel Beech wore a black knit cape with the hood drawn up, and a long, dark-green wool skirt beneath the hem of which showed worn, black, stovepipe boots.

Severance doubted he'd seen the woman in twenty years. Believed to be a recluse or suffering from some malady, possibly arthritis, Mrs. Beech usually made herself scarce and left the range work to her drovers. She preferred her harsh reputation precede her and speak for itself. That made her more mysterious and threatening. When there was especially dirty work to be done, however—like hanging nesters or rustlers—she usually led the way.

She was rarely seen in town but couldn't resist leaving her ranch for a good, old-fashioned necktie party. She had more than a bit of the she-wolf in her.

Anger rose in Severance, as did chagrin. How had he let a dozen riders shadow him without his knowing about it? Had he been living at the Half-Moon long enough without trouble that he'd grown careless? Or maybe he'd been distracted by sentiment, with wool gathering, remembering the good ol' days when he and Roy had been young, when they'd still been brotherly with no unspoken chasm between them...

He shifted his gaze from Garrett to his mother and gave a caustic chuff.

"You think I'd ride up here lookin' for the loot in broad daylight?"

"I don't know," Ethel Beech said, blinking those black, crow's eyes once, slowly, then drilling her gaze into him from across the forty yards between them. "Are you?"

"No." Or was he? What if he'd had the claim paper?

Ethel Beech glanced to her left then to her right and nudged her cream forward. The others booted their own horses forward, as well, moving slowly but steadily toward Severance. Fear touched him. He knew what Ethel Beech was capable of. He wanted to swing the black around and run. But he wouldn't have done that even if he had anywhere to run to but into the canyon, where he'd surely be run down.

He was done running. Even from Ethel Beech.

He sat the black tensely. The horse could sense his anxiousness. Severance felt it tense its muscles beneath the saddle. It shook its head, nearly throwing the bit.

"Easy, boy," Matt said, maintaining a mild expression as he watched the twelve riders including the old matriarch herself move toward him, several of the riders at each end of the procession curving around him to partway encircle him, so he couldn't escape if he tried.

The old, crow-like eyes of Ethel Beech bore into him

as she rode toward him, her long, pale craggy face, framed by the cape's black hood, as hard as stone.

She drew rein ten feet away from Severance. The others checked their own mounts down then, as well, at nearly the same distance away from him, nearly surrounding him. The day had suddenly turned dark. Severance had thought it was his mood reflecting the appearance of this droll woman and her uncompromising riders, most of them practiced killers as well as cowmen. But no. He glanced up to see that flat, steel-gray clouds with scalloped edges had moved in, blocking most of the sunlight.

Ethel Beech sat ramrod straight in the saddle. She couldn't have stood much over five feet tall nor weighed more than a hundred pounds, but she commanded the authority of men much taller than she, and with twice as many pounds. Bags hung beneath her eyes as she gazed darkly at Severance as though waiting for his gaze to waver.

It didn't.

The other men sat silently, slouched easily in their saddles. Most looked grave or disinterested while a couple of others, including Garrett Beech, smirked at him, as though they knew a secret they were just about bursting to share.

Finally, the old bird croaked out, "I hear you're back at Half-Moon."

"That's right. It's my home."

"I've claimed it as my own."

"You have no legal grounds. I paid the taxes on it while I was away. I worked hard, saved my money."

"Still, I've claimed it."

"Not legally."

She had no response to that, knowing that the law in

Del Norte, Bloody Joe Mannion, would not back her play. Most lawmen she could have bought or cowed, but not Bloody Joe. That no doubt graveled the old hen something fierce.

"I doubt you've come to stay, anyway," she said, her voice so gravelly and raspy that it made Severance's own throat hurt to hear it. She turned her head slightly to one side and narrowed a suspicious eye at him. "You just came back, hoping enough time had passed that no one would notice, for the loot you and your brother stole."

"Like I told your son," Severance said hardening his jaws in frustration, "that's not true. I haven't done any sneaking around."

"Only one way to find out," the old woman said, raising her voice until it became the whine of a dull, steam-powered sawblade. "Boys, draw and quarter him!"

They moved on him quickly, both wings of the semicircle breaking away from the old matriarch, their horses closing tightly around Matt. Severance was momentarily stunned by the command. Then it hit home what she'd ordered, and in a panic, he rammed steel against the black's loins.

The horse lunged off its rear hooves but before it had taken more than two steps, Garrett Beech, grinning maliciously, slid the butt of his rifle out in front of Severance. Matt's head slammed against it. The blow sent him tumbling straight back over the cantle of his saddle. He turned a backward somersault over the black's arched tail and struck the ground hard on his chest and belly, the black's rear hooves kicking dirt and gravel on him as it bolted, fleeing.

Matt rose to his hands and knees, shaking his head to clear the cobwebs.

Birds sang in his ears, and his vision was blurry.

Still, he lunged to his feet and as two men closed on him, he struck one with a haymaker. But then the ever-grinning Garrett Beech came up on his right and rammed the butt of his rifle against the side of Matt's head. Severance's knees buckled and then a warm darkness enveloped him from a time before he managed to swim up through the cloying unconsciousness and open his eyes.

Horror kicked him like the hoof of an angry horse.

He looked up to see Ethel Beech, still sitting her cream horse, gazing down at him with a slight, self-satisfied smirk quirking the corners of her thin-lipped mouth. Matt's arms and legs were spread wide. He looked down the length of his spread-eagle body to see that his boots had been removed and that rope had been tied tightly around each ankle. He looked up to each side to see that a length of rope had also been tied to each of his wrists.

The ropes tied to his ankles and wrists stretched away from him, the opposite ends dallied around the saddle horns of four horses standing with their rears facing him, each of the four riders hipped around in their saddles, regarding him with malignant grins.

Garrett Beech sat the horse to whose saddle horn Severance's left ankle was attached via an eight-foot length of nearly razor-wire-taut hemp. All four ropes were stretched so tightly that Severance thought if the four horses took a single step away from him, they'd pull his shoulders and hips from their sockets, for such was the grating pain radiating through every inch of his being from each strained joint.

Ethel Beech stared coolly down at him. "Where's the loot, Severance? Where did you and your brother hide it?"

Severance glared up at the crazy old crone, fury and

terror rolling through him in waves. "I didn't ride with Roy that day! I don't know where the loot is!"

Ethel Beech looked at her son. "Ahead just a little."

Garrett grinned and looked at the other three riders with the ropes dallied around their saddle horns. The rest of the men sat in a complete circle behind Ethel Beech, her son, and the three riders who were essentially set to draw and quarter Severance.

"No!" Matt wailed as the four riders put their horses ahead half a step.

He felt the bones of his hips and shoulders grinding, pulling at the sinews holding them in place. Severance glanced at the old crone and bellowed, his voice cracking, "I don't know where it is!"

"Sure, you do," said Ethel Beech in that low, ratcheting voice. "The girl visited you last night. Today, you rode to Thunder Mountain. She's been out here, you know. Looking around herself." The old crone smiled, her nearly lipless mouth stretching in a straight line. "She knows, doesn't she? And she told you."

"No, she doesn't know!" Matt said, panting, grinding his teeth against the pain in every limb, his horror growing now to encompass Cheyenne, as well. Why did she have to find that claim paper? "Just snooping around," he continued, breathing hard, cold sweat bathing every inch of him. "She doesn't know where it is, and I don't—"

He stopped when Ethel Beech shuttled her coolly malevolent gaze from Matt to her son.

"No!" Matt begged.

"Ahead just a little more, son," Ethel Beech said in an almost jovial tone.

Again, Matt wailed, "*No! Stop, you crazy bitch!*"

The horses started to step ahead, sending waves of

misery through Matt as his hips and legs felt as though they were about to be pulled from their sockets, the tendons holding them in place strained to nearly the breaking point. He threw his head back, feeling the rope-like sinews in his neck tightening and standing out, and closed his eyes in unbearable agony. "Damn you, *nooo!*"

A rifle cracked. The thundering report chased the echoes of Matt's last wail skyward. Crows cawed distantly.

Ethel Beech's black eyes snapped wide in sudden fury. She jerked her head around, hipping around in her saddle, to gaze back toward the forested ridge up which she'd climbed with her riders, following Severance.

The other riders swung their own gazes in the same direction. Beneath the high-pitched ringing in his ears, Matt heard the slow thuds of an approaching rider. Turning his head to stare at the ridge through a gap between Ethel Beech's cream and the dun of one of her riders, he saw a single rider emerge from the forest at the top of the ridge and ride slowly toward the scene of savage torture.

The man was tall, broad-shouldered, and with long, salt-and-pepper hair hanging down over the collar of his dark-red corduroy shirt over which he wore a black leather vest. He wore a broad brimmed, high-crowned black Stetson, and he rode a tall, handsome bay. He held a Winchester Yellowboy repeater barrel up on his right thigh.

The upper half of his face was shaded by the brim of his hat, but the steely light shone in the salt-and-pepper mustache mantling the knife slash of his mouth.

Matt saw two of the Triangle Cross riders snap their own rifles into action.

The newcomer's Winchester roared twice, quickly,

throwing both of Ethel Beech's riders over the tails of their horses. Each mount whinnied and fled, buck-kicking, dragging their reins along the ground beside them.

The newcomer cocked his rifle one-handed and came on steadily, holding the rifle straight out from his right hip. A thin tendril of smoke curled from the barrel as he slid the handsome long gun from his right to his left and back again, encompassing the entirety of Ethel Beech's savage horde encircling Matt. The ropes attached to Severance's wrists and ankles were still drawn taut.

When he drew to within ten feet of the matriarch of the Triangle Cross, the newcomer drew rein. As he did, a ray of sun suddenly poking through thinning clouds, slid up beneath the broad brim of the man's Stetson and fairly glistened in the stern, wolfish gray orbs of Bloody Joe Mannion.

Without expression, holding his reins taut in one hand, the cocked rifle in the other, the Del Norte town marshal turned to the old matriarch and said in a mock jovial tone, "Good day to you, Ethel. Up to your old tricks, I see."

# CHAPTER 18

"THIS IS NONE OF YOUR AFFAIR, MANNION," SAID Ethel Beech, glaring over the head of her fine cream mare. "And you owe me for two good riders!"

She slid her dark gaze to the two men piled in bloody heaps roughly fifteen feet away from each other, to her right, Mannion's left. Each had taken a bullet to the heart, dead before they'd hit the ground. That was the price you paid for threatening Bloody Joe.

Keeping his Winchester aimed at Ethel's belly, Joe said tightly, keeping his rage on a short leash, "Tell your men to slacken those ropes *now*. By the time I count to three, Ethel, or you'll take one you can't digest. I mean it! One...two...th—"

"Back up, boys," the Triangle Cross matriarch bellowed out in her tight, grating rasp, throwing her right arm up, keeping her now-fearful, black eyes glued to the maw of Mannion's Winchester.

Matt screamed as the four horses backed toward him and the slackening ropes fell to the ground. He rolled onto his side, bringing his knees to his belly and closing his arms over his chest, rolling back and forth and moaning as the balls of his hips and shoulders eased back into their rightful places.

"Ahh, Christ!" he bit out, glaring up at the back of Ethel Beech, who still faced Mannion, eyeing the Winchester aimed at her gut.

As Severance sat up, pulled his bowie knife from the scabbard on his right hip, behind the Colt that was still in its holster, Ethel said, "You're on Triangle Cross range, Joe. You're trespassing. I'll remember that!"

"This is open range, you old devil!"

"You know I've always claimed this strip for my own!"

Mannion chuckled and leaned forward over his Winchester, jutting his chin at the irascible, old crow sitting her saddle four feet away from him, "Claimin's one thing! Ownin's another!"

He sat back in his saddle. "Now gather your dead and get you and your men back to your devil's lair!"

Sitting his dun near where Severance had just cut the rope tied to his right ankle, Garrett Beech thrust out an arm and admonishing finger at the Del Norte marshal. "Dammit, Mannion, you can't talk to my mother..."

He let his voice trail off as Mannion slid his Winchester slightly to the right, aiming it now at the younger Beech's guts instead of at his mother's.

"Hightail it!" Mannion said, his voice drawn taut as razor wire, his own malevolent gaze on his lips.

Ethel Beech spat angrily, loudly to one side, glared at Mannion once more, then reined her mare around Mannion's bay and, yelling, "Come on, boys. We'll deal with Bloody Joe later!" put the steel to her mount and galloped off toward the lip of the ridge. Her men followed—all but the two who'd dismounted to throw the two dead men over the backs of their horses, behind the saddles and over the bedrolls, and tied them quickly.

Then, casting owly looks at Mannion, they galloped off after the others, who had disappeared into the timber carpeting the steep slope into the canyon beyond.

Mannion looked at Severance. The younger man was limping around, rubbing his wrists, trying to get the blood back into his grieved joints.

"Mister," Mannion said, "I always took you for way smarter than you obviously are. Wild as hell, a cattle-rustlin', stagecoach robbin' firebrand for sure, but smart. Smarter than Roy. Now I see I had you wrong."

"Oh, hell, Mannion." Severance limped over to where his hat lay on the ground. He picked it up and slapped it against his knees, causing dust to billow. He squinted up at Joe. "Don't add insult to injury, will you?"

"You must have known she was having the Half-Moon watched. You must have known she...or *someone*... would follow you to Thunder Mountain. But still, you did it. In broad daylight, no less."

"You followed me, too?"

"Yep. Saw one of the two Triangle Cross men watching your place from the southern ridge—I was on the north one—skedaddle over to fetch his boss. I followed her followin' *you*."

Severance reshaped his hat then scowled up at Mannion, incredulous. "Then you must've seen them take me down and tie me up."

"Yeah, I was holed up just beneath the lip of the ridge." Joe jerked his chin to indicate the forested slope dropping away behind him. "Watched the whole thing through my field glasses."

"You might've intervened a little sooner!"

"I might have," Mannion allowed, nodding.

"But you didn't!"

"No, no—I intervened just when I figured they were

about to turn you into a human wishbone." Mannion grinned. "And make a wish."

Severance stuffed his hat on his head and planted one gloved hand on his hip. "You were waiting to see if I'd spill my guts about the loot."

"That's about the size of it, yep."

"I was about to pass out!"

"I seen that. That's when I climbed up on old Red and came ridin' to your rescue." Joe frowned and narrowed one eye. "Say, I haven't heard a thank you yet."

"Oh, Christ, Mannion." Severance shook his head and gave a droll laugh. "You believe me now?"

"That you don't know where the loot is? I always did. I just wanted to make sure. "Again, Joe gave an ironic smile. "Now, I know for sure. I'll sleep a whole lot easier. Been preyin' on me, you see."

Severance gave a caustic chuff then stared at his black standing about a hundred yards away, idly cropping grass. Its saddle and bedroll hung down its side. Severance clucked. The black lifted its head then walked toward Severance for several steps before breaking into a trot, reins bouncing along the ground to each side, the saddle hanging a little lower.

"Well-trained hoss," Joe observed.

"Gentled him myself. Took him as pay from Lyle Littleton."

"From outside of Hayes?" Mannion said. "Big rancher. I remember the name. He paid you with a good horse, must've appreciated your work."

"He did," Severance said matter-of-factly, watching the black approach.

"You're smart about horses, not so smart about staying alive."

"Yeah, well," Severance said as the black stopped

before him and turned its left side to him, "I needed a ride to blow the stable green out of both the black an' me. Just found myself headed this way and couldn't stop."

"Figured you'd poke around for it, too, did you?"

Severance didn't seem sure how to answer. He turned his thoughtful gaze to the bold, forbidding formation of Thunder Mountain. He glanced at Mannion and, shaking his head, said, "No. No, I didn't. Can't say as I've never been tempted to take a look, but I knew that if someone saw, I'd just rekindle the old suspicions."

"Which you just did."

Severance winced as he righted his saddle on the black's back. "I have to admit, Marshal Mannion, I'm not always the sharpest tool in the shed."

Mannion knew it was more complicated than that, but as Severance reached under the horse's belly to tighten the cinch, Mannion said, "No, that's obvious. But you're here now, and the word is as good as out."

Grunting as he tightened the strap, Severance looked up at the lawman, a question in his eyes.

"Want to go take a look around?" Joe asked him.

Severance canted his head toward Thunder Mountain. "In the canyon?"

Mannion hiked a shoulder.

Severance stood regarding him thoughtfully. He said, "I always did wonder where you shot him. The place my brother died. You'll show me?"

Joe nodded. "Let's go." He suddenly realized he was as curious about that loot as anyone else. He really did want to take a look around. Hell, for all he knew, he might find those saddlebags behind a rock at the bottom of the formation atop which he'd killed Roy. Likely, not. He and Rio had searched the area thoroughly two and a half years ago.

But you never knew. And there was a sizable reward for the return of the money to the mine to which it belonged.

Mannion silently laughed at himself. Hell, he was thinking the same way all the other fools who'd scoured the canyon had been thinking.

On the other hand, one of them might have found it. Of course, he'd likely have heard about it by now. Word of something like that spreads fast. Whoever might have found it would have blabbed by now or revealed themselves by spending the money too fast and ostentatiously.

How did the old Spanish saying go?

"Gold and love affairs are difficult to hide."

Severance mounted his black and he and Mannion rode down the gentle slope and into the canyon, the shadow-limned formation of Thunder Mountain leaning over them like the most belligerent of sullen gods.

---

AN HOUR LATER, DEEP IN THE CANYON AS WELL AS DEEP in the shadow cast by Thunder Mountain, Mannion rode around the base of a large escarpment and drew rein. Severance followed him around the scarp and stopped his black to Mannion's right.

"That's it," Joe said, dipping his chin to indicate a column of rock roughly a hundred yards away and up a sharp, rock- and gravel-peppered rise. The column was on the far side of the mouth of a narrow, secondary canyon scoring the forested pedestal of Thunder Mountain.

"That's where Roy held up," Severance said, sliding a grave look to Mannion. "Tried to bushwhack you?"

Joe nodded. "On the backside of the formation is the slope he climbed to get to the top and holed up in the rocks up there. He slapped his horse on ahead. Rio and I were following the tracks when I...I don't know what it was, but I got an uneasy feeling. I felt we were being watched. Roy must have seen us slow our pace, hesitate, and get edgy. I saw the sun flash off his rifle when he hauled down on us. I whipped around with my Yellowboy. His first and only shot went just a hair wild. Both of mine struck Roy in the chest."

Mannion lowered his gaze to the base of the column maybe twenty feet up the gravelly slope. "He fell, landed there."

"He didn't die right away?" Severance asked.

Mannion shook his head. He'd never talked to Matt about his brother's death. The information Severance had must have come secondhand.

"Not right away," Joe said. "It was quick, but not right away."

"Did he say anything?"

"He told me to go to hell."

Severance snorted a wry laugh, nodded. For a long time, he stared at the natural stone column deep in the shadow of Thunder Mountain. Then he glanced at Mannion, said, "I have to take a closer look."

He booted the black ahead and drew rein at the base of the gravelly slope. Joe stopped Red beside him. Severance dismounted and walked along the curve of the slope's base until he'd disappeared in the shadows on the other side of the column, which rose roughly fifty feet above the bench it was mounted on.

Mannion sat Red, looking around the canyon, the dark shadows in contrast to the bright, lens-clear light. It was almost like the difference between the darkest hour of the night and the brightest one of the day. From somewhere came the ratcheting cry of a hunting hawk. A faint breeze stirred, nibbling at the brim of Mannion's hat. Those were the only sounds save for the slight rustling sound of sage branches rubbing against each other.

Joe considered taking a look around but nixed the idea. He and Rio had been the first to scour the area for the loot and hadn't found it. If it hadn't been found by now, it likely never would be. Unless by someone who knew its location...

Mannion looked down to see that his right hand was closed over the walnut grips of the Russian holstered on his right thigh. It was then he realized he felt nearly the same edginess he'd felt the last time he'd visited this remote, storied place. Not only its up-and-down terrain and remoteness made it dangerous. Other men, those on the run from the law, as well as wildcats and grizzly bears made it a perilous place be, especially after dark. Some said the ghosts of the men who'd died here, white men as well as those known only as "the ancient ones," haunted this dinosaur's mouth of steep cliffs, deep canyons, forested slopes, and ancient riverbeds.

Maybe that knowledge was what had filed the edge on Mannion's nerves.

Or...maybe he and Severance were being shadowed.

He whipped around in his saddle. He couldn't see very far back along the canyon's twisting course, so he wasn't all that relieved not to see anyone on his back trail.

He shunted his gaze to the top of the column. Severance was up there, gloved thumbs hooked behind his cartridge belt, looking around. A stray ray of gold sunlight angling through a gap in the four peaks comprising Thunder Mountain touched the brim of the younger man's black Stetson.

Mannion gave him some time to consider the place

where his brother had breathed his last, shot by none other than the man he'd ridden into the canyon with— what a mix of contrasting emotions must be awash in the younger's man mind—then, not needing to raise his voice much to be heard in the canyon's ethereal silence, Joe said, "You see anything from up there? Anything *unusual?*"

Severance dropped his chin to stare down at him then lifted his head to gaze back along his and Mannion's back trail. He returned his gaze to Mannion, shook his head, and said, "No. You think we were followed?"

"I don't know. I always think I'm being followed." Again, Joe looked around. Then he looked at Red. The bay didn't seem to be overly bothered. Still, he looked at Severance, and said, "If you'd had enough time, we'd best pull foot. Gets mighty dark down here of a night."

"Don't I know it."

Severance turned, walked toward the far side of the column, toward where it formed a corner with the granite wall, then dropped down out of sight. A couple of minutes later, he reappeared walking along the base of the gravelly apron slope. His eyes looked bleak, haunted.

"Hard thing to do," Joe said. "Seeing where your brother was killed. Being led to it by the man who killed him."

Severance grabbed the black's reins, toed a stirrup, and swung up into the saddle. "I don't blame you for Roy's death, Mannion. Despite your rather uncompromising reputation, I know it was either you or him. Roy would have pushed it to that."

He grimaced as he and Mannion swung their mounts around and began riding back in the direction from which they'd come. They rode slowly, for the ancient riverbed that had scored this part of the canyon was made treacherous by rocks and boulders that had fallen from above as well as by large chunks of driftwood deposited by previous spring floods.

When they'd ridden in silence for a few minutes, Severance said, as though completing his previous thought, "I just wish...that Roy and I hadn't...hadn't had what we had between us." He turned to Mannion as the thought seemed to clarify itself. "I wish we hadn't drifted apart. Hell, I don't think we'd talked in nine months before he died."

They followed the course of the canyon around a sharp bend and into bright, copper sunlight. Red's shod hoof rang off a rock he kicked, sending it rolling, then Mannion glanced at Severance and, having weighed whether he should mention it or not, said, "Did he know she was yours?"

## CHAPTER 19

SEVERANCE TURNED AN INCREDULOUS LOOK AT Mannion.

He studied the lawman for several stretched seconds then gave a dry grunt and turned his head forward. "Since you know...and likely most of the Animas country...probably. Yeah, I have a pretty strong feeling Roy knew. That was the unspoken wedge between us."

"Not too hard to figure it out—who the girl's father is."

"No, I suppose not."

"Does the girl know?"

Severance shook his head. "I don't think so."

"How 'bout her mother?"

"Eva's always refused to talk about it, but she knows."

Severance paused as they rode down into a dry wash. Their horses climbed up the opposite bank, pushing through willows and stunt cedars. The wash and a broad stretch of the area around it were liberally littered with shards of ancient bison bones. The northeast rim of the canyon had been used by ancient Indians as a buffalo jump for several centuries. The spring floods that turned the wash and the ancient riverbed into a torrent each spring had deposited the bones in some places as far as fifty miles away. They could often be spotted in the creeks around Del Norte.

Almost every kid in the area had a bison tooth or part of a bone or horn adorning his bedroom dresser. Likely, the Severance brothers had, too. It was before Mannion's time, but he'd been told that when the boys were younger, they'd been nearly as much a part of the canyon around Thunder Mountain as the ancients had once been, not unlike the wolves, wildcats, and grizzly bears.

Roy had likely stowed that loot good and deep.

There were plenty of nooks and crannies in these rocks. The last two spring floods might have even discovered those saddlebags and washed them away.

Severance must have been reading the lawman's mind.

"Looking for the loot, Marshal?" The younger man gave a foxy smile.

"Hell, no," Mannion said. "It's gone. Your brother as good as took it with him."

"I think you're right."

"Sort of makes me wonder, though," Mannion said, as the two riders, riding side by side, followed another bend in the trail and rode into a broader section of the canyon.

"What does?"

"Why Cheyenne rides out here so often."

Severance looked at him sharply. Mannion had wondered what kind of a reaction his question—which he'd been holding like a missing ace or a jack of diamonds close to his vest—would be. Severance didn't like the query.

Any special reason? Mannion wondered.

"It's where her father died," Matt said, a note of pique in his voice. "I think a little morbid fascination is understandable—don't you, Marshal?"

"I suppose so."

"What else would it be?" Severance asked, the note of pique remaining in his voice. He kept his dark-eyed gaze on the lawman, brows furrowed beneath the pulled-low brim of his hat.

"I don't have any idea," Mannion said, manufacturing an off-hand air. "I guess I was just thinking out—"

He cut himself off abruptly. He and Severance had just rounded another bend in the canyon. The broader section had continued to open, the canyon walls pulling farther back and lowering slightly. Where it narrowed again roughly sixty yards straight ahead, five riders sat facing Mannion and Severance—five bearded, sun-seasoned, and obvious toughnuts in worn trail clothes sitting their five mounts side by side and roughly eight feet apart, blocking Mannion's and Severance's access to the narrow section of canyon farther ahead.

"You were right, Mannion," Severance said, brushing his fist across his nose in frustration. "We were followed."

"You know, if I don't spot somebody on my back trail," Mannion said, leaning forward to give Red's left wither a rough pat, "my horse usually alerts me."

As though in response, Red whickered and shook his head.

"Yeah, my black does, too." Severance glanced at Mannion. "Do you recognize 'em?"

"Two of 'em." Mannion shucked his Winchester from his saddle boot and cocked it one-handed, keeping his gaze on the five hardcases spread out ahead. They each held a rifle of their own and appeared ready, if not eager, to use them. "The man with the white beard is Jack Kittredge. The man to his left, with the eye patch, is Leonard Potts. Both are bounty hunters out of Laredo. The short one with the black beard I think is Faraday. Luke or Luther or some such. The other two I haven't had the pleasure of meeting in person, but they look like bounty hunters, as well. All five likely up from Texas."

Mannion cut a quick, ironic glance at his trail partner. "You're right famous in these parts, Severance."

"All the way up from Texas, you figure?" Severance glowered, shook his head. "I knew I'd draw interest but only local interest."

"Forty thousand dollars is forty thousand dollars." Mannion lifted his chin, and yelled, "We didn't find it, Jack, so you're wastin' your time, pard! Didn't even come looking for it. Severance here just wanted to see where his brother died."

The white-bearded Jack Kittredge, clad in all smoke-stained buckskins, a knife jutting from the top of one of his mule-eared stovepipe boots, rose up tall in the saddle, and said, "I figure he came back fer it an' offered to split it with you for help locating it again"—the bounty hunter grinned—"after so much time has passed!"

"Due for retirement—eh, Joe!" This from one-eyed Leonard Potts, a savage bounty hunter and former Comanchero from the Brazos River country sitting astride a big bay like Mannion's Red. He opened and closed his black-gloved right hand around the neck of the Winchester he held on his beefy right shoulder. "Thirty thousand's a nice nest egg!"

Potts worked up some chaw and spat a long stream of it to one side. His horse didn't seem to like the smell of it; it looked at the long stain in the rocks and gravel, made a face, and shook its head. Mannion inwardly chuffed. He would have thought the bay would have been accustomed to the juicy expectorations of its rider as well as its rider's likely stench. Unless it was new to the man. In that case, poor beast.

Mannion revised his thinking.

These men hadn't followed him and Severance into the canyon. They'd already been here. Likely hunting a man or men with sizable bounties on their heads. When they'd spied Mannion and Severance, they'd likely decided to come inquiring, and, having heard about the missing forty grand in payroll loot, had formed the theory the one-eyed Potts had just given voice to.

Even if Mannion and Severance turned out to not have the loot, at least, they could give Mannion some grief. As with most men, there was no love lost between Joe and these men. Joe hated bounty hunters for the gutter-crawling scum most of them were. And they hated him for his notorious, intransigent ways. Also, like most with reputations, he was a challenge. Killing him would give them all extra credibility in their hard-bitten trade.

Mannion grinned without mirth.

Some days it wasn't easy being Bloody Joe Mannion. Some days were less easy than others.

This was piling up to be one of the less easy ones.

Sitting the black to his right, Severance raised his voice to yell: "One of you ride over and check our saddle-bags if you want. We didn't find the loot, and I have no idea where Roy hid it. I wasn't with him that day!"

"So the story goes..." said the middle-aged Jack Kittredge with a slow, cunning smile.

"It's no use, Severance," Mannion said. "It's gonna be a fight."

"I know it."

"You ready?"

Severance took the black's reins in his left hand, unsheathed his .44, and clicked the hammer back. "Yep."

"*Hi-yahhh, boy!*" Mannion shouted at the bay. "Let's go, Red. Bring it to 'em!"

The bay lunged off its rear hooves and into an instant, ground-chewing gallop straight at the five men who just then put the steel to their own mounts, heading straight for Mannion and Severance galloping the black eight feet to Mannion's right.

Holding Red's reins in his left hand, Joe brought the Winchester to his shoulder with his right hand and, holding the rifle with both hands, commenced triggering and levering, the long gun roaring and bucking. Mannion tried for Kittredge first, but his jouncing purchase caused his shot to merely blow the man's leather hat off his head, so that Kittredge's long, thin, white hair blew wildly in the wind as he shouted and fired at Mannion and Severance with a Henry repeater.

Gun blasts thundered, echoing off the canyon walls, hot lead whistling and whining around Mannion's head.

One bounty hunter screamed as Mannion blew him out of his saddle just as the man had ridden up to within six feet ahead of Mannion and on his left side. Kittredge had ridden on past Joe, one blue whistler carving a fine, hot line across the back of Mannion's neck. The smell of cordite was heavy in Mannion's nose as he rode through a thick, pale cloud of it and then drew back sharply on Red's reins, stopping the horse and curveting him.

Looking back the way he'd come, he saw two bounty hunters down.

One lay still while the other just then rose to his hands and knees and began crawling toward the cover of a low hummock.

The other three men—Kittredge, Potts, and a man

Joe did not know—were dismounting and heading for cover of their own roughly sixty yards away from Mannion. Severance had just then stopped and turned the black to gaze back at the bounty hunters.

Mannion swung down from Red's back and levered another round into his Winchester's action. He bore down on the wounded bounty hunter crawling toward the hummock. The man looked back at him, fear in his eyes, sweat glistening on his bearded cheeks, sliding a revolver from the soft leather pouch hanging from double cartridge belts.

The man shouted, "You go to hell, you bloody devil!" and raised the revolver.

The six-shooter bucked, smoke and flames lapping from the barrel.

Mannion's Yellowboy had spoken a half second before, causing the bounty man's bullet to screech high and wide as Mannion's slug plunged into his forehead, just above his left eye. He rolled onto his back and lay spread-eagle, twitching and kicking as he died.

Mannion fired two more quick rounds at the other three bounty hunters taking cover behind rocks. Then he turned to see Severance return fire from one knee, as well. Red and the black had wisely run out of the bullet path, Red to the west, the black to the east. The bounty hunters' horses had scattered, as well.

Mannion yelled, "Hit the wash! Hit the wash!"

He fired one more round, as did Severance, and then both men rose and ran down the canyon toward where willows sheathed a wash thirty yards away, where the canyon narrowed significantly and was deeply shaded by its looming western wall. Bullets kicked up sand and gravel around Mannion's boots just before he flung himself into the willows, piling up in the wash just beyond them, gritting his teeth against the jarring of his old joints, muscles, tendons, and bones.

As a young man, he'd never realized how many of those he'd had.

He knew now.

"Christ," he said, shouldering up against the cutbank and seeing Severance doing the same twenty feet to his left as he gazed through the willows toward the bounty hunters, whose bullets were still sizzling through the willows, clipping branches and leaves and sending them flying into the wash over Joe's head. "Getting too damn old for this."

"What's that?" Severance said.

Mannion turned to him. Severance was looking at him. Mannion hadn't realized he'd made the declaration about his age loud enough for the younger man to hear. But then, young men had better hearing than older ones, damn their younger, less achy joints, muscles, tendons, and bones, anyway...

"I said I'm getting too damn old for this!"

"Me, too!" Severance rested his rifle atop the bank before him and sent two rounds hurling back in the direction of the bounty hunters, whose own shooting had slowed down to short, sporadic bursts.

Mannion turned his head away from the younger man then turned it back, frowning.

Severance lay on his right side, his right leg bent so that the knee was toward Mannion. Then Joe saw why the odd position. Blood glistened on the younger man's right thigh, just above the knee.

"You hit?" Mannion said, as Severance thumbed fresh cartridges from his cartridge belt into his Winchester's loading gate.

"Yeah, I caught one." He racked a fresh round into

the rifle's action and rested the barrel atop the low bank, sliding it from left to right, looking for a target. "I'm all right."

Mannion reloaded his own rifle, jacked a live round into the breech, and peered through the willows. He could see none of the three remaining bounty hunters. Shadows were stretching long over the two dead men lying roughly between Mannion and the rocks behind which Kittredge, Potts, and the other man whose name Joe thought might be Faraday—Blane Faraday, a cold-blooded killer out of Austin.

Mannion cursed. He didn't like that he saw no movement over there, that none of the bounty hunters were shooting at him, trying to keep him and Severance pinned down. They might know that one of them had pinked Severance and, knowing that the movements of one of their two targets was limited, were trying to work around him and Mannion, trying to get them in a whipsaw.

Mannion thought it over quickly. As he did, the sun slid behind one of the four giant, looming pylons comprising Thunder Mountain, casting him and Severance in shadow. Not liking the funereal silence settling over the wash, Joe climbed to his feet, wincing at the ache in his knees, and ran crouching toward where his partner lay as before, aiming his Winchester through the willows, looking for a target.

"You're not all right." Mannion dropped to a knee beside Severance, leaned his rifle against the bank, and unknotted his neckerchief. He bent his head to peer at the other side of the younger man's thigh. "The bullet's still in there, and you're bleeding good."

Blood was trickling from the ragged entrance wound, out the hole in Severance's denim- and chap-clad right thigh, staining the sand and gravel around his bent knee.

Severance kept his gaze directed toward where their shadowers had gone to ground, said in a fateful tone, his cheek pressed up against the rear stock of his rifle, "Not much to be done about it out here. Roy and I always knew that."

Mannion wrapped his neckerchief around Severance's leg. "You think I'm just gonna let you bleed out?"

"Like I said..."

"Well, I'm not."

"Sentimental Bloody Joe."

"Yeah, well." Mannion leaned forward and grabbed the collar of Severance's shirt, and said quietly but tightly, "We have to get the hell out of here. I think they know you're wounded and are trying to work around us. It's too damn quiet over that way."

Mannion canted his head to indicate where Kittredge and the other bounty hunters had taken cover.

"Have to admit I kinda got that notion myself." Severance grunted as he turned so that his back was resting up against the cutbank. Mannion started to wrap the younger man's arm around his neck, to help him up, but stopped when in the corner of his left eye he saw a small jackrabbit dart out of the brush where the wash curved sharply to the north.

"Hold on."

He picked up the Yellowboy and fired three shots quickly from the hip.

A man screamed and came stumbling out of the willows.

Dropping his own Winchester as he stumbled down the shallow bank, the one-eyed Leonard Potts dropped to his knees, wailing, as he held both hands over his belly.

Mannion finished him with one round to the forehead then grunted as he jerked Severance to his feet.

"Come on!"

They stumbled together across the narrow wash and into the brush on the other side.

## CHAPTER 20

EARLIER THAT DAY, JANE FORD MANNION HAD JUST started down the broad, carpeted stairs in her very own San Juan Hotel & Saloon after an uncharacteristic nap following lunch, which she'd had little appetite for, when a familiar face standing at the bar in the main drinking hall below and to her right, caught her eye and made her stop.

The post-lunch crowd had thinned. There were only four customers standing at the bar and she saw that one of them was Rio Waite. Jane had just seen Rio's face in the backbar mirror. Rio raised a dimpled schooner to his mouth, and, in the mirror, Jane saw the glowing orange of an egg yolk lolling at the bottom of the glass. Rio tipped back the schooner—it was still about a third full—and downed the rest of the beer as well as the egg in three uninterrupted swallows.

In the backbar mirror, Jane watched the craggy-faced, potbellied, former-cowboy-turned-deputy set the schooner back down on the bar. He ran the back of his right hand across his mouth, smacked his lips, then, staring into the mirror, pulled his battered Stetson down lower on his forehead, covering up the pale strip the sun never found, and picked up the double-barreled shotgun from where it leaned against the bar to his right.

He dropped some coins on the bar, nodded to the lone bartender, then swung around and began making his way through the room toward the batwing doors.

Six or seven tables were still occupied. As he passed between two such tables at which over a dozen drovers lounged in post-lunch dolor, a few playing poker, one with one of Jane's doves straddling his knee, one of the men sitting at one of these two tables stuck his leg out casually but quickly. Before Rio could see it, the man drew his leg back under his table as Rio gave a shocked "*Ohhh!*" and, having caught the toe of his left boot under the drover's left ankle, went stumbling wildly forward, pinwheeling his arms wildly and dropping the Greener before he got his feet tangled and piled up on the floor.

The men sitting at the two tables around Rio laughed loudly.

Staring down over the stair rail, Jane saw the middle-aged deputy roll onto a hip and stare up in shock and exasperation. Humiliation lifted a bright red flush in Rio's fleshy face. He'd lost his hat; a lock of thinning hair hung over one eye. Glaring at the men sitting at the two tables nearest him, he gained his knees. He curled his upper lip and gritted his teeth, casting his malevolent gaze around at the two nearest tables that had erupted into loud, unabashed laughter. One of the drovers even clapped his hands together once and turned to say something to the laughing drover sitting beside him.

Rio staggered to his feet. He seemed to have trouble getting his boots set beneath him. Jane surmised he'd had more than just the one beer. Maybe a boilermaker before that. All he'd likely had for lunch was the egg in the second beer. He staggered forward, stooped down, and picked up his shotgun. He staggered to his left then stooped again to retrieve his hat. He stuffed the battered topper on his head and shifted his angry, mortified gaze around at the chuckling men at the two nearest tables.

"Who did that?" he yelled, raspily. "Who did it? Come clean now, ya damn jaspers!"

The laughter, which had infected nearly the entire room but had started to dwindle, grew louder once more.

Rio raised the double-bore to his right shoulder and shifted it around, including in his aim the laughing men at the two nearest tables. "Who did it, goddamn the lot o' ya! Come on, now—don't be a damn coward. Who tripped me? You can't treat me like that, goddamn it— I'm Bloody Joe Mannion's senior deputy!"

That evoked even louder laughter. Every customer in the room was laughing. Even the dove sitting on the drover's knee was tittering into her hand. Only the bartender decked out in a black bowtie and paisley vest was not. Merle Pugh was as sober as a judge.

Rage burning in Jane, she was about to continue down the stairs and lay into the laughing men but stopped again when Rio whipped around suddenly and, still gritting his teeth, the front ones showing like those of a dog about to attack, stumbled across the room and out the doors, the batwings swinging into place behind him.

The humiliation she felt fairly radiating off of the shamed man caused Jane to shiver, chomp angrily down on her bottom lip with her upper teeth, and clench her fists at her sides.

While the laughter continued though the heat of it

was beginning to dwindle, Jane marched down the stairs. She ignored the fluttering of her weak heart and, unable to look at any of the insolent fools around her, knowing she'd go into a very unhealthy and doctor-proscribed rage if she did, she marched over to the bar.

Merle Pugh walked down the bar to her and leaned across the mahogany as she said into his ear, "Merle, did you see who tripped Rio?"

Pugh shook his head.

Jane said, "It was Hartley Skinner of the Box W-8. Send for the bouncers. I want him thrown out of here, and Merle...?"

"Yes, ma'am?"

"I want Mister Skinner to know how very much I disliked his behavior this afternoon. Do you understand?" Jane blinked once, slowly.

Pugh nodded. "Yes, ma'am, I understand. I will convey that to Grigg and Thor."

"Thank you. Now hand me down a bottle of our best Irish whiskey."

Pugh raised his neatly trimmed black brows in surprise. "Yes, ma'am."

Holding the bottle in both hands before her, Jane swung around. As she headed for the batwings, she glanced at Hartley Skinner lounging back in his chair, a spurred boot resting on one denim-clad knee, a smile of supreme self-satisfaction spreading his thick-lipped mouth as he absently spun the spur with his fingers. Skinner saw the withering look on the face of the most powerful woman in town...maybe the most powerful businessperson in Del Norte, in fact...and fashioned an expression that assured Jane the thirty-a-month-and-found, raggedy-heeled cow nurse was thoroughly cowed and likely suspecting the rough justice he was about to be dealt by Jane's notoriously tough bouncers.

She pushed through the batwings, swung to her left, and marched along the street to the north. Heads swung toward her in surprise to see the beautiful redhead, dressed for an afternoon in her hotel, saloon, and hurdy-gurdy house rather than for the street. Carrying a bottle, no less, and wearing a most oblique expression on her lovely patrician's face with her classical nose, firm jaw, and wide, full lips.

Where in hell was Miss Jane heading this time of day with a bottle?

Several pairs of eyes followed her when she left the west side of San Juan Avenue near Dunham's Tonsorial Parlor and made her way at an angle over to Hotel de Mannion. Oh, she was heading over to the jailhouse to see her husband, Bloody Joe himself...but, wait, didn't Joe ride out of town early that morning? No one had seen him since. Only Rio Waite was over there now, having staggered half-drunk from the San Juan—word about that was making its way up and down the street—carrying his notorious double-bore Greener across his chest as though he were fixing to use it!

Now, here Jane was.

Hmmm.

Maybe they'd both gone totally off their rockers!

The word going around town about Jane was she didn't have long—well, best not make no mention of that lest they wanted to face the wrath of the fiery Miss Jane her ownself...

Jane strode up the stoop's three steps and paused at the closed door to knock twice quickly with the backs of her knuckles before opening the door and looking inside. Rio turned his rheumy eyes to her. He sat in Joe's swivel chair at Joe's desk, his boots crossed atop the desk, his fat black-and-white cat, Buster, standing on his lap. Buster was meowing softly and stiffening his raised tail as Rio petted him with an absent air. The cat's mood seemed to reflect that of its master—troubled, to say the least. Only, Buster likely hadn't been hitting the bottle the way Rio was.

A bottle of Mannion's preferred rotgut whiskey, which Joe usually kept in his desk, stood on the desk beside a dented blue, white-speckled tin cup, near Rio's right elbow.

Rio's eyes snapped wide, and he dropped his boots to the floor. "Miss Jane!"

"Don't get up! Don't get up!"

Rio had started to rise but now he settled back in his chair, sheepishness now mixing with the humiliation still burning in his fleshy face. He brushed a fist across his nose, sniffing. He removed the battered hat from his head and tossed it onto Joe's cluttered desk. As Jane drew the door closed behind her, blocking out the bright afternoon sunlight as well as some of the din of horse and wagon traffic on the street, Rio said, "You heard, didja?"

Jane shook her head once and stared grimly down at him. "Saw."

Rio gritted his teeth. "Helkatoot!"

Jane hauled a couple of tin cups down from a shelf on the wall to her right, where there were a half dozen cups stacked haphazardly and a burlap pouch of Arbuckles as well as coffeepots and frying pans and various other eating utensils including silverware bristling from a stone mug—most of it looking only half clean. She set the bottle down on the desk, set the cups down beside it.

"If you want to get drunk, let's do it in style."

Jane gritted her teeth as she popped the cork on the bottle.

Rio frowned up at her. Buster, still standing on Rio's lap, looked up at her, too, and gave an inquiring meow.

"If you're gonna tie one on, don't do it with Joe's rotgut. That'll sear a hole through your insides."

Jane splashed several fingers of the Irish whiskey into each of the cups sitting on a small pile of coffee-stained wanted circulars. She handed one of the cups to Rio then picked up the other one and drew a chair out from the table abutting the opposite wall, to the right of the door leading to the basement cellblock. She turned the chair around, sat down in it, and crossed her long, fine legs behind the long skirt she wore.

She took a deep sip of her whiskey, swallowed, lifted her head and shook her hair back from her cheeks. "Mmmmm! Now, that's good. Try it."

Rio looked down at his cup with uncertainty then drew it to his lips and took a tentative sip. He held it in his mouth for a few seconds, frowning, and swallowed.

He widened his red-rimmed eyes. "I gotta admit it's a whole lot smoother than Joe's Who-Hit-John."

Jane took another deep sip, swallowed, and set her cup on her knee. "Why are you drinking in the middle of the day, Rio? I know you come in for a breakfast mug of beer and an egg, but it usually stops there. You rarely imbibe in the afternoon. Oh, you might steal a swallow of Joe's rotgut now an' then, but...Why?"

Rio sighed and looked into his cup as though for the answer. "I'm old an' washed-up. And now I look like a bigger fool than I did before...when Colvin an' Sugar jumped me in the alley behind your place." He took another bigger sip of the Irish whiskey. Buster sat down on his thigh and stared up at him while Rio absently ran his hand down the cat's stout body with his thick, brown left hand, rope burned from his years punching cows.

"Yes, I heard about that," Jane said.

"Ah, hell, the whole town's heard about it. Likely, the whole county by now!" Rio frowned at her. "Why are you drinkin' in the afternoon, Miss Jane?"

Jane leaned forward over her crossed legs, holding the cup on her knee. "I'd been looking for a reason all morning. When I saw you in the San Juan, I thought, ah...I can get drunk with Rio. After all, that's what old friends are for...when they're both feeling bad."

"Why are you feelin' bad?"

"Because I'm dying, Rio."

Rio's frown deepened. He stopped patting Buster but left his hand on the cat's broad back. "Ah...now, Miss Jane..."

"It's true, Rio. I married the man of my life twice. I love him more than life itself and now I feel it all slipping away from me. Slowly but surely. Him and Vangie, the lives we built together."

Rio just stared at her. He seemed to have no words with which to respond to what she'd said.

Jane tossed back the last of the whiskey, rose from her chair, and crossed to Joe's desk. She splashed more...a lot more...into her own cup and then she refilled Rio's as well. Nearly to the brim.

She lifted her cup from the desk.

She smiled bittersweetly, raised the cup high. "Let's get drunk, Rio. Let's do it in grand style. Let's feel sorry for ourselves in grand style. And then tomorrow when we wake up feeling as though our heads were being used for target practice by bow-and-arrow-wielding Ute warriors, let's leave the pity on our pillows." The bittersweetness left her brightening smile. "Let's rise and go about our day with our heads held high, shoulders back, chests out. Shall we?"

Rio stared up at her, lower jaw hanging.

Slowly, a smile spread across his lips and twinkled in his eyes.

"We shall, Miss Jane!"

They clinked their cups together and drank.

## CHAPTER 21

"LEAVE ME, MANNION," SEVERANCE SAID. "LEAVE ME here. Gonna be dark soon. Hell, it's *almost* dark. You don't wanna get caught down here overnight. This canyon's dangerous at night. Roy an' I can tell you—"

"Just keep your feet moving." Hooking the younger man's right arm around his neck and Joe's left arm around Severance's waist, Mannion kept them both moving. Slowly but relatively surely.

Severance had directed Joe into this secondary canyon Severance remembered from the days when he and his brother had explored practically every nook and cranny of the badlands skirting the base of Thunder Mountain. The secondary canyon had forked off to the left of the main canyon roughly a half a mile away from the wash they'd taken cover in.

So, a half a mile they'd walked, one slow step at a time, blood trickling down the younger man's right leg, staining his leather bull-hide chaps. Severance was right. It was almost dark down here in the massive shadow of the four spires forming the mountain looming over them now to the west.

Severance lifted his chin to gaze at the sky, which was dark green between the black spires of the massive bulwark of Thunder Mountain. "Too late. You ain't gonna make it. Even if you knew your way out, it would take you an hour to find the way out."

"That's right," Joe said. "So stop flappin' your gums about it. Where's this cave you told me about?"

As Severance opened his mouth to speak, Mannion stopped suddenly. "Hold on!"

Severance looked at him, frowning. "What is—"

"Shh!"

Mannion turned his head to the side, pricking his ears. Quietly, he said, "Heard something."

It came again—the clomp of a hoof, then another and another, the clomps growing gradually louder until they were followed by a low horse's whicker.

"Damn, they're behind us!" Severance said.

Mannion reached across his belly for the cross-draw Russian. He closed his hands around the grips but left the hogleg in the leather.

"No," he said. "No...I don't think so." He'd recognized the whicker. Even the tread of the hooves was somehow familiar.

Mannion turned them both around to face the direction in which they'd come. A shadow moved roughly twenty feet away in the rocks, scrub brush, and sage. Then two shadows moved, growing larger and becoming the silhouettes of two horses—one following the other.

"Red!" Mannion said, keeping his voice low, not sure how far the bounty hunters were behind them. *If* they were behind them. Mannion hadn't seen or heard any sign of the two surviving hunters—Kittredge and the man he believed to be Blane Faraday—after he'd shot

Leonard Potts in the wash. "Red, you old devil, you followed us. Look, your black, too!" he told Severance.

"Yeah, but if they followed us..."

"Yeah." Mannion winced. "Kittredge and the other fella might have followed us, too. Might have seen the horses on our trail." He began leading Severance to the black, who followed Red from about eight feet off the bay's tail. "Let's get you in the saddle if you can ride."

"I can ride."

"Where's the canyon?"

Severance got mounted with a groan. Even in the badly failing early twilight of the canyon, Mannion could see the sweat glistening on his forehead. He was weakening fast due to blood loss. "Not far now. We just follow this canyon. It climbs some. When it flattens out, you'll see it on the left."

Ten minutes later, riding Red behind Severance and the black, he saw the black oval of the cave in the cliff wall to his left, roughly twenty feet up from the cliff's base. Severance didn't point it out. He rode slumped over his horse's poll, half asleep in the saddle. Mannion rode behind him in case he tumbled off the black.

Twenty minutes after spying the cave, Mannion had helped Severance up the gravelly slope that gave access to the cave and eased him down against the cave's back wall. The cave smelled gamey and sour from the animals that had called it home, but none of the tracks or the dung littering the cave floor appeared fresh, so Joe didn't think he and his partner would have any unwelcome visitors.

He tended the horses, draping feed sacks over their noses, and tied them to a short picket line strung between two cedars in some rocks at the base of the cliff wall. Then he gathered wood, formed a stone ring in the middle of the cave, near the entrance, and built a fire. He knew the flames might only attract unwelcome visitors in the form of Kittredge and Faraday, but he needed to keep his wounded trail partner warm. Also, the flames would keep away the carnivorous beasts that hunted here— wolves, wildcats, and grizzlies.

When he'd stacked their gear around the fire, he turned to Severance.

The man appeared asleep, darkly handsome head turned to one side, chin resting on his shoulder. His legs extended nearly straight out before him. His Winchester rested across his thighs; his slack, gloved hands rested on top of it. The brim of his black hat shaded his face from the short, dancing orange flames of Mannion's fire.

His chest rose and fell heavily as he breathed.

Joe boiled water in a pan, produced cloth from his saddlebags as well as a small sewing kit with needle and catgut thread. He fished out his skinning knife, set it in the flames until the blade glowed red then set it on a rock away from the fire.

He went over and nudged Severance, who woke with a start, right hand closing around the grips of his low-slung .44.

"Easy, easy," Mannion said. "Need to get you over to the fire. Have to dig that bullet out. You won't survive the night if we don't."

As Mannion helped the younger man to his feet, Severance said, "You a sawbones now, too, Mannion?"

"No, but I'm all you have."

He eased Severance down against the saddle, positioning him for easy access to the wound. The bullet had gone into the side of his leg roughly eight inches up from the knee. Mannion removed the bloody bandanna, tossed it into the fire, then, using his Barlow knife, he cut a patch out of the denims around the wound. He cleaned the wound with the cloth and the warm water then pulled a flat, brown bottle out of a saddlebag pouch and gave it to his patient.

"Take a pull. Take two. This is gonna hurt."

He moved to the fire and retrieved the disinfected skinning knife. He paused to peer out of the cave and into the near-total darkness of the canyon beyond. He frowned as he probed the darkness, an anxious nerve firing, for an orange glow flickered out there against the velvet black of the canyon night.

A long, low ridge rose only forty yards beyond the cave. The cave was high enough that Severance could see over the top of it. Beyond it was another, narrow canyon. The fire burned on the ridge over that canyon, beyond the lower ridge dividing that canyon from the one housing the cave in which Mannion crouched now, staring out into the canyon night where other men had built a fire—likely in a cave similar to Mannion's, in the side of that ridge maybe a hundred, hundred and twenty yards away.

Kittredge and Faraday.

Had to be. Most likely, anyway.

Were they working their way over here?

"What is it?" Severance's voice was a low, raspy growl.

Mannion glanced at the horses he'd tied down in the rocks below the cave. He'd removed their feed sacks, and both stood still as statues, heads down, resting, unalarmed.

"Nothing." Squeezing the knife in his right fist and glancing at his Yellowboy leaning against his saddle, Mannion returned to his patient.

He pulled the .44 from Severance's holster and set it down beside him.

"I'll hold on to that for now."

Leaning back against his saddle, hat pulled down over his eyes, Severance showed the white line of his teeth as he smiled. Stories of men involuntarily shooting other men cutting bullets out of them were well known.

"Want something to chomp down on?"

Severance gave his head a single shake.

Mannion picked up the bottle, poured a little whiskey over his left index finger, took a pull, then one more, smacked his lips, and set the bottle aside.

"All right, then—here we go."

Mannion slid the tip of the knife into the wound. Severance's jaws hardened. He tipped his head back and to one side and groaned. Mannion slid the knife deeper into the wound, following the blade with his left index finger, probing as gently as he could until he could feel the bullet resting against Severance's thigh bone.

Severance groaned again, stretching his lips back from his teeth, the chords in his neck standing out.

"I can feel it," Mannion said, grimacing as he tried to work the bullet with his finger against the knife's razor-edged blade.

When he had a firm grasp of the bullet, he eased the knife and his finger out of the wound, the flattened chunk of lead, dripping blood, held taut against the blade.

"Got 'er!"

Smiling with great satisfaction, Joe set the knife on a rock and held the bullet up to show Severance.

To no avail.

Severance's head was tipped to his left shoulder. His hat had fallen off to lie crown down by the fire. His face was slack, and deep snores rumbled up from his chest, making his lips flutter.

Mannion's patient was out like a snuffed wick.

———

Keeping an eye skinned on the night outside the cave, as well as on the horses, both of whom seemed unperturbed, Mannion cleaned Severance's wound with the whiskey then sutured it closed with the needle and catgut as best he could.

He was not a credentialed medico, but, when finding himself out far from credentialed medicos, he had sewn up deputies, posse members, and even himself a time or two. He gave the sutured wound one more splash of the whiskey, evoking another groan from the uneasily slumbering Severance, then wrapped it tightly with the cloth he always kept in his saddlebags for just such occasions.

He cleaned the knife and needle, returning both to his saddlebags, then removed his spurs, set his hat on his head, and picked up the Yellowboy. He stepped out of the cave and to one side, where he would not be outlined against the short, flickering orange flames. He'd let the fire die now. Maybe build it up later after his work was done.

Holding the rifle low so the glow from the fire wouldn't reflect off the brass receiver, Mannion looked down at the horses. The black held its head up, ears pricked tensely. Red had craned his neck to stare off down the canyon, back the way Mannion and Severance had come, and then the black did, as well, whickering softly.

Mannion's lips quirked a grim smile, his wolfish gray eyes drawing up at the corners.

Trouble was afoot...

He moved slowly, carefully down the gravelly slope. In the canyon below, he raised the Yellowboy up high across his shoulders and strode down the slope to the south, retracing his and Severance's path. He didn't know these badlands anywhere near as well as the Severance boys did...or, in Roy's case, had...but he was guessing the only way into this narrow canyon was back at where the two canyons forked, divided by the long, low ridge between them, a third of a mile back in the direction in which Mannion and Severance had come.

That was the direction trouble would come from. Red's owly gaze corroborated the lawman's theory, though of course the horses might have been sensing prowling wolves or a wildcat, too. Mannion didn't think so. He'd bank on his own senses, honed by years of lawdogging, as well as on those of the horses.

He'd walked only a hundred feet before he saw the pale line of what appeared a game trail climbing the ridge on his left at an angle. He looked around carefully. The night was silent and dense, stars sparkling in the sky over the canyon. A nightbird cooed nearby. More distantly, a coyote gave a long, mournful wail; it paused as though awaiting a response but, not receiving one, howled again, mournfully.

Mannion stepped up onto the trail and began climbing, crouching low and keeping his right hand closed around the rifle's brass receiver. There was no moon, but the light of the stars made for relatively easy going. Also, he'd been on the manhunting trail enough times after dark that his night vision was keen.

He gained the rocky spine of the ridge, dropped to a knee, doffed his hat, and looked around.

Over his left shoulder he could see the weak glimmer of the fire he'd built in the cave. On the other side of the ridge before him, he could see the also weakening glimmer of the fire in the ridge wall on the canyon's opposite side, roughly twenty feet up from Mannion's position, maybe two hundred feet away.

No wood had been added to that fire in several minutes. The flames were small and feeble.

Mannion waited, listening for the tread of a boot on gravel, looking around for the flicker of any moving shadow. He didn't like leaving Severance alone in the cave unconscious but from here he had a good view of the canyon he'd left behind. If Kittredge and Faraday got around behind him, he'd know about it. Or he'd cut them off at the pass.

Maybe the very one he was on, down on one knee, surrounded by rocks, hat off, peering over the rocks, shuttling his gaze around him, watching...listening.

Minutes passed. The night grew chill. The eerily still air smelled like cooling rocks and sage.

From somewhere nearby, he could hear the faint scratching of some burrowing night creature—a rabbit or a mouse, maybe.

The coyote started to give its distant howl once more but cut itself off abruptly.

The nightbird screeched, the screeches dwindling, echoing as the bird lit from its perch and winged off into the night.

Mannion drew a breath, held it.

A soft crunching sound came from down the slope before him and on his right.

He peered that way, saw a brief glimpse of a shadow move between two large rocks roughly two-thirds of the way down the slope. Mannion rose to a crouch, moved soundlessly to his right, and shouldered up against a large rock, staring down the slope, holding the Yellowboy straight out from his right hip.

Again, the shadow slid between two rocks.

Mannion stepped out around his covering boulder and moved slowly to his right, on an interception course with the shadow moving nearly straight up the ridge. When he'd moved twenty feet, he stopped. The shadow was moving up the slope nearly straight at him now. Starlight glistened off a rifle barrel. When the shadow took the clear shape of a man wearing a broadbrimmed hat, and when Mannion could smell the rancid sweat of the man now fifteen feet away and straight down the slope below him, he said quietly, "Faraday?"

A startled grunt. The broadbrimmed hat came up, revealing two eyes peering up at Mannion, bright with anxiety. "Oh, shit!"

The rifle came up, the man jacking it loudly.

Mannion had just racked a round into his own Winchester. His three blasts shook the ground beneath his boots. Faraday fired a round toward the stars as Mannion's first bullet picked him up off his feet and hurled him straight back as two more of Mannion's rounds cut into the bounty hunter, one just before and one just after he'd struck the ground with a resolute, crunching thud and a final sigh of expectorated air.

The man's thrown rifle clattered on the rocks.

Mannion ran forward then dropped to a knee, pumping another cartridge into the smoking Yellowboy's action. His heart hammered as he stared down the slope, looking for Kittredge.

No movement down there except the wafting of his own pale powder smoke in the darkness. Silence.

Then a horse's high whinny cut shrilly through the otherwise quiet night back in the direction of where Mannion had left Severance.

*They'd split up!*

Mannion picked up his hat and scrambled down the

slope too quickly, dropping to his knees once and on his hip just before he'd gained the bottom. He ran hard, ankles aching against the rocks he stepped on in the darkness. At the top of the slope, he paused to stare up at the cave on his left. It was brightly lit, shadows dancing across the walls and ceiling.

Both horses were whinnying and nickering, their wildly jostling figures silhouetted against the bright light of the fire above and to their right.

Mannion's heart leaped into his throat as a man-shaped silhouette just then gained the top of the slope outside the cave. Mannion could see the long, white beard of Jack Kittredge just as the man turned away from the canyon to face the cave, poking his rifle straight out from his right hip and loudly jacking a round into the action.

"No!" Mannion started to run forward, fairly leaping out of his boots.

He stopped when a rifle blast sounded. It was followed by another...another...and another...

Mannion stared in horror at the cave.

Kittredge wailed and leaned forward just after he fired a round straight into the cave. He dropped the rifle, staggered forward then backward to go tumbling down the slope before the cave and into the darkness of the canyon.

Mannion stared, his thudding heart gradually slowing its pace.

"What in holy blazes...?"

He jogged forward, yelling, "Severance?"

When he gained the top of the slope, he stared, breathless, into the cave in which the fire blazed. His trail partner lay back against his saddle, black hat pulled low over his eyes.

Mannion glanced at the fire then at Severance again, scowling. "Why'd you build up the fire?"

Severance poked his hat brim up. "I was cold."

Then he pulled the hat brim low over his eyes again and crossed his arms on his chest.

## CHAPTER 22

MANNION DRAGGED KITTREDGE OUT AWAY FROM THE cave so the man's fetid carcass, which smelled as bad as Faraday had smelled, far enough away from the cave wouldn't invite any unwanted, four-legged, carrion-eating guests.

Then Joe emptied his bladder, calmed the horses, and returned to the cave in which the fire had died to a more appropriate size. He removed the leather ties from Severance's bedroll and draped both sewn-together blankets as well as the rain slicker that was part of the bundle over the slumbering man. Maybe he wouldn't wake up cold and toss enough wood on the fire to allow it to be seen from as far away as Del Norte.

Mannion wanted no more guests tonight.

He took a hit from the bottle, unrolled his own soogan, kicked out of his boots, coiled his shell belt around his guns, leaned the Yellowboy close enough for an easy grab, and rolled up in the blankets that had that distinctive smell of horse and past fires built in remote canyons not unlike the one in which he found himself now. Almost instantly, his breathing slowed. He felt the sandman drag his lids down over his eyes.

Ah, sweet slumber...

He woke at dawn's first pale wash. He'd been up only a few minutes, making coffee and cooking beans, when Severance woke and rose, albeit stiffly. He immediately started moving around, gathering his gear, readying it for the long ride back to the Half-Moon.

"Easy there," Mannion warned him. "I didn't suture that wound closed just so you could open it up again."

"I'm fine as frog hair split four ways."

"The hell you are. You oughta rest that leg here another day. Then I'll take you back to the Half-Moon and summon one of the medicos from Del Norte."

Severance shook his head as, gritting his teeth against the invisible, rabid dog chomping into his leg, he rolled his soogan and tied it. "I'm good. Once I'm home, I'll rest up."

Mannion chuffed his reproval and stirred the beans.

Severance had sand, he'd give him that. But once the younger man had directed Mannion out to a part of the canyon the lawman was familiar with and could find his way out from on his own, Severance started having a hard time staying awake atop his black. Several times he almost fell out of his saddle. After the fifth or sixth time, and when they'd arrived at the bottom of the trail that would take them up and out of the canyon, around ten thirty in the morning, the sun blasting down on them, Mannion stopped and tied the man's wrists to his saddle horn and his boots to his stirrups.

Severance was so weary from blood loss and likely pain that he only muttered a few half-hearted protestations. Then Mannion climbed back up on Red's back and led the black by its bridle reins. Two hours later they clomped across the bridge spanning Elk Horn Creek and into the Elk Horn Ranch headquarters, which, Joe was sorry to see, had gone to hell in a handbasket though a couple of hands—old-timers, judging by their wizened faces and potbellies—were fiddling with one of the place's two corrals.

Chickens strutted around the yard, foraging, yielding for the horses and riders heading for the cabin. A long rope line was strung between two ponderosa pines to the right of the shack, and two large, oval, braided hemp rugs hung from it. A large pot of water, likely for doing laundry, was steaming over a fire between the cabin and the rugs, where more Barred Rock and Rhode Island Red chickens clucked.

Boots clomped inside the cabin. The door opened and the thin, blond matriarch of the tumbledown place came out onto the badly sagging stoop and raised a hand to shield her eyes against the sun. A large wooden bucket banded in rusty steel sat beside her atop the porch, mounded with sheets and badly faded and tattered quilts.

"What is it? Who's there?"

"It's Joe Mannion, Mrs. Severance. I have Matt here. He's been shot and needs tending."

From inside the cabin came a loud gasp that was half a scream. Footsteps sounded and then the tall, trim, dark-haired, dark-eyed daughter came out onto the stoop, her lower jaw hanging, Cheyenne's eyes wide with concern. She, too, shaded her eyes with a hand and she strode across the porch, brushing past her mother.

"Uncle Matt? He's been *shot*?"

"Cheyenne—hold on!" Eva Severance grabbed her daughter's arm, but the girl jerked it out of her hand and hurried on down the steps and into the yard, dust puffing up around the low hem of her worn, gingham day dress, the sleeves of which were rolled up her slender, nut-brown arms.

Severance stirred on the black that had stopped just behind Mannion. The black gave a start, whickering, as the girl ran toward it.

"Hold on, hold on—easy!" Mannion said, not wanting the black to rip the reins out of his hand and make a run for it. Joe gripped the reins tightly.

Severance lifted his head from where it had long since sunk down against the saddle horn. He shook his head as if to clear it, blinked his eyes groggily. He saw the girl running up to him and glared at Mannion.

"Damn you, Mannion. What the hell do you think you're doing? We were heading for the Half-Moon!"

"That wound needs tending. Take a look yourself. My stitches have opened up and I'm guessin' you might've lost another half-gallon of blood."

While Cheyenne fussed over Matt, half sobbing and regarding with shock the fresh blood staining Mannion's bandage and the already blood-stained denims, Mannion turned to Mrs. Severance. "Will you help? Can I leave him here while I fetch one of the medicos from town?"

The look Eva Severance gave Mannion could be described in no other way—it was a bone-chilling, cold-eyed, pinch-mouthed glare. She shook her head slowly and for a minute Mannion thought she was going to refuse, but then said, coldly, "Well, you've brought him here now—haven't you?"

"No, no—leave 'em," Severance said to Cheyenne, who had plucked the man's bowie knife from the sheath on his belt and, rising onto the tiptoes of her scuffed ankle boots, was sawing at the ropes binding his wrists to his saddle horn. "Cheyenne, no—*leave* 'em!"

"Go to hell, Uncle Matt! What is with you?" Then she

cast her wild, dark-eyed glare at her mother. "What is with *both* of you?"

Suddenly, the girl froze.

Her face slackened and her eyes grew even wider in sudden realization.

She stepped back away from the black. The knife dropped out of her hands. She shuttled her awestruck gaze from Matt to her mother.

"No," she said, shaking her head. "No—it's *not* true!"

"Oh, Christ!" Severance said, barely able to hold his head up.

"Cheyenne!" Eva Severance said and hurried down the porch steps.

"No!" Cheyenne whipped around and, lifting the hem of her day dress, ran toward the bridge spanning the creek, her long, sunlit, dark-brown hair jouncing on her shoulders.

Severance turned his head and shared a long, dreadful look with Eva. Then his head sagged. He tried to hold it up to no avail. It sagged lower until his forehead rested against his saddle horn.

Mannion walked over, picked up the man's Bowie knife, and cut Severance's feet free of his stirrups. When he cut the ropes tying his hands to his saddle horn, he slid the knife into its sheath on Matt's belt, drew the man toward him, and let him sag into his arms. Mannion pulled his legs down off his saddle and snaked his right arm under them and, grunting under the man's weight, turned to Eva Severance, who stood staring after Cheyenne who was just then running across the bridge spanning the creek. She was running hard, as though to or from a fire.

"Show me where I can take him," Mannion said, Severance a dead, groaning weight in his arms.

Eva turned to him, looked at Matt. Mannion would be damned if the expression he saw on the woman's worn, drawn face, which was once so pretty, wasn't one of tenderness. Maybe even old longing. Then she turned quickly, hurried up the steps and across the porch, drawing the door wide, letting Mannion pass into the cabin with Severance in his arms. She closed the door then stepped around him, crossed to the back of the cabin, and opened one of the two halved-log doors in the rear wall.

"In here. You can put him in my room."

As Mannion sidled into the room, Eva lay an old, thick, wool blanket down on the four-poster bed then stepped back. Mannion eased the groaning man down on the bed then winced when he saw the fresh blood glistening on the man's right thigh, soaking the bandage.

"I'll fetch one of the doctors."

"No," the woman said. "If he can be helped, I can help him. I've sewn him and Roy up, set their broken bones, more times over the years than I can count on both hands. That wound needs to be cleaned and cauterized."

"How can I help?"

"Fetch wood from outside, stoke the range."

Mannion fetched the wood, stoked the range, and set a pot of water to boil. He went into the bedroom, helped Eva remove Matt's soiled sweat-soaked clothes then stepped back while she cleaned the wound with the water and fresh cloths. When the wound was relatively clean, he held Severance down while she lay the glowing blade of a meat cleaver, heated in the stove's firebox, across the wound and wrinkled his nose against the stench of scorched blood and skin.

Severance bucked hard, like one of the mean broncos he'd broken for area ranchers.

But he never woke up.

Even in sleep, he groaned and muttered and grunted in pain.

"I'll finish up now," Eva told Mannion, stepping past him, carrying the basin of bloody water into the kitchen and dumping it over the porch rail. "There's coffee on the warming rack there," she added, as she prepared a poultice pouch from various jars she pulled down from kitchen shelves.

There were various root and bark powders which she mixed with spit and molasses.

When she'd gone back into the bedroom with the poultice, and closed the door, Mannion was seated at the table, sipping a stone mug of hot, black coffee. He'd unsaddled both Red and the black, rubbed them down, grained, watered, and corralled them, leaving them munching hay from the crib.

The two old cowpunchers watched him almost suspiciously, silently as they continued fiddling with a corral rail.

Now Mannion savored the soothing elixir of the coffee.

What a day.

What a past couple of days.

When he'd ridden out here to check on Severance, and seen him riding away from the Half-Moon, and followed him from a good distance, he hadn't expected to be out here two whole days. Even if he started back to Del Norte now, he wouldn't make it until after dark. He couldn't start for at least an hour. He and Red both needed rest.

He built a cigarette and was smoking it when Eva stepped out of the bedroom.

She came into the kitchen and washed her hands in warm water.

Mannion watched this tired, sullen woman who was dressed more for punching cows than tending a cabin. But that was likely mostly what she did now. She said nothing until, toweling her hands and forearms dry, she turned to him.

"More coffee?" She seemed out of breath. But then, she always seemed a little breathless with weariness when Mannion rode out here to check on her and Cheyenne.

Mannion glanced at his nearly empty mug and nodded.

Eva brought another mug and the pot over. She filled Mannion's cup and then her own, the steam washing up from above the two mugs and glowing in the late afternoon light angling through a dirty window behind him. She returned the pot to the range, opened the door to let the excess heat out, propping it open with a rock, then returned to the table.

She leaned forward and placed a hand on Mannion's makins sack. "May I?"

"Sure."

She deftly rolled a smoke and Mannion lit it for her. She sat back, blowing a plume of smoke at the rafters.

She looked at him. "What happened?"

Mannion told her. He gave her all of it, starting with Ethel Beech and finishing with Kittredge and Faraday.

Eva sat sideways in her chair, denim-clad legs crossed, one arm hooked over a spool of the spool-back chair. "She'll be back. She won't give up." She took another quick, nervous drag on the quirley and blew the smoke toward the open door.

Mannion frowned. "How do you know?"

"She's ridden in here a time or two. She told me I was still here not by divine grace but because she allowed me to be here. The grieving widow. She told me I could be a lot more certain of my future if I told her where the money was."

"She thinks you have it?"

"Or knows where Roy might have hid it. She's seen Cheyenne ride out there. Have to admit, I rode out there a time or two myself." Eva laughed drolly. "What I couldn't do with that much money, and why not?"

She chuckled and took another puff from the quirley.

"Why is Ethel Beech so interested in the loot?"

Eva looked at him, thin blond brows arched in surprise. "Oh, she's not rich. No, far from it. Stock prices are down. Leastways, she's not as rich as she once was. I've heard she's hemorrhaging money due in no small part to cattle rustlers. Some of the smaller ranchers have gotten right bold. Thinning her herd for her, Ethel."

Eva gave a little devilish, delighted smile.

"She wants to sell out, move to Denver, find her a senator to marry. But she can't afford to. No, she's bound here...unless she can find a handy forty grand to help her pay her debts."

Mannion sipped his coffee. "I'll be damned. I didn't know that."

"We have our own community out here, you might say." Eva canted her head to indicate the bedroom in which Severance lay. "Now he's back part of it." Her voice acquired some pique. "Complicating...matters."

"Now everybody's thinking about the loot again," Joe said.

"Yes." Eva was staring out the window behind Mannion.

Joe turned to see Cheyenne sitting on the other side of the creek, knees drawn up behind her dress, arms around them. The sun glistening like molten copper in her hair, she stared at the shallow, flowing stream.

———

CHEYENNE STARED AT THE RIPPLING WATERS OF ELK Horn Creek, but it wasn't the water she saw. What she saw was the crazy rush of years that comprised her life. Or at least what she'd thought was her life. Now, she wasn't sure who those years belonged to. Because she was no longer the person she'd once thought she was.

She was no longer Roy Severance's daughter.

No.

His place in her memory now was a lie.

Her actual father was the man she'd known and loved as her uncle.

Now not only her father...or who she'd thought was her father...had been taken away from her. But the man she'd thought was her uncle—her handsome, horse-loving Uncle Matt.

She should have known, she scolded herself. She'd realized that she and "Uncle" Matt had shared the same Indian-like traits of Matt's mother and Cheyenne's grandmother, Louise. Cheyenne thought that was what had made her feel so close to him, to her so-called Uncle Matt. She'd felt a special, rarefied kinship with him, not knowing of course that he was her father.

She'd been lied to. All these years, she'd been lied to by the two people she'd loved the most in this world— her mother and the man she'd thought was her Uncle Matt. She'd loved her father, too, of course. But not as much as she'd loved Matt. Now, oddly, she felt a stronger kinship with a dead man, Roy Severance, than she did with the only two people in her family still alive.

Two people who were not who she'd thought they were.

Two people who'd betrayed her father and then her, Cheyenne, as well.

A bird cooed somewhere behind her. She only vaguely heard it, but then she heard it again, louder. This time it nudged her from her reverie. From her sadness, anger, and confusion.

She welcomed the familiar signal.

She turned her head, saw the horseback rider sitting on a low rise behind her, silhouetted against the sky.

Cheyenne looked at the cabin. Both her mother and Marshal Mannion were still inside. She hoped they weren't looking out the window in her direction. She rose, letting the skirt of her cambric dress fall down over her legs. She glanced once more, cautiously, at the cabin, then turned and walked quickly up the rise and down the other side where the rider now waited for her, standing beside his horse, holding the steeldust's reins in one gloved hand while it cropped wheat grass behind him.

"Oh, Garrett!" Cheyenne said, running into his arms. "Oh, Garrett. I'm so glad you're here. I need you so much right now!"

She wrapped her arms around him. Garrett Beech, Ethel Beech's only son, wrapped his arms around her, leaned back, picked her up off the ground, and kissed her hungrily. He set her back down, smiling warmly.

"Well, I'm here now, honey. You know me. I can make anything right!"

———

THE TWO WERE SO HAPPY TO SEE EACH OTHER, THEY did not see yet another horseback rider sitting on a rise a hundred yards away, to the west, also silhouetted against the west-angling sun. A pretty, blonde rider sitting astride a handsome brown-and-white tobiano stallion.

Only, she was not so pretty just now.

Jodi Miller's eyes were too hard, her jaws too rigid, her lips pinched too tightly in barely contained fury as she stared at the two lovers embracing in the sage-stippled swale below her.

"Oh, you think so, do you, *Mister* Beech? You think so, do you, you half-breed *whore!*" she said tightly, blue eyes sparking rage. She reined the tobiano around and booted him down the rise with a snarl. "We'll see about *that!*"

## CHAPTER 23

WALKING ALONG THE BOARDWALK ON SAN JUAN
Avenue in Del Norte, his shotgun resting on his shoulder,
Rio Waite paused to pull his hat brim down lower over
his eyes. The sun was on its westward journey toward the
far side of the San Juans, but there was still enough power
in those rays that they pierced his tender eyes like minia-
ture javelins.

The brunt of his hangover had abated, but his eyes
were still tender, and there remained a grievous little,
invisible man pounding his brain plate with an invisible
ball peen hammer, albeit with less vigor than he'd been
wielding it earlier that morning, when Rio had awakened
in his cabin behind the jailhouse, his mouth feeling like a
rat had wandered in overnight and died.

He and Miss Jane had had quite a time of it, not
ending the day until well after midnight over at the San
Juan Hotel & Saloon. Rio wasn't sure how he'd gotten
home, but he had a vague recollection of being half
carried outside by two of Miss Jane's burly bouncers and
being more or less poured into a carriage. That was the

end of his recollection, but that was enough to tell him he'd likely been driven home by those bouncers, half carried into his cabin, and more or less poured into his bed.

It had been a long day. He was glad it was coming to an end and that the mountain-sized Cletus Booker would take over for him and Mannion's youngest deputy, Henry McCallister. Rio needed a good, long night's sleep. His nerves were frayed. He was just glad the day had gone relatively smoothly and he hadn't had to take on any toughnuts in his frail condition—both physically and... well...yes, emotionally. All day, he'd felt that old, black-eyed demon, self-doubt, lurking in the back of his mind like a thief waiting in the bushes under cover of darkness.

Only half darkness.

Rio could see him there—beady-eyed, horned, and with talons for fingers—peering over the bushes, grinning, showing his long, curved fangs, waiting to spring.

Continuing his stroll along the boardwalk out front of the All-Nighter Saloon, Rio shook his head to clear it of the nettling thoughts and doubts about his courage. No sooner had he done so than three men clad in trail gear, and obviously drunk, came clambering out the All-Nighter's batwing doors, laughing and shoving each other, one slapping the side of one of the other's head with his hat, jokingly calling him a card cheat and a swine.

As they did, the first one who'd emerged from the saloon, bumped into an elderly lady wearing an elaborate yellow gown and matching picture hat and carrying three twine-bound parcels wrapped in brown paper. The parcels went flying and the lady, whose name was Cora Rose, Rio knew—she was a widow who worked as a seamstress at Mrs. Harrison's Dress Shop—stumbled sideways and likely would have fallen if she hadn't run into a square-hewn awning support post.

She gave a startled cry as she grabbed the post as if it were the mast of a ship negotiating choppy seas.

The laughing men ignored her as they went scuffling, shuffling, and jostling off down the boardwalk. The man who'd run into the lady—Bryce Wheatley—inadvertently kicked one of the parcels off the boardwalk and into the street where several horses were tied to a hitchrack fronting the All-Nighter.

Rio sucked back a knot of dread that automatically lodged itself in his throat. His feet grew heavy, but he let a wave of anger as well as obligation to duty propel him forward, and said, "Hey, you three—get back here! Didn't you see what you just did?"

The three stopped and swung around, frowning incredulously.

"What the hell's got your drawers in a twist, Rio?" said Wheatley.

Rio stepped forward, scowling, holding his lingering anxiety at bay and saying tightly, canting his head to indicate Mrs. Rose, "You ran into Mrs. Rose here, you big galoot. Knocked her parcels out of her hands!" He took another step forward and stopped just three feet in front of Wheatley, who had a good four inches on him. "You pick up those packages and give them to the lady and apologize—understand?"

Rio tipped his head back to jut his chin at the taller man, liking the steel, the resolution and bravery he'd heard in his voice.

"Oh...oh..." Mrs. Rose said, weakly, one arm hooked around the post, gazing fearfully at the roughhewn, rustically clad toughnuts facing Rio.

Wheatley screwed up his face, shoved it down close

to Rio's, and said, "Suppose I don't, Rio? What're you gonna do about it?"

He cut a sneering smile at his two partners standing to his left. They returned the look with sneering smiles of their own.

Of course, they'd all heard about Rio getting jumped in the alley beside the San Juan Hotel & Saloon and then about the humiliation he'd endured just the day before in the San Juan's main drinking hall. His breakdown and bout of cowardice that had sent him fleeing the place amid a wave of mocking laughter.

Now Rio found himself smiling almost benevolently up at the taller man before him. He'd brought the shotgun down off his shoulder and was holding it in both hands. Now he lowered it, grabbed it by the barrel, and swung the forestock up between Wheatley's spread legs, ramming it soundly against the man's crotch.

Wheatley staggered backward a step or two and jack-knifed forward with a loud exhalation of expelled air. Closing his hands over his privates, he dropped to his knees as though in prayer. His hat tumbled onto the boardwalk. Groaning, he tipped his head back to glare—red-faced above his scraggly, sandy patch beard—up at Rio.

"That's just for starters!" Rio barked, swinging the shotgun to aim the double-bore at Wheatley's trail pards—T-Bone Price and Hector LaPaz. All three rode for the same outfit out toward the Sawatch Range. They'd probably come to town on a supply run. "How this is gonna end, you see, Wheatley—if you don't do what I just told you to do—is you three becoming the newest guests at Hotel de Mannion and not getting out till you each pay a twenty-five-dollar fine. That's the goin' rate for drunk 'n' disorderly, don't ya know!"

Rio shuttled his wolfish grin from the man on his knees before him to his two cohorts, both of whom had closed their hands down over their six-guns' grips but had wisely removed them when Rio turned the savage double-bore on them, both likely imagining the damage a double dose of ten-gauge, double-ought buck would inflict on their bellies.

"Oh," said Mrs. Rose. "Oh...oh, my..."

"What's it gonna be, Wheatley?" Rio said, almost enjoying himself. No, he was downright enjoying himself! His confidence was coming back full force! "You wanna spend the night at Hotel de Mannion. We got a couple fellers from the Cloud Tickler in there. You fellas can sit around and swap big windies till you can come up with those fines!"

Again, he grinned down at Wheatley.

It was almost as though he'd separated into two Rio Waites, and the fearful one, the one with the dark specter of cowardice hiding in the bushes, was watching the old, brazen, fearless, some might even say *pugnacious* Rio Waite dressing down three toughnuts half his age. The fearful one couldn't believe what he was seeing, but he sure as hell was enjoying it as well as hoping against hope it wouldn't end badly...that the fearless one wouldn't lose his nerve, merge with the fearful one again, and run off down the street yowling like an old coyote with a pack of rabid curs on his tail.

Wheatley glared up at Rio again. "You hurt me, damn you. You had no call to do that. I got rights!"

Rio's fearful self couldn't believe what he saw his fearless self do next.

Why, his fearless self rammed the brass butt plate of his Greener right smack-dab against the dead center of Wheatley's forehead!

Wheatley crumpled onto the boardwalk, howling, one hand closed against his forehead, the other one cupping his throbbing oysters.

Again, his trail pards, Price and LaPaz, closed their hands over the grips of their holstered six-shooters.

Again, Rio aimed the shotgun's double bores on them and grinned, feeling a forked vein in his forehead swell in devilish delight. "Go ahead," he said to Price and LaPaz. "Jerk them six-shooters. I'd like you to, though I would hate to make such a mess in front of the lady."

"Oh," said Mrs. Rose. "Oh, dear..."

Price and LaPaz removed their hands from their six-shooters.

LaPaz dipped his chin to stare down at Wheatley, and said in his Spanish-accented voice, "*Dios mio*, Bryce. Maybe you better do what this old *gato montés* says—eh, amigo?"

The Mex puncher glanced at Rio's double-bore with a warily slitted eye.

Inwardly, Rio grinned. The Mex had just called him an old wildcat.

Outwardly, he gave the two hardcases standing before him his best poker face.

"Oh, hell!" Wheatley clambered to his feet. Grunting and casting hateful glances at Rio shifting the double-bore around at the three hardcases, he stooped to retrieve Mrs. Rose's first parcel, which one of the horses at the hitchrack was nosing around curiously. He staggered over to the next parcel, picked it up, picked up the third one, stacked them neatly, and extended the stack to Mrs. Rose. "Here ya are...um..." He glanced at Rio who kept a threateningly narrowed eye on him. "...ma'am," he added.

"And...?" Rio said.

Wheatley turned back to Mrs. Rose who stood holding the three parcels now as though each had a rattlesnake in it. She regarded warily the hardcase towering over her, Wheatley still flushed and grunting with the soreness of his nether regions.

Wheatley drew a deep breath, doffed his hat, and gave a courtly bow. "Ma'am—"

"Her name is Mrs. Rose," Rio told him out the side of his mouth.

"Mrs. Rose," Wheatley said, bowing once more, holding his hat in his hands, "This big galoot wants to apologize for his"—he cut a sour look at his partners and then at Rio—"uncouth ways and clumsy, public drunkenness and for knocking your packages out of your saintly hands. I do hope you will find it in your no doubt bottomless heart to forgive this unwashed sinner!"

"Oh," Mrs. Rose said, glancing from Wheatley to the Greener-wielding Rio and back again. "Oh, well, yes...yes, thank you. You are...you're forgiven, young man." With that, badly flustered, the lady trundled off down the boardwalk, holding the parcels out away from her, distastefully, as if they'd somehow been tainted during the dustup, heading in the direction of the post office.

Wheatley gave a deep sigh of relief and exasperation then stuffed the battered topper on his head. He turned to Rio. "How was *that*?"

"Bryce, I do believe you missed your callin'. You should be back east actin' for the New York stage! I reckon that'll do, since I don't feel like emptyin' your slop buckets over in the hoosegow. From now on, you three mind your p's and q's or you'll each get another little kiss to your unmentionables from my double-bore, and, as

Señor Wheatley here can attest, it ain't near as sweet as Miss Jane's doves over at the San Juan! Now, skedaddle—the lot o' ya!"

The three wheeled and strode quickly off down the boardwalk, casting cautious looks over their shoulders, half expecting a load of double-ought buck blasted into their backsides.

Inwardly, Rio grinned.

Outwardly, he grinned, as well. He chuckled as he shouldered the double-bore, pulled his pants and gun belt up higher on his hips, puffed his chest up, pulled his shoulders back.

"I'll be damned," he said, as he continued his walk up the street toward the north end of town. He laughed. "I'll be da—"

"Hey, Rio!"

He looked straight ahead to see the tall, slender Henry McCallister long-striding toward him, a grave, anxious look on the young man's long, narrow face, a wing of sandy-red hair hanging wing-like over his left eye. He held his Winchester carbine in one hand and poked his tan Stetson up higher on his head with his other hand. He stepped around two miners chinning on the boardwalk, soapy beer mugs in their hands, and stopped in front of Rio.

"Rio!" Henry said.

"Yes, we done already got that far, Hank. What in holy blazes is it? That new schoolmarm in town lose her cat down an old mine shaft again?" Rio laughed, brimming, near overflowing with renewed confidence.

Uncorrupted by irony, the wide-eyed Henry McCallister shook his head. "No, it's way worse than that, Rio. One of the clerks from over at the Territorial Bank just come over to the jailhouse. He'd been pistol whipped an'

was in a bad, bad way, but somehow, when the desperadoes were distracted, he slipped out the bank's back
door. Rio, a passel of gun-hung desperadoes in long
cream dusters and flour-sack masks is robbin' the bank,
and we gotta get over there!"

## CHAPTER 24

"THE TERRITORIAL, YOU SAY?" RIO SAID, BREAKING HIS shotgun open to make sure the Greener was fully loaded. Ignoring a sudden tightening in the back of his legs, he snapped the shotgun closed, dipped his chin resolutely, and added, "All right, then—let's get over there an' put the kibosh on them greedy devils!"

He swung around and he and the taller, younger Henry McCallister ran down the street to the south. The Territorial Bank sat on the corner of San Juan Avenue and a cross street, on the avenue's west side, adjacent to Wilfred Drake's Mercantile. Rio and the deputy he called Hank ran one block south then crossed the broad avenue at a slant, leaping the train rails, heading toward the mercantile. Sure enough, Rio saw seven horses tethered at the hitchrack fronting the saloon on the other side of the cross street from the mercantile—short, leggy horses built for quick getaways in rough country.

These were professionals, Rio absently, silently opined as he and Hank slowed their pace as they headed past the mercantile toward the bank—a squat, boxlike building built of brick and with a flat, corrugated tin roof.

A mustachioed man in a long, cream duster, red-brown hat and wielding a double-barrel shotgun stood outside the bank's double front doors, a cigar dangling from between his teeth. Seeing Rio and Hank running toward him, he turned to the bank, rammed the shotgun's butt against one of the doors three times, hard, and bellowed, "Trouble, boys! Two tin stars lookin' to be heroes!"

He laughed as he ducked under the hitchrail, strode quickly into the street between two of the horses, stopped, spread his feet a little more than shoulder-width apart, and extended the Greener straight out from his left hip.

"Double-bore, Rio!" Hank said, throwing himself hard to his right.

"Oh, hell!" Rio said, throwing himself hard to his left just as the mustachioed gent, grinning around the cigar in his teeth, cut loose with one of his double-bore's barrels, blowing up a pumpkin sized chunk of the street where Rio had been standing half a second before.

The mustached gent turned slightly to his left and again the double-bore thundered, spraying double-ought buck into the stock trough behind which Hank had gone to ground.

Rio rolled onto his left shoulder and tried to bring his own double-bore up, but suddenly it was a lead weight in his hands. The mustachioed gent tossed away his own, empty Greener, unsheathed one of his two matching, silver-chased Colts, crouched, extended the hogleg toward where Hank was just then rising onto one knee and loudly jacking a round into his Winchester's breech. The mustachioed gent and Hank exchanged a couple of rounds and then Hank rose, ran ten feet to his right, and dove behind a second stock trough fronting the side of Drake's Mercantile just as the mustachioed gent, still grinning around the cigar, put a couple of .45 rounds into it.

Rio lay where he'd lain a few seconds ago, still trying to get his damn Greener up, wincing and grunting with the effort. For some reason he couldn't pull the damn thing up off the street. His hands were shaking, and the double-bore suddenly seemed to weigh as much as an anvil.

As men came running out of the bank behind him, shouting, a girl screaming, the mustachioed gent swung the big .45 toward Rio. He smiled around the cigar as he aimed the .45 straight out from his left shoulder, clicked the hammer back, and slightly narrowed his left eye.

Time froze for Rio, or slowed to a snail's pace...

Frozen in place, his heart beating a war rhythm against his breastbone, Rio stared in mute horror at the .45's maw, which grew larger and larger until he felt as though he was staring down a large, deep, night-black well that led all the way to hell. He saw the man's left index finger pull back against the trigger. He saw the hammer drop.

Rio squeezed his eyes closed, awaiting the bullet.

No blast came.

What he heard instead was a sizzling sound and a hushed pop.

He opened his eyes to see the mustachioed gent scowling incredulously at the big .45 in his hand.

A misfire!

Rio's heart hiccupped.

Suddenly he realized that the other six robbers were mounting their screaming, jostling, wide-eyed horses, exchanging gunfire with Hank and several men who'd run out onto the mercantile's loading dock, above and behind Rio. The mustachioed gent shoved his .45 into its holster, picked up his shotgun, and ran over to a chestnut, the reins of which one of the other robbers tossed him. The robbers were firing carbines or six-shooters at Hank, whom Rio could see pinned down behind the stock trough roughly thirty feet away from him. Hank's hat was lying on the boardwalk behind the younger deputy, a bullet hole in its crown.

Hank was staring, his face pinched with the gravity of the situation, toward Rio and waving wildly with his left arm. "Rio, get the hell out of the street. *Rio!*"

Suddenly seeing himself the way the kid was seeing him, like some cowering damn fool—what had happened to the brave Rio he'd watched dress down the three hard-cases only a few minutes ago?—silently, Rio shouted, "Gallblastit!" and clambered to his feet. He scooped up the shotgun and as several of the robbers reining their dancing mounts away from the hitchrack took wild shots at him, he ran as hard as his weary, old legs would carry him, took a lunging dive, and landed hard on the other side of the stock trough Hank had first taken cover behind.

"Damn!" the oldster bellowed, feeling as though he'd busted a half dozen ribs inside the thick layer of tallow he cushioned them with.

As the shooting and screaming continued, he lay flat on his back behind the trough. He raised his right hand. It was shaking like a leaf in a stiff breeze.

"Not again, dammit," he snarled at himself, closing his fingers over his palm, making a fist. "Not again!"

Gritting his teeth against the dogs of cowardice that had somehow found him again and were gnawing on him savagely, he grabbed the double-bore, heaved himself up onto his knees, picked out one of the robbers just then putting the steel to his black-and-white pinto, and tripped one of the Greener's two triggers.

Ka-BOOM!

The man on the pinto screamed and, his duster winging wildly out around him, went flying off his horse. He fell into the path of one of his brethren and was thoroughly trampled. The man on the horse trampling the first man turned to Rio, eyes widening as he bunched his mustached lips around his cigar—he was the mustached son of Satan who'd been standing guard with the double-bore—and swung his second, smoking .45 at Rio.

Rio aimed his Greener at him and said, hardening his jaws and flaring his nostrils, "You an' the devil done had your chance, amigo."

Ka-BOOM!

The second barrel of ten-gauge, double-ought buck shredded the chest of the mustachioed gent and punched him off his horse, making him lose his hat and cigar and triggering his .45 skyward. He hit the ground and rolled a few feet away from the man his horse had trampled and left in a quivering heap in the street.

Rio heaved himself to his feet, resting the smoking barn blaster across the stock trough and unsheathing the .44 from the soft leather holster tied down on his stout right thigh. The five remaining robbers were just then galloping around the corner of the side street onto San Juan Avenue, heading south. Rio was about to trigger a shot at them but then he saw two girls riding double with two of the riders, screaming and casting terrified, pleading looks back behind them.

One was a blonde, maybe twelve, the other a brunette, maybe fifteen.

"Hold your fire!" Rio shouted, throwing his arms up high and waving them at the half dozen men behind him at Drake's Mercantile and in various positions around the main avenue and the cross street who were shooting at the robbers. "Hold your fire—they have the Williams girls!"

As the thudding of the robbers' horses dwindled and the gunfire became sporadic before stopping entirely, a man shouted, "Nancy! Connie!" Rio swung his head around to see a man in a three-piece, charcoal-colored suit come staggering out of the bank, holding a white neckerchief to his bloody nose, his head thrown back. He staggered into the street and lowered the bloody neckerchief to his side, and yelled, "Those brigands have my girls—Nancy and Connie!" The man—in his early forties and with mussed but usually well kempt brown hair and a thick, walrus mustache—dropped to his knees with a warbling sob and yelled in a breaking voice, "They have my girls! Oh, *God*!"

With a strangled wail, Carlton Williams, president of the Territorial Bank of Del Norte, dropped forward onto his hands, blood dribbling from his likely broken nose into the finely churned dust and horse manure of the street.

"Oh, fer Pete's sake!" Rio cast his anxious gaze at the men and women standing around on the street, staring toward the bank. There was almost no moving traffic on either the main street or on this side street the bank was on. "Someone, send for the doctors!" he shouted, then hurried over to drop to one knee beside the sobbing bank president. "We'll get 'em, Mister Williams," he said, placing a hand on the man's shoulder. "Don't you worry—we'll get 'em back! Did you recognize any of those devils?"

Rio thought a couple might have looked familiar, though he hadn't gotten a good look at any of them.

Things had been happening too fast and he, to his lingering horror, had been too froze up with fear to make much sense of any of it. Now, however, he had his senses back, and he, by God, was going to run those jackals to ground.

Williams spat a large gob of blood and looked up at Rio, rage and fear in his eyes. "One was that card cheat, Ed Colvin!"

"Ahh," Rio said, feeling as though the man had just slapped him across the face. Since Colvin was one of the seven, his sidekick Bob Sugar likely was, too.

Williams's eyes blazed in horror at Rio. "Colvin beat me even after I opened the safe for him. He took Nancy and Connie—they were with me at the bank because their mother is visiting relatives in Denver—and he told me that if he saw any sign of a posse on his back trail, I've"—the man glanced away with a shudder and when he looked back at Rio, a sheen of emotion glistened in his eyes—"he said if he saw a posse, I've seen the last of the girls!"

He lowered his forehead to the street and sobbed.

"Don't you worry, Mister Williams," Rio said, patting the man's back reassuringly. "We'll get 'em back. He won't know we're behind him, no sir, but we'll get 'em back all right!"

"*We'll* get 'em back!" said a man's deep-throated voice. "We'll get 'em back, and I'll get my money back. I made a deposit just a few minutes before those brigands robbed the bank!"

Rio turned to see a tall, gray-haired man in a tall, cream Stetson and fringed leather vest standing on the loading dock of Wilfred Drake's Mercantile. Mine owner Duke Winston swung around and began striding toward the front of the dock, toward the four horses tied there and where an older gent sat in a supply wagon, holding back tightly on the reins of the frightened mount in the traces.

"Come on, boys!" Winston called to the three other younger men who'd been firing with Winston at the robbers and whom Rio recognized as Winston's mine guards who helped the mine owner make bank deposits and pickup supplies every two weeks in town. "Let's run 'em down before they cross into New Mex—"

"Hold on, Winston!" Rio said. "This ain't your call. It's mine. With Bloody Joe gone, I'm the law in charge. If you want to join a posse with me an' Deputy McCallister, we'd be happy to have you. But I'll be leadin' it up and you won't be ridin' after those scurvy devils half-cocked. You done seen they had those girls as plain as I did!"

Winston stopped and swung toward Rio. His three men stopped, as well. They, too, turned toward the deputy. "You?" Winston said, through a sneer, showing his white teeth beneath his thick, salt-and-pepper mustache. "Why, you're nothing but old and dried up. You're fat and, what's worse, you're a damn coward. I won't be led by such an old fool as you, Rio Waite!"

Rio winced against the assault.

He felt as though he'd been punched in the gut. Hard.

He looked around at the suddenly silent street where the breeze lifted thin curls of dust, nibbled hat brims, and jostled the women's hair around their cheeks. All faces were turned toward him, regarding him with barely concealed disgust and...what?

Pity.

Even the banker, Williams, regarded him sourly.

"There you have it!" Winston said, and started down the loading dock to the horses at the hitchrack, saying to the older gent in the wagon, "You head on back to the mine, Curly. Put those supplies away. With any luck, we'll be back—"

A rifle barked.

Rio jerked with a start. Winston stopped halfway down the loading dock steps and swung around, his brown eyes hard and exasperated beneath the broad brim of his cream Stetson. Rio turned to see Hank McCallister standing on his left, holding his carbine one-handed high above his head. Smoke curled from the octagonal barrel.

"You heard Deputy Waite, Mister Winston," Hank said. "If you wanna ride after the robbers, be part of a posse, that's fine. But we'll lead it up—Deputy Waite an' me." He turned to the twenty or so other folks standing around the sides of the main street and the cross street, and added, "That goes for the rest of you. Anyone want to be part of a posse, meet Deputy Waite and me in front of the jailhouse in fifteen minutes. No one rides out ahead or they'll be arrested for interfering with two lawmen in the commission of their official duties under the territorial statutes. That there's an offense Marshal Mannion would frown upon. An' you all know how the marshal can frown!"

The younger deputy dipped his chin resolutely.

All eyes were on him now. So were Winston's, the man's heavy jaws set hard.

Men muttered to each other. Women looked up curiously at the men.

The late afternoon sun glinted in the dust curling up in several places along the street over which shadows grew long.

Winston's hard eyes returned to Rio. "All right—we'll play it your way, Waite. But I don't think you're good enough. The first time I see you start to freeze up, me an' my boys will be going after those robbers alone!" He stepped down off the steps and turned to his men, beckoning angrily. "Come on, you men. Let's get these horses water and grained—ready to ride!"

The crowd dispersed.

Dr. Ben Ellison had appeared and was gently helping the banker, Williams, to his feet.

Winston and his men galloped off toward a livery barn.

Rio turned to Hank. "Thanks. I hope you haven't just made a big mistake. At least, you still have a reputation in this town."

Hank smiled. "Oh, I don't think so."

Rio shaped a wan smile then frowned curiously up at the taller, younger deputy. "Uh...'interferin' with two lawmen in the commission of their official duties under the territorial statutes'...?"

"Did you like the sound of that, Rio?" Hank said. "I did, too." He patted the older man's shoulder. "Let's fetch our hosses!"

## CHAPTER 25

CHEYENNE OPENED HER EYES, BLINKED SLEEP FROM them.

Realizing she was not home in her own bed in her own bedroom, she gasped and rose to a sitting position, making the army cot creak beneath her shifting weight while holding the moth-eaten wool army blanket against her breasts.

"Oh, my God!" she exclaimed, staring at the young man gazing back at her from over his steaming coffee cup where he sat at a square eating table scarred over the years with the initials of all the drovers who'd spent nights in this remote line cabin near Thunder Mountain.

"Whoa! Whoa! What is it, honey?" asked Garrett Beech, rising from his chair.

"We're still here!" Cheyenne exclaimed. "You let me fall asleep. Garrett, you told me you wouldn't!"

"I fell asleep, too." Garrett chuckled as he squatted beside the cot and, holding his steaming cup in one hand, used his other hand to slide a lock of mussed, nearly black hair back from Cheyenne's left cheek. "You're dang near a full-grown woman. You can do what you wanna do."

Cheyenne couldn't help but smile. She placed her right hand along Garrett's left cheek. "I can't go out spending the night with wayward cowpokes." She leaned toward him, rubbed her nose against his, and pecked his lips. "Ma's gonna tan my hide really good this time!"

"Don't you worry—I'll doctor it for you." Garrett's lips spread but the oddly cobalt eyes staring back at Cheyenne through the coffee's steam remained without expression.

Cheyenne stared at him. Chicken flesh rose across her shoulders. Why did this man—ten years older than her but seeming younger, still half wild—seem to regard her like prey? Like he was thinking something not quite right about her. Not quite right in his head...

Suddenly, the skin wrinkled above the bridge of his nose. "What is it, pet?"

Cheyenne gave a little, involuntary shudder. "Sometimes that's how you look at me, Garrett. I'm a little pet of yours...and you don't always treat your pets right."

He held her look with a level one of his own. Then his lips spread a smile again, and he chuckled and said, "Why, that's the strangest thing I ever heard leave your lips. And I've heard some strange things over the past several months, Cheyenne. You're a strange one. You might think I am, but you're just as strange." His smile broadened. "Maybe that's why we get along so well."

He winked, lifted his cup to her as though in salute, then brought it to his lips, and sipped, the steam bathing his large, handsomely sculpted, clean-shaven, lightly freckled face. She was glad he didn't look anything like his mother, who, while only in her fifties, looked closer to eighty. Cheyenne had never met his father, Owen Beech, but it was said that Garrett got his handsome looks from him. Handsome except for those oddly flat, cobalt eyes, that was.

What had attracted her to him?

She supposed it was because he was older and that he'd courted her so desperately hard, and there weren't many handsome men—handsome aside from his eyes, of course—in this remote country. And Cheyenne's mother rarely let her ride to town—at least, not without Eva at her side, riding shotgun, so to speak.

"You're gonna get me kicked off Wolf Creek," she warned, though the notion didn't seem so terrible right then, after all that had happened. Even before she'd found out that her Uncle Matt was really her father, life with Eva Severance had been no picnic. Her mother hardly ever spared her a warm word; her tone was always rigid and she was always giving orders, scowling as she moved breathlessly about the cabin and the ranch head-quarters, working...always working. It was as though she was afraid to slow down lest she should give her overly active mind time to think.

Before, Cheyenne had thought her mother was just ashamed of what had become of her husband, and all the suspicions about the missing loot washing through this section of the mountains, along the Animas River.

Now Cheyenne knew what Eva Severance had really not wanted to think about.

"You can come live with me at the Triangle Cross," Garrett said.

"I don't know which would be worse—your mother or mine."

"My mother would love to have you."

Cheyenne narrowed one eye, suspicious. "Why?"

"You know."

Cheyenne gave a knowing smile. "As leverage so she can get my and Ma's ranch." Cheyenne looked at the window on the other side of the tiny cabin where morning was an intensifying gray wash. "Can't say I'd mind. As long as she gave Ma a good price. Ma should get off the place, go live in town." She turned back to the handsome young man squatting beside her cot. "You'd marry me? Take me off this range...out of these mountains...?"

She wrinkled her nose in disdain for the hard, lonely life she lived here, which, as of only one day ago, had turned so much worse.

"Why, sure." Garrett looked down at his coffee. "If we had the money."

Cheyenne gave a snort. "I don't know where Pa's loot is. I promise—for the seventeenth time! I swear, Garrett —sometimes I think that's all you see in me. The money my pa stole!"

Garrett looked up at her quickly, rested his hand gently against her cheek. "Now, you know that's not true," he said, with quiet tenderness. "Why, there's no prettier, sweeter girl in these mountains than you. That's all I see in you. And, yes, I'll marry you, honey. Take you far away from here. Heck, you think I don't want off this range as bad as you do. Workin' for my ma is not an easy job, and...well...I've done told you she's goin' broke. Every time she goes to town to see the bank, she comes home even more colicky than before she left."

Suddenly, Garrett frowned at her. "What's wrong, honey?"

Cheyenne sat staring at the window. Just a second

ago, in the corner of her eye, she'd thought she'd seen something move just beyond the dirty, warped pane. She thought she'd heard something, too. A quickly drawn breath?

"I thought I saw something in the window."

Garrett turned to it. A branch swept across it, nudged by the dawn breeze.

"Just the wind," Garrett said. "Don't worry—I made good 'n' sure we weren't followed. Wouldn't want our secret place discovered by anyone else—now, would we?" He pecked Cheyenne's cheek.

Satisfied they were alone, Cheyenne returned to the topic at hand. "Your ma's acquiring Wolf Creek isn't going to help her much."

"Every little bit helps."

"Pa's loot would really help—wouldn't it?"

Garrett gave a sheepish laugh. "It sure would. But it would help us even more...to leave her...maybe start a whole new life in St. Louis or San Francisco, some such a place..."

"I want to go to New York and be an actress!" Cheyenne said with dramatic flair. She shook her hair back from her face and stuck her chin high in the air. "Don't you think I'd like it fine in New York City, Mister Beech?"

Garrett laughed. "I sure do, honey!" He laughed again. "I sure do. Fine. Mighty fine!" He frowned suddenly. "You wouldn't get a big head, though, would you? You wouldn't leave ol' Garrett for some rich railroad magnate, would you?"

"Never in a million years, my sweet!" She laughed then turned to where a coffeepot hung from an iron tripod in the fireplace at the far end of the cabin. "That coffee sure smells good."

"I'll bring you a cup."

"Will you?" Cheyenne said in her spoiled little girl's voice. Now, she felt good about him again. They couldn't get together very often, but when they did, they had a fun, easy way of talking to each other. She was thinking now about telling her mother about Garrett. She hadn't been ready before, because she'd had her suspicions about him. But she thought she was ready now.

Thoughtfully, she watched him pull a tin cup from his saddlebags hanging over the back of the chair he'd been sitting in, fill it, and bring the cup to her on the cot.

"Thank you, kind sir."

"Anytime, milady." He walked to the table, plucked his black hat off it and, yawning, glanced back at her. "I reckon I'd better saddle my horse. You probably best get back to—"

"Wait." Cheyenne sat up higher on the cot, rested back against the log wall, and drew her knees up against her breasts, tenting the blanket over them. "I'd like to ride over to my uncle..." She stopped, reconsidering what she should call him now. No, she couldn't think of him as her father. At least, not yet. Maybe never. She drew a breath, shook her hair back from her face again, and continued with, "I'd like to ride over to my uncle Matt's. I left something with him. I'd like to share it with you."

Garrett turned full around to face her, frowning. "What is it, honey?"

"It's a paper."

Garrett returned to the cot, squatted down beside it, and regarded her curiously. "What kind of paper?"

Cheyenne blew on her coffee, sipped. "It's a mine claim."

"Oh?"

"My father's claim. I found it in an old trunk in his

and Ma's room." Again, Cheyenne sipped from her cup, swallowed. "Turns out he had a secret claim somewhere at the base of Thunder Mountain."

"Oh...?"

"I'm thinkin'...well, I'm thinkin' he might have hid that loot at his claim. It'd make for an easy way to find it again. I gave it to Matt. I figure it might still be at the Half-Moon. I doubt he'd have it on him. I don't think he wanted to have anything to do with it. I should have taken it back, but I left it with him, hopin' he'd come around. It's probably still on his table at the Half-Moon."

"Hmm." Garrett nodded, thoughtful. "Well, then, let's go look for it."

Cheyenne nodded as she stared down at her cup, tapping her thumbs against the rim.

Sudden urgency rising in his voice, Garrett said, "You get dressed. I'll saddle my horse."

As he headed for the door, Cheyenne stopped him again with: "Wait." She shuttled her gaze from her coffee to Garrett, frowning. "He had something scribbled on the side of the claim. I doubt it means anything. He was probably just doodling, but..."

"What?"

"It looked like a helmet. One of those old conquistador's helmets. You know...like the ones they find around here from time to time...with shields and breastplates and other such old Spanish stuff."

Garrett rubbed his jaw. "You don't say." He thought in silence for a minute and then said, "You know what?"

"What?" Cheyenne said, brightening hopefully.

"We might not have to ride to the Half-Moon."

When she said nothing but just frowned at him curiously, Garrett said, "Get dressed. I'll saddle my hoss."

He grabbed his saddlebags and carbine and went outside. When he brought his steeldust gelding around to the front of the cabin from the stable and corral behind it, Cheyenne was waiting on the small worn patch of ground fronting the cabin's door, holding the wool blanket around her shoulders against the mountain morning chill. She stepped forward, and Garrett reached down with his left hand to pull her up onto the horse behind him, onto his saddlebags and bedroll.

He clucked to the steeldust and Cheyenne leaned forward to look up into his face. "Garrett, where are we going?"

He gave her a little coyote grin, slitting those too-blue eyes, and said, "You'll see. Let's make it a surprise."

An hour later the sun was well up and they were dropping down the steep trail into the canyon, the four spires of Thunder Mountain painted a gauzy copper lemon as they jutted back against the western sky. The canyon was still filled with deep-purple shadows. A knife-blade chill remained in the air, making Cheyenne shiver even though she drew the blanket taut around her.

Just as they reached the bottom of the canyon, the steep walls rising a good two hundred feet around them, Cheyenne felt a strange reverberation. It seemed to be coming from all around them. Garrett drew the gelding to a sudden halt and the beast, feeling the strange shivering sensation, also, lifted its snout and chewed the bit, frightened.

"Whoa, now. Whoa, boy," Garrett said, leaning forward to pat the horse's left front wither. He got the horse stopped as best he could and looked around, saying, "Do you feel that?"

"I sure do," the girl said, also looking around, feeling

anxiety dribble up her spine. "What is that? Sounds like thunder but there's not a cloud in the sky!"

"No, it ain't—"

Garrett cut himself off abruptly when the rumbling grew louder in the west. There was a great crackling sound, deeper than a thunderclap. He and Cheyenne turned to see a secondary spire lean out away from the north side of the first of the four columns comprising Thunder Mountain. It was a finger of rock dwarfed by the column it was part of—maybe only a hundred feet tall. As it leaned away from the main column, Cheyenne saw a great, black crack form at its base and grow larger the farther the secondary column leaned out away from the primary one.

Then suddenly the secondary column broke clean away from the larger one and, in a great explosion of dust and rock, tumbled down the side of the larger spire, breaking into smaller rocks and boulders until those rocks and boulders were all tumbling down toward the canyon south and west of the two witnesses sitting the steeldust, lower jaws hanging in shock at the minor cataclysm they were watching. A great mushroom cloud of dust rose around the falling rocks, obscuring them until they were completely hidden from view.

"Wow!" Cheyenne exclaimed.

"Did you...did you see *that*?" Garrett said, holding the reins of the nervous gelding taut in his black-gloved hands.

As the rumbling dwindled, the rocks and boulders of the secondary spire now settling on the canyon bottom back and to the west of Cheyenne and Garrett Beech, the former, steady rumbling grew silent. No longer did the earth shake beneath the steeldust's dancing hooves. Gradually, then, as silence once again filled the canyon, the horse settled down, giving one last stomp and an incredulous shake of its head.

"Never seen anything like that before in my life!" Cheyenne said.

"Earth tremor," Garrett said. "Never felt one before, but I heard about 'em."

He clucked to the reluctant gelding and on they rode, Garrett seemingly following a path in his head, taking a series of intersecting canyons then riding up and over a pass and through the sunlight of the warming day. As they started down the pass's other side, back into the shadows, heading roughly northwest, Cheyenne saw a cracked, horned buffalo skull embedded in the sandstone ridge to her right, only a few feet off her right thigh as they passed it. Pictures drawn by the ancient ones, most faded with time but some still bright as though they been painted only a few years ago, appeared in the cliff walls to either side of the ancient Indian hunting trail they were following. At least, that's who Garrett thought probably carved most of the trails through these canyons—Natives and the ancient streams that were likely related somewhere back in time to the Animas that cut down through the eastern side of the San Juans.

He and Matt and Cheyenne's father, Roy, had ridden through here when they'd been friends, scouring cattle that had wandered into the canyon from above, and sharing lonely campfires.

When they reached the bottom of the pass, a rumbling sounded again.

The steeldust stopped, shook its head, and whinnied.

"Uh-oh," Cheyenne said. She could feel the earth's reverberations through the gelding.

The rumbling didn't last long this time—only a few seconds.

Still, Cheyenne was wary. "Are you sure we should continue, Garrett?" She looked at rocks and boulders littering the steep walls of the canyon to either side, imagining them rolling down those ridges and turning her, Garrett, and the steeldust to red jelly.

"Pshaw," Garrett said, and booted the steeldust ahead.

## CHAPTER 26

SUDDENLY THE SUN NO LONGER SHONE AT THE TOP OF the canyon. A chill wind picked up, spiced with rain. A squall was on the way.

Cheyenne drew the blanket tighter around her, shivered. She saw a rock painting of a stick figure stabbing a red-tipped spear into the belly of another stick figure convulsing on its back in the stone wall to her left. She frowned, anxiety nettling her.

"It almost feels like this canyon doesn't want us here."

"Pshaw," Garrett said, and suddenly stopped the steeldust.

"Why're you stopping?"

Garrett smiled over his shoulder at her. "We're here."

He swung his right leg over his saddle horn and dropped to the ground.

Cheyenne dropped into his arms. The wind blowing her hair, feeling the first drops of wind-driven rain mixed with snow, she looked around. They were in a deep cleft in the larger canyon. Badly eroded rocky slopes rose around her. A narrow, intersecting canyon rose on her left, cutting through the rock-littered slope on that side, rising, choked with rocks and boulders so that she could see only a few yards along its course.

"I don't see anything," Cheyenne said. "But rock."

"I know." Garrett smiled at her. "That's why it's such a great place to hide loot." He winked. "Follow me!"

Frowning curiously, she watched him climb a steep slope of gravel and rock ahead and on her left. She started to follow him, keeping the blanket closed tightly about her shoulders, wishing now she had more than just the blanket as the rain was turning to snow, the large, gauzy flakes coming down heavier. As Garrett leaped from rock to rock, Cheyenne spied a quick flicker of movement in the corner of her left eye.

She whipped around quickly.

Nothing but rocks as the canyon rose to the pass they'd just ridden down.

She would have sworn she'd spied someone moving behind her, maybe ducking out of sight. She shivered. She was just getting spooked was all. All she really wanted now was to get out of the canyon. She no longer cared much about the loot. She kept seeing that spire come crashing down as though it had been given a savage flick by the oversized finger of an angry god.

If it kept raining, this canyon would flood.

Beneath the wind, she heard a whistle.

She looked up the slope to see Garrett poking his head out from behind a large, flame-shaped rock, a big grin on his pale, blue-eyed face. He beckoned, frowning impatiently, then pulled his head back behind the rock.

Shivering against the growing chill—snowstorms were not unheard of this high in the San Juans this time of the year—Cheyenne picked her way up the slope, climbing, sometimes dropping forward to use her hands. She stepped up to the flame-shaped rock and saw Garrett standing to her right, gazing into a dark opening, partly hidden by the stone wall of the cliff it had been cut into. The wall and the flame-shaped rock standing before it had hidden the jagged-edged opening from below.

Garrett turned to her. He had an almost ethereal look, his cobalt eyes dancing with mischief, with an evil glee.

"Come on over here, honey," he said, just loudly enough for Cheyenne to hear him above the wind. He turned his head forward to stare into the cavern. As he did, he thrust out his left hand straight out from his shoulder and opened it wide.

Cheyenne hesitated, off-put once again by the look of evil in his too-blue eyes. But then she moved toward him, accepted his hand, and stepped beside him to stare into the jagged, shadowy opening in the cliff wall before them.

An involuntary gasp escaped her lips.

Her heart fluttered.

The cave floor dropped steeply before flattening into a maybe ten-square-foot area. There was a charred stone fire ring in the middle of it. But what Cheyenne's disbelieving gaze held on was the skeleton slumped back against the wall to her right. The skeleton was clad in the steel breastplate and combed steel helmet of the ancient conquistadors. That's all it wore. The rest was white, dusty bone. The head was turned and tipped to one side so that the large, black, empty eye sockets seemed to be boring right through Cheyenne from where the long-dead man—several hundred years dead, most likely—stared as though with silent, ancient yearning toward the cave's entrance and freedom.

In the man's bony lap, his bony arms and hands cradling them as though lovingly, sat a pair of dusty, grimy, brown leather saddlebags. They could have been a baby in the man's fleshless arms.

Garrett chuckled and glanced at Cheyenne. "That's your old man's sense of humor, right there. He reined up below, ran up here, and set the saddlebags on that old Spaniard's lap. Probably had him a good chuckle, too, as he ran back into the canyon, mounted up, and rode on...with Bloody Joe and Rio Waite hot on his trail."

He turned his head forward to stare down at the dead conquistador and the saddlebags once more. He shook his head, and said in a droll tone, "Just my luck."

Cheyenne tore her anxious gaze from the coveted bags to frown up at Garrett. "What do you mean?"

"That he got shot before we could split the loot." Garrett frowned down at the Spaniard. "I just wonder if he meant to split it with me...or if he thought he was gonna keep it all for himself." He glanced at Cheyenne again. "Your old man couldn't be trusted, truth be known."

Cheyenne felt her lower jaw sag in shock.

Her already-fluttering heart fluttered more violently, kicking against her breastbone.

Words were slow to shape themselves on her tongue. "You...you were..."

Again, Garrett grinned at her, those too-blue eyes again glinting evilly. "The second robber. Yep."

She felt as though she'd run a long way. She found it hard to catch her breath. "Oh...you thought...I'd eventually..."

"Lead you to the bags? I sorta thought so. After I seen you snooping around the canyon yourself. I thought you mighta had a clue about where he hid them. I never woulda thought of this place. This place here...that old Spaniard...scared plum heck out of us when him an' me an' Matt stumbled on it, tryin' to get outta the rain while the arroyo out there was fillin' up with water. We built a fire an' spent a chilly, spooky night, the lightnin' flashin off the old fellow's helmet, making his eyes look red. We were superstitious. That's why we never took the helmet or breastplate. We had no truck with a dead man, especially one who'd been so well preserved. Why the wildcats and wolves never scattered his bones to kingdom come! That was downright spooky its ownself. No, we left him alone an' after that long night, we vowed never to return."

He smiled at Cheyenne again. "I ain't so spooked nor suspicious anymore. Never woulda thought of this place, though, if you hadn't told me about that helmet your old man doodled on that claim paper. His mine's around here somewhere, I'm sure—that helmet helped *him* find it. He was illiterate, Roy was. He wouldn't have been able to read the claim. When you told me about the helmet, I knew right away where he hid the loot. Folks mighta found his mine, but no one ever woulda found the loot here."

Cheyenne stared up at him in shock.

In fear.

His evil was on full display in his eyes, in his voice.

She found herself backing away from him, the snow now clinging to her hair.

"Where you goin', honey?" he said, frowning at her. "Bad weather out there. Bad footing for the gelding. We're gonna have to stay in here till it clears."

"No," Cheyenne said. "No, I...no..."

She turned to run but he grabbed her quickly, thrust her back toward him before giving her a violent push into the cavern, yelling, "Didn't you hear me, honey? We'll be spending the night in here with the old conquistador!"

Cheyenne hit the floor of the cave and rolled up against the charred fire ring and the ashes from a long-dead fire. Old ashes. The ashes of her father, Matt's, and Garrett's fire...from years ago.

Cheyenne rolled onto her hip and watched Garrett walk into the cave and crouch over the saddlebags. He unbuckled one of the flaps and peered inside. He whistled, slowly shaking his head.

"It's all here. All...right...here..."

"You don't love me," Cheyenne said. She'd lost her blanket in the fall, but her trepidation kept her mind off the cold as well as the chill wind howling outside. The weather that would make escaping this man, this canyon impossible, even if she had a horse, which she didn't. "You never intended to share the money with me. You're gonna kill me now, aren't you?" She heard her voice tremble with fear. "That's the only way you can make sure I won't tell who the second robber was...and who now has the loot."

She stared at him staring into the saddlebags, her heart hammering.

She waited, wanting him to tell her that, no, she was wrong. She waited, but he said nothing. He stared into the open flap of the second saddlebag, grinning. She didn't know if he'd even heard her. His mind was likely on how he was going to spend that money he'd waited for two and a half years for.

"Aren't you?" she demanded, silently pleading with him to spare her.

She'd never known such fear. Why had she come after the loot, anyway? It was worthless to her now...unless.

She eyed the .44-caliber revolver holstered on his right thigh.

Unless she could somehow get her hands on his gun...

He looked at her suddenly. He followed her gaze to the walnut-gripped gun then raised his eyes to hers as she quickly lifted her own gaze from the weapon. Chagrin and a deepening, even more penetrating fear chilled the marrow in her bones. He looked at her with those cold, flat, blue eyes. They were a snake's eyes, if a snake's eyes were blue. They regarded her indifferently for several seconds, and then he smiled and closed his hand over the butt of the holstered revolver.

"Want me to do it now?" he asked, almost too quietly for her to hear above the wind howling and moaning outside, blowing snow up behind the rock concealing the cave and a few inches into the cavern itself. "Get it over with?"

She looked at those cold, blue eyes.

She looked at the gun.

Suddenly, fury rose in her. Fury and defiance.

Defiantly, she said, "Yes." She sat on one hip, propped on one hand against the cave floor. "Yes. Do it now. Get it over here. Leave me here...for the rest of time..." She glanced at the revolting specter of the skeleton that had haunted him all those years ago. "Leave me here with him. Then try to forget what you did. Try, every time you spend a dollar of that loot you and my father stole, to not think about what you did to me. About me lying here, moldering away with the old Spaniard."

Tears filled her eyes as her rage, defiance, and terror rose to a crescendo. Her lips quivered as she said, "Do it, Garrett!"

He brushed his right thumb across the keeper thong fastened over the revolver's hammer, releasing it. That hand tightened around the Colt's grips. Cheyenne's heart shuddered as he slid the gun from the holster, his hard, flat, lunatic eyes riveted on her, chin dipped slightly so the gaze up at her from beneath his brows such a washed-out blond, he didn't appear to have brows at all.

He was calling her bluff!

He smiled at her then. He tossed the gun in the air, caught it with his other hand. He tossed it again, caught it with his right hand.

"If you insist," Garrett said, drawing his thumb back against the hammer, cocking it.

He aimed the barrel at her.

She sat frozen in fear, ears ringing, her mouth suddenly as dry as an old boot.

"Don't," she heard herself mutter. "Please, Garrett..."

"Might as well get it over with," he said, holding the Colt steady on her, aimed at her chest.

He smiled at her from beneath his brows.

Outside, beneath the howling wind, the steeldust whinnied.

Garrett frowned, turned his gaze toward the cavern's entrance on his left.

She saw her chance. It might be the only one she'd get.

She sprang off her left hip, throwing herself at Garrett, wrapped both hands around the gun, driving it down. Its roar was deafening. She saw the orange flash and smelled the burnt powder as the bullet ricocheted off the cave floor to hammer into the ceiling above and to her right.

Garrett bellowed.

He raised the gun up and his face was a red mask of narrow-eyed fury as he said, "Why, you...!" He brought the gun back behind his left shoulder then thrust it forward, smashing the side of it against Cheyenne's right temple.

She screamed and flew several feet to her right.

Again, she rolled, her head reeling, ears ringing.

She lay flat on her back, badly dazed. She dipped her chin to watch Garrett rise, turn toward the cave entrance, and ratchet back the Colt's hammer. Holding the gun half out from his right side, he moved straight ahead, stepped to one side, and left the cave.

Cheyenne heard something.

She couldn't identify it with the wind blowing and her ears ringing. Maybe a man's grunt...?

Garrett appeared again, stepping back into the cave.

He'd lost his hat. He held the Colt straight down against his right leg. Blood oozed from a long, deep cut on his right cheek. It dribbled down to the corner of his mouth. He stopped just inside the cave entrance. His eyes rolled back in his head as he dropped to his knees.

"Oh...*mercy!*" he said and felt flat on his face.

Another figure appeared in the doorway, long, curly blond hair hanging down around the girl's slender shoulders clad in a snow-flecked, yellow rain slicker. Moisture dribbled off the brim of her cream Stetson. Light from behind her winked off the barrel of the pearl-gripped, silver-chased revolver she held in her hand, aimed at Cheyenne.

## CHAPTER 27

"Rio, you certain-sure them curling wolves rode this way?" asked Deputy Henry McCallister.

On one knee beside him, Rio Waite scrubbed his jaw with a gloved hand and, scowling down at the gravelly ground, said, "Well, not certain-sure, I gotta admit. The ground's too dang hard through here to hold much of a print. But I did spy horse apples a ways back, and they were relatively fresh. That rock there has a scrape mark on it, and I think it was made by a shod hoof kickin' it."

"Those horse apples could've been dropped by one of Tater Gleason's men. The scrape mark made by them, too. Gleason runs horses in this country, you know, Rio."

"I know, I know," Rio said, scratching his ear, hating his lack of confidence. He glanced back at the small posse comprised of the mine owner, Duke Winston, his three mine guards, and three townsmen—a grocer, a druggist, and the big Chinaman whose name everyone pronounced "Zang" because they couldn't pronounce his real name. Zang, almost as broad as he was tall, and with long, mare's tail mustaches running down both sides of his mouth, ran a laundry; he, like Winston, had just made a sizable deposit in the Territorial Bank a few hours before it was robbed. He was as piss-burned as the other townsmen whose money had been plundered from the bank.

All seven men were standing in the rocks lining the trail, resting their horses and smoking, or, in Zang's case, biting off bits of tobacco from the big braid that hung around his neck from a leather thong. One of his big, brown cheeks fairly bulged with the stuff. A couple of the horses drew water from hats on the ground before them including one drinking from Zang's low-crowned, frayed-brimmed sombrero from the rawhide band of which a red crow feather poked up. The bank had been robbed the day before, and Rio had pushed the posse hard overnight, as the quarter moon had offered enough light to follow the robbers' trail without injuring the horses. That trail had played out, however, just after dawn, when Rio had led the catch party around the east side of the Rattlesnake Buttes roughly twenty-five miles south of Del Norte, nearly into New Mexico Territory. The Sangre de Cristos rose behind the blue-green mist of distance to the east.

It was noon, the sun high, the sky a clean cerulean blue and cloudless except where a late-summer snow squall had settled over a peak of the San Juans to the northwest. Here it was hot, likely in the eighties. In the mountains, it was likely cold. Rio would have preferred to be in the higher reaches, but here he was, toiling earthly, trying to prove his worth and to save a couple of innocent young girls in the bargain.

The seven posse men stared toward Rio and Hank, none looking overconfident in the deputy-in-charge, either. The broad-shouldered, red-faced, mustached Duke Winston, leaning one hip against a rock and holding a smart-looking Henry repeater across his lap, looked downright peeved, his broad cheeks puffed up, his eyes narrowed impatiently.

Rio turned to Hank again and, trying to inject more confidence into his voice, said, "They went this way, all right. We'll keep skirting the wash where it wraps around the bluffs." He glanced at the deep, broad, cedar- and sage-bristling dry wash curving on his right as he stood gazing south.

Hank nodded, but he didn't look overly certain. But he did look hopeful, at least. Rio would give him that. The others just looked skeptical and not so vaguely impatient to downright hostile.

"You know why I think they rode this route, Hank?" Rio said, wanting to convince himself now as well as his junior deputy.

Hank pulled the brim of his slouch hat down lower on his forehead. "Why's that, Rio?"

"Because that's what I'd do, gallblastit!"

He swung around and, the mule ears jostling around his stovepipe boots, strode in his bandy-legged fashion back toward the waiting posse.

"It's about time, Waite," Duke Winston said, pushing away from the rock. "You ever hear the expression 'we're burnin' daylight'? Well, that's what we're doing, all right. While those bank robbers get farther and farther into New Mexico. Hell, they probably swung west by now and are pret' near in Arizona!"

"The horses needed a rest and so did we." Rio walked up to his dun and tightened its saddle cinch. "Now we'll mount up and continue south."

"West," Winston insisted, walking up to Rio and resting his rifle on his shoulder. He flipped away his cigar stub, and said, "Heading south is a waste of time. They didn't skirt these bluffs." He glanced at the craggy, red buttes rising a half mile to the west of the wash. "They rode right through them."

"I don't believe they did," Rio said, turning to the man, not enjoying having to look up at him; Winston was a good four inches taller than he. "I believe they headed west and south. They wouldn't have ridden through the middle of those buttes at night. Too hard on horses and too many places for other owlhoots, seeing them two girls and the overstuffed saddlebags they're carrying, to effect an ambush."

"Just before *you* lost their trail, they'd swung west," Winston said. "Southwest!"

"They were just tryin' to throw us off."

Winston pointed with the Henry. "I say they headed straight through the middle of those buttes, Waite. Shortest way through them...shortest way into New Mexico, around the Black Range and into Arizona, headed for Mexico...with *my* money!"

"You're wrong, Winston. And I call the shots." Rio gave the man his best steely-eyed, confident look and thumped himself in the chest. "I call the shots!"

Winston smiled coldly down at Rio, showing his big, horsey teeth. "I think you're scared. Yeah, that's it— you're scared we might overtake 'em and you might have to prove your worth...and freeze up again!"

Rage filled Rio. He clenched his fist at his side, resisting the urge to punch the bigger man. "I don't give a good goddamn what you think of me, Winston. But you heard me back in town, and you hear me now. I call the shots, or you go home!"

"Go to hell!" Winston turned his big, red-angry face to the others flanking him, all looking uncertainly on. "Who wants to ride with me and my men through the buttes—fastest way to the New Mexico border? That's the way they headed with our money and those girls. If we keep following this tin star's route, we'll never catch up to them, and they'll get away scot-free, likely sell those poor little girls to a flophouse down in Mexico!"

The grocer, the druggist, and the Chinese laundryman, Zang, silently conferred.

The druggist, Mortimer Arthur, a short man in his late thirties whose salt-and-pepper beard hung nearly to his paunch, looked at Rio. A former military man, he sighed, adjusted the black felt slouch hat on his nearly bald head, and said, "Sorry, Rio. I think Winston's right. My life savings was in that bank, and, well..."

He glanced at the grocer, Layton Waters, a tall, pale, thin Englishman in his early forties. Rio had heard he'd done some fighting for France in Prussia and had a long saber scar on his right cheek to prove it. Waters glanced guiltily down then gave one, waxed corner of his thick, brown mustache a nervous twist, and said, "Yep, I agree. Sorry, Deputy."

He pulled his gun and shell belt higher on his lean hips from which his broadcloth trousers sagged. "We have to catch up to 'em, all right. Take the bloody beasts down before nightfall or they'll lose us, for sure." He shot a vaguely defiant look at Winston and pulled the narrow brim of his black bowler hat down lower on his sunburned forehead. "It's the girls I'm most worried about, though. Not the money."

"Be that as it may," said the mine owner, defensively, turning his hard, commanding gaze to Zang. "What about you?"

Zang rose from the sun-bleached log he'd been sitting on, cast his watery, dark-brown gaze to Rio, and wagged his head. "Zang go with R'o...Depitty 'Callister." He spat a long wad of chow into the gravel beside him. "Zang go with law!"

"Zang go with law," laughed Winston, turning to the others. "The yellow man's going with the yellow lawman. That sounds right fitting—doesn't it, gentlemen?"

Only Winston's men laughed.

The riders split up, mounted up, and Rio stood watching as they crossed the wash, climbed the opposite bank, passed through some willows, and dwindled into the western distance. Their own rising dust obscured them. The Rattlesnake Buttes rose, craggy and redly ominous, beyond them.

"They might cut some time off," Rio allowed. "But not by much...if they don't get shot out of their saddles before they know what hit 'em. That's bushwhack country."

He pulled his pants and gun belt up higher on his broad hips and grabbed his dun's reins. "Let's get moving, gentlemen. I would like to overtake 'em before nightfall." He glanced at Hank who was just then stepping aboard his own mount. "I don't know about yours, but my old ass is beginnin' to chafe!"

He laughed but there was no real humor in it. He was just trying to laugh off his injured pride, his continuing humiliation. He knew that and he knew the others did, too. Silently, he cursed Winston's defiance and betrayal. But most of all, as he and the others booted their mounts off along the wash to the south, he cursed himself and what had happened to him. His loss of nerve.

He wondered if he had any left.

He had a feeling he was about to find out.

———

TWO HOURS AFTER THE POSSE HAD SPLIT UP, RIO glanced down at the ground, glanced away, then glanced down again and drew abruptly back on his horse's reins.

"Whoa! Whoa!"

"What is it?" Henry asked, stopping his own mount off Rio's horse's left hip.

"Got somethin'."

Rio swung heavily down from the leather, wincing at the ache in his chafed behind. It had been a while since he'd sat a saddle for as long as he had over the past two days. Dropping his reins and moving slowly forward, he swept his gaze across the ground, his heart picking up its pace.

He poked his hat up on his forehead, whistled, and dropped to a knee, regarding the several sets of shod hoof tracks scoring the ground here, which accepted a print much better than did the terrain a few miles back. He looked from his left to his right then on up the old horse trail he and Hank and Zang had been following.

"Five shod horses," Rio said. "Sure enough—four shod horses riding in from the east." He glanced up at Hank and then at Zang and back again, his confidence returning. "They swung east a ways, likely trying to throw us off their trail again. But they rode back this way then headed straight south. Just like I said! Well, sorta like I said, anyways. But anyways..." He straightened, shucked up his trousers and gun again then removed his hat and sleeved sweat from his brow. "We're on their trail!"

"How far ahead, R'o?" asked Zang, from where he slouched forward on the beefy chestnut he rode, a livery rental, and spat a wad of chaw to one side.

Rio set his hat back on his head then moved forward, scouring the ground, enjoying the confidence creeping back into his heart. "Judging by them prints and...and..."

Then he found what he was looking for and crouched down once more. He scooped up a handful of green horse apples flecked with parched corn the animal had consumed, and sniffed then pinched some bits of the manure between thumb and forefinger and sniffed again. He glanced in delighted surprise at his two fellow possemen sitting their horses behind him. "I'd say only an hour or two. We must've gained on 'em overnight and then they lost more time tryin' to give us the slip by ridin' farther east."

"Dang lotta good it did 'em—eh, Rio?" said Hank, grinning down from his saddle. "You're smarter than they are. I knew you were all along!"

Rio gave a dry chuckle then swung back up onto his horse's back. "Yeah, me too; me, too," he said, with another wry laugh and booted the mount forward.

An hour later, when they were out on a flat stretch of desert bristling with sage, creosote, and patches of prickly pear, the Black Range lumping darkly ahead and to their left, Rio again reined to a halt. Again, his gaze scoured the ground.

"What is it this time, R'o?" asked Zang, stopping the beefy chestnut to Rio's right. He took another hard, hungry bite off the tobacco braid hanging from his neck.

"I'll be hanged if they didn't swing dead west from here," Rio said, his voice betraying his surprise. "But that don't make no sense." He stared off along the old stagecoach trail that angled westward. "That would take them into the southern edge of the buttes."

"Why would they head that way?" Hank said. "The best trail west is farther south."

"That's what I'd like to know," Rio said. "Makes no sense less'n...less'n..."

"Less'n what, Rio?" Hank asked.

Rio's heart picked up again, this time with dread.

"Less'n," he said, "they figured we'd be stupid enough to go that way an'...they'd catch us in a bushwhack..."

As if to corroborate his theory, there rose a sudden, angry crackling of distant gunfire.

## CHAPTER 28

"Sure enough—that's what happened, all right!"
Rio said. "I'd bet double eagles against navy beans! Let's
go, Hank! Zang!"

"Behind you, Rio!" Hank said, as Rio spurred his
coyote dun into a ground-churning run.

"Behind you, R'o!" Zang chimed in, spurring his own
mount after Hank and Rio.

As the gunfire continued, Rio pulled his hat brim low
so the wind wouldn't blow it off then reached forward
with his right hand to shuck his Winchester repeater
from its worn leather sheath. His double-bore twelve-
gauge was fine for close-order work in town, but it was
no good for distance shooting whereas his old, battle-
scarred repeater was just the ticket for out here in the
rocks and brush.

He rode crouched low as the dun tore up the old
stagecoach trail which hadn't been used in years, so rocks
had fallen onto the trail from the banks on both sides
and clumps of sage and grass had grown up, as well. The
dun was surefooted, however, and picked his way with
nary a missed step. As the trail made a long, gentle curve

north, to Rio's right, the gunshots grew louder and beneath the rataplan of his horse's galloping hooves he could hear men shouting.

When Rio could see individual shooters lined out on a rocky rise three hundred yards away, and see the shooters' long, cream dusters, he knew a brief hesitation, an inward wince.

"Nope, dammit," he growled, giving his head a stubborn wag. "Not again. Deputy Waite, you got a job to do, an' if you make like a yeller dog again, you're hangin' up your badge an' gun an headin' out into the desert with your tail droopin' to die alone in a blame cave. Hell, you won't even be fit for ol' Buster's company!"

He, Hank, and Zang rode up a rise then down into the rocky wash on its other side. Rio drew back on the dun's reins and raised his rifle, indicating to Hank and Zang to stop, which they did off Rio's right stirrup. They blinked against their dust wafting over them from behind, and Hank said, "How we gonna play it, Rio?"

"The robbers are on the rise just ahead, on the other side of this one," Rio said, indicating the rocky dike ahead with the Winchester's barrel. "The posse must be pinned down just beyond them."

"Judging by the gunfire, they're makin' a fight of it, anyways!"

"I don't think the robbers saw us, so we'll scout the situation from up yonder and come up with a plan." Again, he indicated the dike with his rifle then swung down from his sweat-lathered horse's back.

He dropped the reins and he, Hank, and the big Chinaman climbed the side of the dike. When they were ten feet from the crest, they dropped to crouches and removed their hats. They hunkered down behind two large rocks between which grew a gnarled cedar, offering more cover.

Rio cast his gaze across the stretch of relatively flat but rugged terrain between him and his two partners, where the robbers were hunkered in the rocks atop the next ridge. At least, three appeared to be hunkered in the rocks. Rio couldn't see much more of them than the crowns of their hats, swathes of cream duster, and the smoke puffs made by their rifles. With his gaze, he followed the cries of a girl down into the rocky flat roughly halfway between his and Hank's covering dike and the next one the shooters were on. Some dusty cottonwoods stood in a pale wash to the left. Because of rocks and the trees impeding his view, Rio couldn't see much save the brown tail of a horse and maybe another patch of cream duster through the cottonwood leaves.

"It appears two of the robbers have the girls down there to our left," Rio said, stretching his lips distastefully back from his lips.

A man's hard voice, pitched with warning, cut through the girl's cries, and the cries faded a little.

The shooting was growing sporadic, telling Rio that the bushwhacked posse must be pinned down well. A couple might have taken lead—he didn't think he was hearing the shooting of six rifles from that direction.

"Damn fools," Rio mused aloud, rubbing his jaw.

"This is gonna be tricky, Rio," Hank said. "If those robbers see us, they're liable to kill the girls."

"I got a feelin' that's Colvin and Sugar with the girls. Think I recognized Sugar's voice. Heard it plenty the other night."

"They're branchin' out from poker, eh?"

"Appears that way." As the shooting continued, albeit sporadically, Rio turned to Hank and Zang. "I'm gonna

steal down this slope. I'm gonna take down Colvin an'
Sugar before they can hurt the girls. You two stay here
and keep down. Don't let them bastards see you...till
we're ready."

"When you've taken down Colvin an' Sugar."

Rio nodded. "You cover me. When I have the girls up
here out of harm's way, we'll lay the lead to them three up
yonder."

He caught Hank giving him a quick, ever so vaguely
skeptical glance. Hank tried to turn away fast, but Rio
had seen it.

He narrowed an eye at his junior partner. "Don't you
worry, amigo." He grinned and nodded with forced confidence. "I got this."

Hank looked at him, smiled. "I never doubted you for
a minute, partner. Hell, it's been you all along who started
doubting."

Zang smiled then, too, and spat a long wad of chaw in
the rocks.

Rio peered over the crest of the dike, between the
cedar and the rock on his left. The other three robbers
were still hunkered on the far ridge, still shooting toward
the north where the posse was pinned down. Rio thought
only two, maybe three of the possemen, were returning
fire at their bushwhackers.

He could hear the girl crying between gunshots fired
from the ridge beyond her.

"Here we go—time to dance." Rio rose and scuttled
over the crest of the dike, hoping against hope the three
shooters on the next ridge didn't see him. If they did,
Colvin and Sugar would likely kill the girls. He was pleas-
antly surprised that so far, they hadn't. Maybe that was
just too nasty a job even for bottom-feeding vermin like
Colvin and Sugar. Rio had no doubt they'd use the girls as

human shields, though, if they discovered they were being flanked.

Staying low, he picked his way carefully down the slope, not wanting to stumble and fall and make himself look an even bigger fool than he already looked...and felt. He kept the cottonwoods between him, the two men, the girls, and the horses, hoping the horses wouldn't wind him and give him away. A thumb of stout rock jutted up out of the shoulder of the dike, roughly twenty feet from the bottom. Rio quartered toward the formation, shouldered up against it, and hunkered on his haunches, holding the Winchester across his knees.

Here, he was concealed by the trees from the slope on which the shooters were still shooting once every five or six seconds. Bullets of the possemen's return fire spanged off rocks. The girl was still sobbing. Rio peered between two of the cottonwoods. A shallow wash lay on the other side. Flames flickered in a fire ring over which hung a coffeepot, steam rising from the spout.

The two girls, the little blonde and the slightly older brunette, sat on the near side of the fire, their backs to Rio. Their wrists and ankles were tied. The little blonde hung her head, sobbing. Both girls' gingham day dresses were worn and dirty and their hair was badly disheveled. Otherwise, they appeared unhurt.

So far.

Rio had been right. Two men guarding them were Colvin and Sugar.

Anger burned in Rio. He'd enjoy taking those two down.

Both were hunkered on their haunches, holding steaming cups of coffee and peering toward the ridge beyond which their brethren had the posse pinned down. One horse stood to the right of the fire, the other to the left, facing each other. They were each tied to a branch of the cottonwoods, edgily switching their tails at the rifle fire coming from the ridge.

"Just keep looking away," Rio said, as he quietly, slowly levered a round into his Winchester's action. "Just keep lookin' away," he sang to himself as he rose and continued down the slope.

He'd taken three steps and was about to take a fourth when his right foot suddenly grew heavy. He looked at the booted appendage hanging there in midair as he held his rifle and his left arm out to his sides for balance.

His heart drummed in his ears.

His throat went dry.

*Oh, no, you don't, Rio Waite. Not again. Not now!*

He stretched his lips back from his teeth, stared at his foot, willing it down.

It dropped to the next rock on the slope. He placed his left foot on another rock, both feet feeling like he had lead in his boots. He lowered one foot again and then the other until he gained the bottom of the slope. He paused to sleeve the cold, stinging sweat from his forehead then continued forward and down, counseling himself to continue.

*No matter what happens, don't you stop, gallblastit, you clay-spined, ol' mosshorn!*

Heavily, heart hammering, he walked to the trees. He shoved a branch aside. Now he had a clear view of both girls and both men as well as both horses, though the girls sat between him, Sugar, and Colvin. He had to get closer, so he had surer shots at both owlhoots.

One more step...

One more.

He squeezed the rifle. His hands were slick with sweat inside his gloves.

Suddenly, the horse on the right side of the fire turned toward him. It gave him the woolly eyeball, switched its tail nervously.

Rio stopped, sucked a breath through his clenched teeth.

*No, no, no, no, no. Don't you—*

The brunette turned her head to one side, peered over her shoulder at Rio.

Her eyes widened in horror at the man standing with a rifle behind her. Her mouth opened. She screamed.

Colvin stood on the left side of the fire. Sugar, to the right. Colvin yelped with a start and swung toward Rio, dropping his coffee cup. Sugar dropped his own cup as both men swung toward Rio, astonishment widening their eyes and reddening their faces, the flaps of their dusters winging out around them.

"*It's Waite!*" Colvin yelled.

Each man's right hand was a blur of quick motion as they shoved that side of their dusters back and dropped their gloved hands to the six-shooters jutting from their holsters. Rio had no idea what just then happened, but time suddenly stood still. Or at least, it slowed down so that the next second passed with the slow, purposeful plod of a minute.

His heart slowed, as well.

He felt himself grin with a sudden, profound, improbable but glorious confidence as he extended the Winchester straight out from his right side, lined up the sights on the dead center of Colvin's chest, and squeezed the trigger. Colvin went stumbling back, triggering his six-shooter into the air. He'd only just started to fall when Rio jacked another round into the Winchester's action, lined up the sights on Sugar, and shot Sugar, as well. The outlaw's pistol went flying out of his hand as he twisted around and went stumbling backward, yelling like a gut-shot coyote.

He nearly got his boots planted and was reaching inside his duster for a shoulder rig when Rio shot him again and then shot Colvin again for good measure, though the man was already down and writhing.

The three men on the ridge had turned toward Rio, one yelling, "They flanked us! They flanked us!"

Rio jacked another round into the Winchester, dropped to a knee and sent three quick rounds caroming toward the men on the ridge as they scrambled for cover. He dropped the Winchester, and bellowed, *"Cover me, Hank! Zang!"* as he scrambled to the sobbing girls cowering where each was tied.

As Hank's rifle began barking on the ridge behind Rio, the older deputy snatched his bowie knife from the sheath on his shell belt, and said, "Hang on, little ladies! I'm Rio Waite, deputy town marshal, an' I'm gonna get you both out of here an' back home to your pa. An' that's bond!"

He quickly cut them both loose then returned his knife to his sheath and picked up his rifle. He turned to the still sobbing blonde, and said, "Little one, I'm gonna give you a horseback ride up that ridge yonder. Can you climb up on my back?"

The girl nodded dully, her sunburned cheeks tear streaked. Rio got down on his knees. The girl leaped up onto his back and wrapped her arms around his neck.

"All right, darlin'," Rio said, rising and pausing to jack a round into his rifle and send a bullet caroming up the ridge where Henry and Zang were doing a fine job of keeping the three surviving robbers pinned down in the rocks. "Take my hand and let's run!"

The brunette, appearing as in shock as the little

blonde, nodded dully then gave her hand to Rio. With the little blonde on his back, the brunette running along beside him, Rio ran in his bandy-legged fashion back through the cottonwoods and up the rocky slope toward where Henry and Zang's rifles spat smoke and flames from between covering rocks. Almost as soon as Rio started climbing the steep slope, leaping from one rock to another, he was out of breath and sweating profusely. A couple of the robbers triggered lead at him, the bullets barking off the rocks around him and the girls, and that kept him running though his lungs ached and his heart drummed in his ears.

The blonde sobbed. He could feel her tears through his shirt, though by now he wasn't sure which were her tears and his own sweat. The brunette ran fleetly along beside him, leaping onto rocks, holding pace, grunting with each lunging stride.

Twenty feet from the crest of the ridge, Rio felt himself slow. His old legs were giving out. His chest burned.

Henry saw from the crest above and to Rio's right, and the younger deputy yelled encouragement. "Come on, Rio. You're almost there!"

Then he fired another round at the distant ridge. Zang fire another round then, too.

Rio pushed on, his swelling knees feeling as though they were about to burst through his denims. He gave a fierce grunt as he covered the last six feet and crested the ridge. Squeezing the brunette's hand in his own, he moved down the slope several feet then on a clear patch of ground he dropped to his hands and knees, drawing great drafts of air into his aching lungs, wincing against the war drum of his heart beating in his ears.

"Winston's on the ridge above 'em now!" he heard

Henry yell above and behind him. "They're tryin' to get to their horses! Let's finish 'em off, Zang!"

"I right behind you!" Zang shouted.

Rio glanced over his left shoulder to see both men leap up from their perches and run across the crest of the ridge to disappear down its opposite side.

Rio rolled onto his back, his round belly expanding and contracting as he breathed. He looked up to see the little blonde staring down at him through her cornflower blue eyes that were suddenly dry. Concern shone in them.

"Are you gonna be almost right, Mister Rio?"

Rio sucked another breath and smiled. "Yeah, I think so."

He saw the brunette carrying the canteen she'd taken off his horse up the slope toward him. She uncapped it, dropped to her knees beside the blonde, and handed the flask to Rio. "Mister Rio," she said, giving her pretty head a single shake, "you saved our lives. Take a big drink."

Then she smiled.

"Why, thank you, darlin'," Rio said, sitting up and accepting the flask. "I think I just will."

He laughed again. He was plum beat to death. But he hadn't felt this good in ages.

## CHAPTER 29

Cheyenne stared up in disbelief at Jodi Miller holding the silver-chased, pearl-gripped revolver on her.

"I...don't...understand," she said. "You followed us here. So...you're after the money, too?"

"Yes, well he promised it to me—to us—if he ever found it."

That nudged Cheyenne ever farther back on her proverbial heels. Sitting on the cave floor, her knees drawn up to her chest, it took her several seconds to find the words before, glancing at Garrett passed out belly down, she said, "You two were..."

"Lovers, yes," Jodi Miller said, tonelessly. "He promised himself to me. My father wanted it. His mother wanted it. Then, yesterday, I followed him over to your ranch. I had my suspicions. A couple of the hands said they'd see him and you riding on the range together, heading for Thunder Mountain." She curled her upper lip as she added, filing an edge on her voice now, "I followed you to the line shack...listened outside. I swear, I could kill you both now!"

On the floor of the cave, Garrett moaned and waggled his head from side to side.

"Shut up!" Jodi walked over and aimed her handsome revolver at the back of the man's head, carpeted in short, straight blond hair. "I could kill you now, you two-timing, double-crossing son of a—"

Suddenly, she screamed as Garrett thrust his left arm out, cutting her feet out from under her. She fell backward hard, in a blur of motion, firing the pistol into the ceiling. She landed with a yowl and a thud flat on her back and lay there, blinking and groaning, stunned. She reached out with her hand, feeling along the floor for the pistol.

"Oh, no, you don't!" Garrett said, thrusting himself up and forward, reaching for the Colt.

"No!" Cheyenne dove forward. She got her hand on the pistol before he did, but he closed his hand on top of hers, pressing down painfully, and then plucked it out of her grasp.

He rose to his knees, the gash in his right cheek leaking blood into the corner of his mouth. His face was a swollen red mask of fury as he aimed the Colt at Cheyenne and then at the still prostrate Jodi then back again. He looked like a wild beast who made his home in these mountains.

Jodi lifted her head from the cave floor. She'd lost her hat and her hair hung partly over her face. She pressed her fingers to her temples and shot Garrett Beech a wild look of her own. "You devil! What're you gonna do now? Kill us both. You'll never get away with it."

There was a low rumbling sound. Cheyenne looked around. The cave shuddered slightly. Some sand dribbled down from the ceiling.

Garrett looked at Jodi then at Cheyenne and smiled

his savage grin. "I'm betting I will. In due time. No one knows where we are. We'll wait out the storm. Then..." He glanced down at Jodi's pistol in his hand then gave both young women an evil, lopsided smile.

"All in good time," he said. "You two sit tight. I'm gonna fetch my saddlebags and gather some dry wood. Oh, I'll be watching the cave entrance, now. Either one of you tries to make a run for it, I'll shoot you before you get three feet." Again, he smiled. "Remember, no one knows where we are. They'll never find you."

"You'll kill us anyway," Cheyenne said, sitting on the cave floor beside Jodi now.

Garrett aimed the gun at her belly. "Want to die now...or later? After a meal and a cup of coffee? Your choice."

Neither Cheyenne nor Jodi responded to that.

He looked at them each in turn then clucked and shook his head. "Cryin' shame. Such a pretty pair, too. I don't see no other way, though. Me—in a couple weeks I'll be in Mexico, dancin' with the señoritas." He turned to the cave entrance. "Sit tight. No tricks or you both die."

As soon as he stepped out of the cave into the blowing snow, Jodi rose quickly and started for the door.

"Don't!" Cheyenne grabbed her arm, stopping her. "You heard what he said."

Jodi glared at her. "What do you care?"

Cheyenne stared back at her. Yes, why did she care?

"Maybe I just don't want to be alone with him," Cheyenne said. "He's obviously crazy."

Jodi looked at the cave entrance. "Yes, I suppose we both should have realized that." She sighed and sat down, facing Cheyenne, drawing her own knees to her chest. "If

I could make it to my horse, I have a carbine in the saddle boot."

"You'll never make it."

"What did you see in him?"

Again, Cheyenne shrugged. "What did you?"

"Same as you, I suppose. He's handsome except for those crazy eyes. I'm a widow. My options are limited. His mother and my father would've worked together, building up both herds. Also..."

"You know he'd ridden with my father. Maybe you thought he'd eventually find the loot."

Her arms around her knees, Jodi pursed her lips and nodded. "It's a lot of money."

"What would you have done with it?"

"Move to town, maybe. Move to Leadville...Denver. Take your pick. Anywhere but these mountains. I'm so sick of them I could die!"

Cheyenne laughed without mirth. "Same here."

"Maybe we're more alike than we thought. Odd, how we never talked bef..." Jodi let her voice trail off when Garrett appeared in the doorway, saddlebags draped over his shoulder, carbine in one hand while holding a load of what appeared relatively dry wood in the other.

He stopped, and said, "Oh, now, look whose gettin' cozy!"

Jodi cut her snarling gaze at him. "Shut up, you demon! We were both wondering what we ever saw in you."

"Gettin' to know each other, I see." Garrett walked over and dropped the wood beside the fire ring. He looked at Jodi, and said, "Get a fire goin'. Some of it's a little damp, but I found it in the lee of rocks and boulders, so there should be something to work with."

"Build your own damn fire!"

Garrett dropped the saddlebags and aimed the rifle at her, loudly jacking a live round into the action. "You wanna reconsider?"

Jodi cursed and turned to the wood.

Garrett reached into his shirt pocket for a small, metal box and tossed it down to her. "There's some lucifers." He turned to Cheyenne. "Gotta keep everybody busy. The snow's really comin' down. We'll be here awhile. You do the cookin'. There's beans an' fatback. I'd have Jodi do it, but she can't boil water for coffee!"

He laughed as he walked away from the two women and sagged down against the wall by the cave entrance. He crossed his ankles and rested the Winchester across his legs. He tapped his fingers on the receiver, thoroughly enjoying himself.

The loot was finally his and he had two women to gloat about it to.

Jodi coaxed a fire to life in the fire ring. As it grew darker outside and the natural light left the cave, the light of the dancing flames made a surreal specter of the dead Spaniard holding the long-sought saddlebags on his lap. He seemed to move slightly, shifting shapes. Occasionally, light slipped into the large, dark eye sockets, glowing oddly, frighteningly red, as though the man were a devil trying his best to return to life and was grinning, showing all his long, wretched teeth, with the effort.

Cheyenne tried to keep her gaze off him. The times she didn't, she shivered.

She boiled coffee on a flat rock in the flames and cooked beans and fatback in a tin pot. Garrett ordered his be brought to him and he smiled when Cheyenne brought the steaming plate of beans and fatback and Jodi delivered the coffee, setting it on the ground a few feet away from him as per his demand, apparently afraid of being assaulted with the hot meal or the coffee.

Returning to the fire, the two women shared a grave look, silently agreeing that sometime tonight, before dawn, they had to make their move.

Neither of them ate. They were too nervous to be hungry. Garrett chuckled when he saw this and really bore down on his food, chuckling and jeeringly telling Cheyenne she should have taught Jodi some cooking skills, though it was too late now.

He laughed again.

The fire died down to glowing coals.

The wind continued to blow outside the cave.

Cheyenne saw that Garrett was getting sleepy. His lids grew heavy and at one point his chin sagged nearly to his chest.

Cheyenne and Jodi shared an anxious look.

But then he lifted his chin again, yawned, and gave them each a bold smile.

Later, his eyelids grew heavy again. Suddenly they closed, his chin dipped to his chest, and he began snoring.

Again, Cheyenne and Jodi shared an anxious look.

As Garrett continued snoring, Jodi tucked her bottom lip under her upper teeth, rose silently, and stole the eight feet to the man. She glanced over her shoulder at Cheyenne, who encouraged her with a look. Jodi bent down and placed first her left hand and then her right hand on the rifle in his lap.

Just as she started to pull the rifle up off his lap, he lifted his chin and opened his eyes, and bellowed, "Gotcha!" He laughed loudly then sobered suddenly, glared at Jodi with those too-blue eyes, and said, "Try that again, I'll gut-shoot you. How'd that be?"

"Can't blame a girl for trying," Jodi said crisply, wrinkling her nose distastefully at the man, then returning to her place by the fire.

Again, he fought sleep and lost.

He'd been snoring for a good three or four minutes when Cheyenne, knowing it was her turn, rose quietly and crept across the cave. Slowly, she bent down. She glanced at Jodi, who raised her brows hopefully. Cheyenne turned her head forward then gritted her teeth, placed both hands on the rifle, and jerked it up off the man's lap.

Garrett howled and lifted his chin, eye red with rage.

Cheyenne stepped back with the rifle but before she could get both feet set, Garrett swung his right leg with savage fury, cutting her legs out from under her. She'd just racked a round in the action but now she fired that round at the ceiling. Garrett reached for the rifle but then Jodi came bulling toward him with an enraged, "*Noooo!*" and rammed into him, throwing him sideways and clawing at his face with her fingers.

They fought like two wildcats and then Cheyenne, recovering her senses, joined the fray. When Garrett got the upper hand, smacking Jodi's face with a savage backhand, Cheyenne got her hands on the rifle. But he was too strong for her. He jerked it out of her grip, yelling curses.

"Jodi, run!" Cheyenne shouted, grabbing the blonde and shoving her toward the cave entrance.

Garrett was shaking off the cobwebs, cursing, and levering a fresh round into the rifle's action when Cheyenne flung herself after Jodi toward the cave entrance. Then they were out the door and finding themselves in the pearl light, cold wind, and damp snow of the early dawn.

"Run!" Cheyenne yelled again as they slipped and slid down the rocky, slippery slope. Only a few wayward flakes were falling now but a good four inches lay on the ground.

"Where?"

"Anywhere!"

They were both spurred on by the enraged shouts behind them. Then a bullet screeched through the chill air to their right. Jodi screamed and fell. Cheyenne helped her to her feet, and they ran off down the canyon, opposite the direction from which they'd come. More enraged shouts and rifle blasts behind them, but bullets plowing into the sides of the narrow canyon to each side as they followed its turns. They followed an especially sharp bend, and then Jodi said, "There!"

She pointed to a dark patch in the stone wall on the bend's far side.

They headed for it. It was a long, deep fissure in the wall, just wide enough to accept two people their size. They moved into it, hoping Garrett wouldn't see it. If so, the cavity having no back door, they'd be dead.

They moved as far back into the eight-foot-deep notch as they could and slumped down against the back wall. Jodi wore her yellow slicker but Cheyenne had only her blouse and vest. She shivered.

They'd been in the cavity only a minute or two when a man-shaped silhouette appeared at the opening.

"Oh, my God!" they both hissed in unison.

The figure moved toward them until they could make out the face of not Garrett Beech but Matt Severance. He held a rifle low in his right hand. He wore a brown-and-green plaid mackinaw. He held his left index finger to his lips then canted his head to indicate the canyon outside the notch.

Cheyenne and Jodi shared a wide-eyed, hopeful look then hurried to their feet. They'd taken one step toward Matt when a bullet barked loudly off the wall of the cleft, to their right, Matt's left. A horse—probably Matt's—whinnied. Matt ducked then crouched to return fire.

A man's voice came from outside, ripped and torn by the wind:

"Hold it, Beech! Come out of there or I'll blast you to kingdom come!"

Despite the wind, Cheyenne recognized the rich baritone of Bloody Joe Mannion.

## CHAPTER 30

MANNION STOOD IN A CLEFT IN THE ROCKS SOUTH OF the notch he'd seen Matt Severance step into, following the girls.

Joe had tracked the man to the canyon after having checked on him at the Wolf Creek Ranch and learning from Eva Severance that, despite his bum leg, he'd tracked the horse and rider that had likely picked up Cheyenne on the far side of the creek from the Wolf Creek headquarters, day before yesterday, after the distraught girl had learned Matt was not her uncle but her father.

He rested his Yellowboy on the rocks before him, gazing down canyon and into a nest in the rocks on its left side. Just a minute ago, he'd spied Garrett Beech slip into that notch and track Severance with his rifle, as Severance rode down canyon on his black.

Beech swung around suddenly and fired three quick rounds toward Mannion, who ducked as the slugs slammed into the rocks around him. Mannion raised his head and rifle and returned fire, sending three rounds of his own toward Beech, who lowered his own head.

Mannion's rounds hammered the rock wall above and behind the man.

An eerie rumbling sounded.

The rocks cradling Mannion shuddered.

Mannion looked up to see rocks tumbling down from the ridge on the canyon's left side. Standing in the rocks just behind the cave he'd emerged from a few minutes ago, yelling and firing his rifle, Garrett Beech looked up.

More rocks tumbled from above, crashing onto the canyon floor beyond Mannion and around Beech.

Joe lowered the Yellowboy, raised his hands to his mouth, and shouted, "Earthquake! Matt, get those girls out of there! I'll cover you!"

Mannion jacked another round into the Yellowboy's breech and fired toward Beech, keeping the man pinned down as Matt Severance and the two girls emerged from the fissure in the canyon's right wall. Severance ran ahead and grabbed the reins of the black standing just down canyon from him. The two girls ran after him. Mannion kept Beech pinned down with his Winchester and then, when he'd emptied the rifle, continued sending lead toward Beech with his two Russians. He was relieved when Severance led the black, upon which the two girls now rode, down canyon, away from the mountain that was about to tumble down around them.

More rocks fell from above, crashing onto the canyon floor ahead of Mannion.

Behind him, down the slope just south of the cave from which Beech had emerged, Red whinnied.

Joe triggered his last shot.

"The loot!" he heard Beech cry among the growing roar of the shuddering earth and slowly disintegrating mountain.

He watched as Garrett Beech emerged from the

rocks he'd holed up in, ran back toward Mannion, climbed the slope forty yards ahead of Joe's own perch, and disappeared into the rocks that concealed the cave he'd emerged from earlier.

"Get out of there, you damn fool!" Mannion shouted.

Too late.

Just then a cabin-sized rock fell from above, crashing into the canyon and effectively sealing off the cave. The ground leaped violently around Joe, who blinked against the roiling dust and flying rock shards. He leaped down from his rocky perch and ran down the slope to the south. Red stood just beyond, dancing in place and whinnying shrilly, reins dangling, eyes wide and ringed with white.

"Hold on, boy!" Joe yelled, running for all he was worth as several rocks falling from above crashed to either side of him. Rock dust mushroomed up from behind him.

He grabbed the bay's reins, hurled himself into the leather, and gave the terrified beast his head.

They galloped hell-for-leather south along the canyon while all hell was breaking loose behind them, Mannion hoping Severance and the two girls had gotten out of harm's way.

He discovered a half hour later, when he'd climbed up out of the canyon, they had. All three stood on the canyon's east wall, Severance's black and a fine brown-and-white tobiano stallion idly cropping grass behind them. Joe rode up to them and stared into the canyon which the top of the mountain straight across had broken off and filled.

Dust still rose in the growing, buttery morning light, as though from the scene of a great, bloody battle.

The snow was melting, glistening in the sunshine along the canyon rim.

Birds chirped in the aftermath of both storms.

Severance turned to Joe, gave a wry half smile. "Never thought I'd be happy to see you, Mannion."

Mannion chuckled. "Where have I heard that before?" He glanced from Severance to the girls staring with beleaguered expressions into the canyon that had nearly become their sarcophagus. "The loot?"

"In there. Buried deep. Along with Garrett Beech." Severance turned to Joe. "Roy's partner."

"Ah." Mannion nodded. "How in holy blazes did you find them down there?"

Severance shook his head. "I was riding blind, just happened to be close enough to hear the shooting. It was then I remembered the cave...and the dead conquistador." He turned to the canyon, smiled ironically, shook his head. "I'll never know why when I saw that helmet Roy had scribbled on the mine claim, I didn't figure it out. Where Roy had hidden the loot. But Garrett did."

"And he paid for it," said Cheyenne Severance, staring dully into the canyon. "I know that canyon didn't want us down there." She crossed her arms on her chest and shuddered.

Jodi Miller turned to her. "We almost paid for it, too. Greed."

Cheyenne nodded. "I'm glad it's gone. Relieved it's gone. Forever."

"Me, too," said Severance. "Me, too."

Mannion saw the blood staining his pants. "Best get you on home, Matt."

The girls helped Severance over to his horse, helped him mount. Severance turned to Mannion and nodded.

"I'm ready to go home. To stay there...for a long, long time."

The girls mounted the tobiano and all four—Mannion, Severance, and the girls—rode away from Thunder Mountain.

Mannion doubted any of them would be back.

Bad medicine down there—a dead man and the money he died for.

## CODA

TWO DAYS LATER, RIO WAITE SAT AT THE DESK AT Hotel de Mannion, contentedly petting his fat, tuxedo-wearing cat, Buster, who was curled snugly on the middle-aged deputy's lap, purring.

Rio felt as content as Buster did.

While two of Duke Winston's men and the druggist, Mortimer Arthur, had been killed when they'd ridden into the ambush set by the five bank robbers, including Ed Colvin and Bob Sugar, the two Williams girls had been rescued and were safely at home with their folks. The money the robbers had stolen had been retrieved. That loot had included the life savings of a good many of the folks in and around Del Norte.

Del Norte was pleased. And so was Rio.

Yes, contentment, Rio thought, smiling down at the cat he was petting and who purred contentedly.

The lawman knew the contentment wasn't meant to last, however. It never did in Del Norte.

From outside, came the sound of running feet. The sound grew louder until it was accompanied by quick, raking breaths. Boots thumped on the porch and then the front door opened and young Harmon Haufenthistle poked his immigrant-hatted, blond, tan-faced head into the office, and yelled, "Rio, come quick! A coupla big Germans from the Cloud Tickler are fightin' over one of Miss Jane's girls, and they're about to turn the San Juan to *matchsticks*! The bouncers can't do nothin' with 'em. Miss Jane said to come fetch *you*!"

"Holy blazes!" Rio complained, rising as Buster thumped to the floor. He grabbed his hat and double-bore gut-shredder, stepped around the desk, and headed for the door. "A lawman's work is never done around here —I tell you, Harmon. It just ain't never done!"

"Come on, Rio! Hurry!"

"Don't never grow up, Harmon!"

"Come on, Rio! Hurry!"

"I'm comin'! I'm comin'!"

In his bandy-legged fashion, shotgun resting on his shoulder, not an ounce of fear in his feet or knees or anywhere else, Rio followed the boy along the street to the south and over to the San Juan Hotel & Saloon and mounted the broad front steps. It was late in the day; shadows were growing long. From inside the saloon came a man's deep, guttural, German-accented voice shouting, "Come on, Herman! Talk's cheap. Come a little closer and I'll rip your throat out with this bottle, you swine! I'll show you whose spendin' the night with Miss Betty once an' for all!"

A girl's shrill voice cried, "Hans, no! Herman, no! Please don't! Please don't!"

"Oh, for pity's sake!" Rio said, as Harmon opened one of the San Juan's stout oak doors and stepped back, holding the door for the deputy.

Rio walked into the saloon and, sure enough, he quickly found two big, wool-and-denim-clad, bearded men swinging broken whiskey bottles at each other, knife-like, while a young, blond doxie clad in a red-and-black bustier, black fishnet stockings, and red high-heeled shoes stood on a nearby table, holding her face in her hands while she watched the two men feinting and ducking and thrusting the bottles at each other. Trepidation shone in the little whore's eyes.

A large crowd stood in a wide, complete circle around the two, big, German fighters—who fought bare-knuckle on Saturday nights on San Juan Avenue. The crowd looked awestruck, fearful. Two big bouncers lay on the floor just inside the door near Rio; they appeared unconscious.

"All right, you two knuckleheads!" Rio said, leaning his shotgun against the wall and stooping to retrieve a hide-wrapped bungstarter lying on the floor near one of the bouncers. "Step aside, everybody! Step aside! Make *way*!"

The crowd parted for Rio who stepped up to the two big men and, tapping the bungstarter in the palm of his left hand, shouted, "Put them bottles down, you hoople-heads, or it's lamps out for both of you and two days in Hotel de Mannion!"

Oddly, the two crouched fighters suddenly straightened and, lowering the broken bottles to their sides, turned to Rio and grinned.

The little doxie on the table to Rio's left lowered her hands from her face and smiled, as well.

The crowd's collective look of concern suddenly dissolved into grins as they all turned to the deputy.

Rio's lower jaw sagged, and his brows beetled, bewildered.

*What the...?*

Suddenly, Miss Jane Ford Mannion's voice cut through

the room's sudden silence. "Just our way of getting you over here, Deputy Waite...to show you the town's appreciation as well as my own! It's a *party*!"

Rio looked up to see the begowned and jeweled Mrs. Mannion standing beside Bloody Joe himself at the top of the stairs running up the wall at the back of the room, smiling down at him from over the banister. Joe's daughter, Vangie, and her young medico husband, Dr. Ben Ellison, were there, too, holding wine glasses. Bloody Joe held up a shot glass in salute and winked.

Rio saw the two "unconscious" bouncers gain their feet behind him. Puffing up their chests in their swollen suits, both big men turned to him, rosy-cheeked, and cut loose with a hearty, "For he's a jolly good fellow! For he's a jolly good fellow...!"

And then the rest of the crowd, including Harmon Haufenthistle still holding the door open and the little doxie atop the table, chimed in until the roar filled the room and Rio thought the backbar mirror would burst:

"WHICH NOBODY CAN DENYYYYY!"

———

THE NEXT MORNING, BLOODY JOE WOKE WITH A splitting headache.

Sunlight edged around the curtained windows, and a rumble of industry rose from the street below his and Jane's suite of rooms on the San Juan's second floor. He turned to his beloved lying belly down beside him, her face buried in her pillow.

"Well, that was a party I won't soon forget," he growled, sitting up and massaging his temples with his fingertips. "How 'bout you, my love?"

Jane did not reply.

Joe glanced at her. "Jane?"

Nothing.

Concern rose in Mannion. He turned and said softly into her ear, "Jane, honey?"

She did not move. He wasn't sure he could hear her breathing.

Mannion shook her gently. "Jane."

When she made no sound, he shook her a little harder. "Jane...please, honey..."

Mannion lowered an ear to her back. He couldn't hear her heart beating.

Terror made his own heart buck. He placed his hands on her shoulders and shook her still harder. "Jane!"

She moaned, moved her legs, stirring.

Beneath the bed covers, Jane rolled over slowly, her thick, copper-red hair spilling across the pillow to make a lovely nest behind her head.

She smiled up at him, sleepily, dreamily, brown eyes catching the light from the edges of the windows, and sandwiched his big face in her pale, freckled hands. "Here we are together. Another day. What a lovely thought, is it not, Bloody Joe?"

She lifted her head to kiss him lightly, tenderly on the lips.

**Bestselling author "Mean Pete" Brandvold has been
spinning classic, action-filled western yarns for the past
25 years. In this Introductory Library, you'll find the
first book from each of 8 bestselling, fan favorite series,
offering you a mere taste of the smorgasbord served up
by the legend himself.**

**The Classic *Sheriff Ben Stillman Series* Begins...**

Playing poker, smoking cigarettes, drinking whiskey—
retirement was treacherous business for ex-lawman Ben
Stillman. The best of life seemed to be past, but then the past
came looking for him... Can the worn-out old lawman live up to
the legendary lawman he once was?

**Peter Brandvold has worked up the grittiest, bloodiest
fast-action western in the *.45 Caliber Series*!**

Cuno Massey's thirst for revenge runs deep. Deeper than his
skills. But when Rolf Anderson and Sammy Spoon killed his
stepmother and his father, nothing would stand in young Cuno's
way. He'd ride straight through hell for the bittersweet taste of
revenge...

**Saddle up for the wildest, bloodiest Peter Brandvold
series yet—*Yakima Henry*!**

Half Indian and half white, Yakima Henry considers himself
lucky to have any job–even if it means just sweeping up the
local brothel. But when four hombres attempt to carve up one
of the house girls, Yakima gives them a taste of their own

medicine with his Arkansas Toothpick. Now, he's become the girl's protector, and is on the run from a vicious bounty hunter.

**A hot and heavy western noir...** *The Saga of Colter Farrow...*

Colter Farrow may be young, but ever since his stepfather was savagely murdered, his blood has boiled with a rage as great as any man's. While trying to exact revenge, Colter ends up on the run from bounty hunters, outlaws, and a sadistic sheriff. Desperate and afraid, Colter is searching for freedom and a chance to return home to live a quiet, normal life.

**This Prophet is riding to hell and back!**

Lou Prophet's life as a bounty hunter has taught him one rule: You don't stop riding till the job is finished. Prophet is repeatedly caught in bloody crossfires and he is determined to show the outlaws that justice doesn't always wear a badge. Join the bounty hunter as he faces seemingly insurmountable odds at every turn...

*The Revenger Series*

Mike Sartain, The Revenger, grew up in the French Quarter of New Orleans where he was taught how to fight by some of the toughest, meanest SOBs in any port. He was taught how to love by some of the most beautiful women in the world...

Now, The Revenger rides for anyone who has an ax to grind...

**Ride the rough, lawless trails of the western frontier with** *The Rogue Lawman*!

Deputy U.S. Marshal Gideon Hawk was respected throughout the Territory as a lawman of principle—until Three Fingers Ned Meade threw him a curve. Meade killed Hawk's ten-year-old boy, and the grisly act drove Hawk's grief-stricken wife to hang herself. Now, robbed of kin, Hawk sets out on a brutal quest to find the man responsible—at any cost.

**Get ready for a dose of action and adventure and a heaping helping of western justice with** *Bloody Joe Mannion*!

"Bloody" Joe Mannion is a town tamer of great renown. His temper is just as famous. Known as the most uncompromising lawman on the Western frontier, he's been the town marshal of Del Norte in the Colorado Territory for the past five years. Now, Bloody Joe will risk everything, including his life, the town, and a hail of hot lead!

*The Peter Brandvold Introductory Library* **includes the following titles:**

**Once a Marshal (Ben Stillman 1)**

**.45 Caliber Revenge (.45 Caliber 1)**

**The Lonely Breed (Yakima Henry 1)**

**The Guns of Sapinero (Colter Farrow 1)**

**The Devil and Lou Prophet (Lou Prophet 1)**

**A Bullet for Sartain (The Revenger 1)**

**Rogue Lawman (Rogue Lawman 1)**

**Bloody Joe (Bloody Joe Mannion 1)**

*AVAILABLE NOW*

**Peter Brandvold** grew up in the great state of North Dakota in the 1960's and '70s, when television westerns were as popular as shows about hoarders and shark tanks are now, and western paperbacks were as popular as *Game of Thrones*.

Brandvold watched every western series on television at the time. He grew up riding horses and herding cows on the farms of his grandfather and many friends who owned livestock.

Brandvold's imagination has always lived and will always live in the West. He is the author of over a hundred lightning-fast action westerns under his own name and his pen name, Frank Leslie.